COMBUSTION

Agents of Ensenada, Book Two

Tess Summers

Seasons Press LLC

Copyright 2019 Tess Summers

Combustion

She was meant to be mine—I knew it the moment we met. Too bad I'm about to kidnap her.

Mason Hughes

As a decorated CIA agent, I know better than to kidnap a former colleague's sister and hold her hostage on a ship in the middle of the ocean. The agency tends to frown on that sort of behavior. But desperate times call for desperate measures; I have my reasons, and they're good ones. I'll be forgiven with a slap to the wrist—at least for that part of the mission.

Until I tie Reagan Jones up and can't resist her when she presses her tight little body against mine. That's probably not so forgivable.

Then there's the issue of falling in love with her and refusing to let her go once the mission is over. Definitely not forgivable.

I have no idea what I'm thinking—we can't be together; it's not safe for her. I'm a spy, and she's a feisty art instructor from Fargo. Not exactly the perfect match.

Or is it?

Dedication

To my readers—thank you letting me share my stories with you.

Acknowledgements

Elayne Morgan—thank you for being such an incredible editor. The care and effort you put into this book is so appreciated.

OliviaProDesigns—thank you for another amazing cover.

Mr. Summers—thanks for taking such good care of me.

Janece Ellers—thank you for continuing to be the best beta reader ev-ah! You've been with me since Ava and Travis, and I can't thank you enough for your valuable feedback.

JM—your feedback on each and every book is so appreciated. Thank you for always encouraging me.

My mom, aunties, grandma, and cousins—you're the best tribe a girl could ask for. Thanks for always being there.

My writing friends—thank you for letting me be a part of your amazing, talented group. Your energy is contagious.

Ric fuckin' Casper and Brian Kurtz—thanks for volunteering to have characters named after you. I hope you like them!

Table of Contents

Combustion
Agents of Ensenada

Chapter One

Reagan Jones

The Ensenada humidity and Reagan's hair were currently at odds with each other as she finished getting ready for her niece's baptism rehearsal, and the humidity was winning. Since Reagan was godmother to little Madison Belle Guzman, the petite redhead thought she should at least try to look presentable, but her curly red hair was not cooperating so now she was running late. The actual baptism was taking place on Sunday, two days from now, and it seemed like it was pretty straightforward, so why on earth there needed to be a practice run was beyond her. But her big sister had asked, and there was no way Reagan was going to tell Kennedy no. Besides, the godfather provided some delicious eye candy, so it wasn't like this was going to be torture.

After putting the finishing touches on her makeup, she took a step back to look in the mirror at her reflection in a pastel green sleeveless sundress and strappy heels. Seeing the opulent Mexican furniture in the background, Reagan took a deep breath and smiled.

She was a long way from her little life in Fargo, North Dakota, where she taught painting at the community center and graphic design at the local college. She wasn't making millions, but she was paying the bills and living on her own without having to rely on anyone else—and that was all that mattered.

Of course, it was a far cry from her older sister's rich and glamorous life. Kennedy Jones, now known as Bella Guzman, was happy with her new husband and baby girl. Granted, Bella had to live under a new identity, so any get-togethers with her family had to be coordinated and clandestine, like this week's carefully orchestrated trip with Reagan and her mother.

Reagan stepped out of the villa walls, past the watchful eyes of the guards, and down the steps into the back seat of the waiting black car with tinted-out windows. A *long way from Fargo*, she thought again. She'd had a driver with her at all times this week, and she was never allowed to go out exploring on her own. It was stifling, and Reagan felt like she was being babysat every time she walked out the beautiful double wooden doors of the villa her new brother-in-law had rented for her and her mother. There were guards at the palatial gates where she was staying, but there were at least triple that at her destination, the mansion her brother-in-law owned. Her brother-in-law owned the estate, but his best friend—and Madison's godfather—John had been living there while Kennedy and Dante stayed in California so her niece could be born in the United States.

The more Reagan learned, the more she swore her sister was living a real-life telenovela. Who had the energy for that drama? *Not this Midwestern girl.*

It wasn't until they drove out the gates that she noticed her driver was new. With his linebacker shoulders under his charcoal grey suit and short, dark blond crew cut, he looked more like a farm boy from North Dakota than a Mexican security guard. And when he tried to answer the question she posed to him in Spanish, his response was awkward and stilted.

Definitely not a native speaker. Maybe her farm-boy assessment wasn't that far off.

"What's your name?" she asked in English.

He looked at her in the rearview mirror through his aviator glasses, the corners of his mouth lifting.

"Mason."

"Mason, I'm detecting an East Coast accent, and I don't mean Veracruz, Mexico-east coast."

His smile got broader, revealing a dimple on his handsome, tanned baby-face.

"You'd be correct, ma'am. Massachusetts, born and raised."

"You did *not* just ma'am me. How old are you?"

"Thirty-three, and it's just part of my upbringing. I certainly didn't mean any disrespect."

"Well, since I'm a year younger than you, you're not allowed to call me ma'am. Reagan will do just fine."

That elicited a chuckle.

"Very well, Reagan. I won't do it again."

"So what's a nice Massachusetts boy doing working security in Sinaloa, Mexico? I mean, you obviously have the physique for it." Boy, did he, from what she could tell by his broad shoulders and arms. "But this is an awfully long way to go for a job."

"I'm only here temporarily. I came to solicit some help from an expert in the area, and managed to pick up this gig in the meantime."

They chatted so much during the drive, she didn't pay attention to the route. So when they pulled into the marina and slowed to a stop near the docks. Reagan looked around, confused, not moving when Mason opened her door.

"Are we picking someone else up?"

Offering her his hand, he nonchalantly answered, "Oh, no. Dante decided to move things to the yacht at the last minute. He thought everyone would enjoy the fresh ocean air. I think we're probably the first ones here."

Now, you'd think that, given the warnings her sister had been hammering into her, alarm bells should have been going off in her head. Red flags waving, neon signs flashing, that kind of thing.

Nope.

None of it. Not with the handsome, blond American holding her hand as he escorted her down the dock and chatted hockey with her while helping her onto the most luxurious ship she'd ever been on.

Which wasn't really saying a lot, since her boating days consisted of drinking and tanning on Ricky Hansen's parents' pontoon boat in the middle of Pelican Lake during her summers in high school.

Mason walked on board like he was familiar with the vessel, while she lagged behind, admiring every detail.

"Wow, this is beautiful," she whispered in awe when she stepped down into the living area with its shiny, dark veneer wood and muted gray furniture, complete with a corner bar with a top that appeared to be made of granite. The ceiling with recessed lighting was higher than she'd expected. Until four days ago, she'd had no idea people really lived like this. Now, this was her sister's fairytale life.

But it came at a cost.

Reagan didn't know the details of her sister's life as an ex-CIA agent; she just knew Kennedy was presumed dead by her agency, and that was a good thing because they wanted her that way. Her family was under strict instructions to never reveal she was alive or going by the name Bella Guzman. Reagan didn't know much about her new brother-in-law, Dante, other than that he made her sister happy. Frankly, she didn't want or need to know anything else. Ignorance was bliss.

Mason offered her a mimosa.

"While you wait," he said with a panty-dropping smile. Damn, he was hot.

She felt so luxurious, sitting on a yacht with a champagne flute in her hand while a gorgeous blond man with blue eyes and adorable dimple watched over her to make sure she was safe. If her friends in Fargo could see her now!

That was the shitty part of this experience. She couldn't even tell anyone about it, much less post pictures on social media of her living the high life. The adage of *pictures or it didn't happen* definitely applied. It was though she was living her life as if it belonged to someone else.

Mason was on the phone, glancing her way, so she walked around the space, glass in hand, and took small sips while examining the art on the wall. *I'm on a ship that has art on the wall.* Reagan couldn't help but giggle.

Her handsome driver/guard/babysitter disconnected the call and came to stand by her side, drinking a bottle of water.

"That was security from Dante's estate. They had a late start; I guess the baby was being fussy, so they're on their way now. Are you hungry? Would you like something to eat while you wait? Another mimosa?"

She drained the contents of her glass and walked over to the sink to rinse it out.

"They have people to do that, you know," he said with a smirk.

"I know, but I don't at home, so it just feels natural to clean up after myself."

"So I'm assuming that's a no on another mimosa?" His adorable smirk was still intact. She had a sudden urge to suck on his dimple.

Whoa, drunk hussy. Calm your hormones.

"No, I think it was a bad idea to drink one without eating yet today. I'm feeling a little woozy."

"Come on, let's get you something to eat," he said, offering her his hand, which she readily accepted. She liked it when he held her hand.

How sad was her life that the most action she'd seen in a year was having the bodyguard hold her hand while he escorted her to the galley? And he was only offering it to make sure she didn't trip.

She sat at the small kitchen island while he pulled a platter of hors d'oeuvres from the refrigerator.

"Do you think we should be eating those? I'm sure they're for the guests."

"You're a guest, aren't you?" he replied with a wink as he removed the plastic wrap.

Oh damn, the matching wink to the adorable dimple. And he's feeding me. I think I might be in love.

"So, how long are you planning on staying in Ensenada?" She tried to sound casual while plucking a cucumber slice with cream cheese and diced tomatoes off the tray.

Mason handed her a small plate and napkin.

"Not long. As soon as I get the expert to buy in on assisting me with my next project, I'll be leaving."

Hopefully he'd be here until she went home. How scandalous would it be if she had an affair with her driver?

She popped the entire snack in her mouth and instantly regretted it as she tried to chew in a ladylike fashion with her mouth stuffed full of cucumber and cream cheese. If he noticed her chipmunk cheeks, he didn't mention it.

Finally, she swallowed and took a sip of the glass of orange juice he had poured for her.

"What's your project? If you don't mind my asking?"

At least that's what she intended to ask him, but suddenly she felt like she couldn't form words. Her brain was telling her mouth to move, but it wouldn't work. Same with her limbs.

She heard him say, "Relax, sweetheart. I've got you," as his arms came around her.

And that was the last thing she remembered until waking up hours later in the middle of the ocean on a beautiful yacht with a man who, turns out, didn't really have her best interests at heart after all.

Chapter Two

Mason Hughes

Goddammit, he wasn't supposed to like this woman. She was supposed to be a means to Agent Jones, and that was it. She was supposed to be disposable should things not go as planned.

Then out walked a knock-out with red hair... why did it have to be red? That was his fucking weakness. Although, given who her sister was, he should have been expecting it. But she hadn't been anything like Kennedy—or any woman he'd ever met. She was enthusiastic about everything and so goddamn genuine it made him want to hug her. Or fuck her. Okay, both.

Looking at her passed out on the bed in the master suite, her pale green dress inching up her creamy thighs, red hair fanned out around her delicate features, he realized she might be hard for him to simply dispose of should the need arise. This was not how the plan was supposed to go.

Shit, shit, shit.

His team had held her sister on this very ship after extracting her via helicopter from Dante Guzman's estate. They had waited in the servant's quarters for further instructions on what to do with Agent Jones. Something about that whole assignment had felt off. He'd read her file before the mission; it was exemplary, so he wasn't sure he'd heard correctly when the orders came to terminate her. It didn't sit well with him, but someone with a higher pay grade was making that call. His job was to carry out orders.

Then dipshit Robinson decided to try and get his dick wet, and she got the drop on him. He'd told everyone he shot her and she fell overboard, but unfortunately for Agent Dipshit, Mason had been watching the security feed and saw what really happened.

But Mason Hughes was smart and knew an opportunity when he saw one, so he shut his mouth and tucked away the knowledge that Special Agent Kennedy Jones was alive and well until he needed it for a rainy day.

Well, it was more than raining right now; it was a goddamn hurricane. And he needed Kennedy's help, or her husband's money, or both.

Getting the real driver for Reagan to give him the gig was a piece of cake. Way cheaper than it should have been, frankly. But Mason hadn't expected a freaking knockout to walk out of the gates, and he definitely hadn't expected to think she was the most adorable creature on the planet within thirty minutes of meeting her. He suddenly understood how Kennedy Jones might have found herself on the agency's hit list. The heart wants what the heart wants and all that bullshit.

He wasn't sure if it was heart or his dick that wanted Reagan Jones, but it was something. And these next four days sailing to Colombia with her, alone except for the small crew, were going to be an exercise of his willpower.

Fortunately, she was going to hate him when she woke up, so that would probably help curb her adorableness. It wasn't going to do anything about her tight little body though. Why couldn't Agent Jones have had an ugly, hairy brother to kidnap instead of this sexy nymph?

Means to an end. That's all she is.

He needed to keep telling himself that. His own dumb, hairy brother's life depended on it.

****

Reagan

Her head was pounding from the worst hangover she'd ever had. How was that possible from one mimosa?

She ventured into the living room on her way to the kitchen in search of painkillers. It was so fucking bright out. Shielding her eyes, she stumbled toward the kitchen—then it occurred to her that there was still no one else onboard.

Squinting hard, she glanced around and realized they were no longer at the dock. They were out to sea, with no land in sight.

A million thoughts raced through her head at once, the most prevalent being that she was on the ship alone, and it had somehow floated out into the ocean on its own. She needed to find where the wheel was and figure out how to get back to shore. But first, she needed to take something for this damn headache.

Reagan entered the galley and stopped short when she found Mason standing at the island, preparing a meal in a more casual t-shirt and jeans than the suit he'd been in earlier. The dark blue in his shirt brought out the cornflower color in his eyes, and his smile disarmed her. Did he know they were no longer at the dock?

"Hey, how are you feeling?"

"Like I got run over by a truck, then it backed up and ran over me again. Um, did you know we're like, in the ocean? No land in sight?"

"Yeah," was all he said as he washed peppers and cucumbers in the sink.

So, being in the middle of the Pacific, just the two of us, isn't a problem? Maybe in her fantasy, but her sister was going to kill her. *What am I missing?*

"What's going on? I'm so confused right now. I swear I can usually handle my liquor. I don't know what happened."

He simply replied, "You need to hydrate," then offered a placating smile like he didn't believe she wasn't a total lightweight—although she kind of really was. Still, he didn't know that and was being rude. She'd only had one mimosa, for Chrissake. It didn't even equate to one glass of champagne.

"I'm serious! What's happening? Where are we? Where is everyone else?"

He paused his dicing and looked at her, his expression solemn.

"I drugged you. You need to drink some water to help get it out of your system," he said, then resumed his veggie preparation like he had just given her an update on the weather.

Her hand went to her chest. "You—you drugged me?"

He nodded soberly.

"Why?" she whispered. "Did you—rape me?"

That made him set his knife down with a thud.

"Absolutely not. I prefer my partners to be active participants when I fuck them."

Well, that was crude.

"Then why?"

He started chopping again with a sigh.

"It was either that or tie you up and gag you until we got of the marina and on our journey. I thought drugging you was the easier, more pleasant, option."

"But why? I—I don't understand."

"Because, my dear, you're now my hostage." He then picked up the salad bowl like he didn't have a care in the world. "Are you hungry?"

Chapter Three

Mason

Her calm voice did not match the panic on her face, and that worried him. He would have preferred she go batshit crazy—it felt safer that way. As it stood, she was unpredictable, and that was dangerous.

"I'm your hostage? Why? This makes no sense. I'm a nobody. I don't even have a full-time job, I work two part-time jobs just to pay my bills. I barely have any savings. My mom..." The realization came to her, and she jerked like he'd struck her, then stumbled backward toward the doorway, frantically looked around as if trying to find an escape.

He hoped she wouldn't dive overboard like her sister had done. They were a hell of a lot farther from shore than when Kennedy had taken the plunge.

Mason came around the galley island and walked carefully toward her, speaking softly and calmly like she was a cornered, wounded animal he was trying to soothe.

"Reagan, it's okay. I'm not going to hurt you. You're just a way to get to your sister."

Tears were streaming down her face, and he had to jam his hands in his front pockets to keep from pulling her into him and holding her. He hated it, but he needed her upset and scared when she made the call to Kennedy. And she needed to stay afraid of him so he could keep her under control.

Then the little sprite lifted her chin in defiance, even as the tears continued to flow, and set her jaw while shaking her head.

"No. My sister deserves to be happy. She's a new mom. I'm not going to let her sacrifice her life for mine. You're just going to have to kill me."

Dammit. Not the best time for his dick to move, but it did. Little Red was spunky *and* adorable.

"Sweetheart, I'm not going to hurt her. I just need her help."

"So why don't you just ask her then? Why did you have to kidnap me?"

"Well... I don't think she's going to be very amenable to helping me without some incentive."

She furrowed her brows. "Why not?"

"Let's just say we used to work together and had a bit of a falling out."

She turned white as a ghost as she scrambled backward. He knew she was getting ready to rabbit.

"You're one of the men who were going to kill her," she hissed just before turning and bolting.

Fuck. You did not plan this through very well, he chided himself, then took off after her. In his defense, he hadn't thought she knew about that. He really needed to stop underestimating the Jones sisters.

Mason got to her before she reached the deck, wrapping his arms around her from behind and pulling her into him. She was a tiny little thing, and his six-foot-one frame completely engulfed her. *Damn, she smells good.*

"Please don't hurt me," she whimpered before going totally limp, a move he was sure she'd learned in a self-defense course. It probably would have worked better if she weren't so little, because the only thing it did was surprise him, then make him scoop her up in his arms.

"I am not going to hurt you," he barked, a little harsher than he'd meant to, as he stormed through the yacht toward the captain's quarters, still holding her.

"I'm sure you said that to my sister, too," she snarled back, straining against his hold on her.

Having her in his arms was turning him on, which pissed him off, and he unceremoniously dumped her on the bed with a thud. Picking up her cell phone from the nightstand, he tried to hand it to her.

"Call your sister."

"No," she said boldly and scrambled to sit upright on the edge of the bed, even as tears streamed down her cheeks again.

He shoved the cell at her. "Call. Your. Sister."

She stood up defiantly with her hands on her hips.

"I will not."

Mason invaded her personal space, towering over her. Unable to help himself, he brought his mouth inches from hers while staring at her lips. Those luscious pink, kissable lips.

"Goddammit, Reagan, don't make me hurt you."

"Go ahead," she taunted, refusing to avert her stare, but he could see the pulse in her neck beating a mile a minute and couldn't help but notice how her chest heaved.

The CIA agent wanted to grab a fistful of her hair and slam her against the wall to kiss some sense into her. His cock was screaming, *Do it!* Fortunately, his training kicked in, and he restrained himself to try another approach.

"Video call your sister so she knows you're all right. Otherwise I'm going to drug you again and call her myself and let her think you're dead. You remember what an awful feeling that was, don't you? Thinking your only sibling has been taken from you?"

He knew he had struck a nerve when she began to sob.

"Call Kennedy," Mason reiterated softly and handed her the phone.

To his relief, she did as she was told. He heard the phone ringing, then a woman answered with concern in her voice, "Hi baby sister, where are you? Is everything okay?"

"No." Reagan's voice shuddered, then squeaked. "I'm so sorry, Keni."

"Hey, whatever it is, it's okay. Tell me what's wrong. Where are you?"

She could only repeatedly mutter 'I'm sorry,' she was crying so hard. Taking the phone from her, he turned the screen to face himself and smirked.

"Hello, Agent Jones. Glad to see you're alive and well."

Kennedy was cool as a cucumber, not a bit of shock registering on her expression when she responded, "Mr. East Coast, to what do I owe the pleasure?"

"Well, we need to talk about you coming out of your... retirement. I need some help in a delicate matter, and you're the first person I thought of."

She narrowed her eyes suspiciously. "What kind of help?"

"The kind you're an expert in."

She nodded in understanding. "So what does my sister have to do with this?"

He shrugged. "Nothing. Other than assuring your assistance. Once you help me, she'll be released unharmed. If not, well... let's just say I hope sweet little sis is as good a swimmer as you are."

"Tell me what you need," she replied, unflinching.

****

Reagan

Watching Kennedy on the screen over Mason's shoulder, Reagan realized her sister was kind of a badass. She'd always sort of known that, but had never truly seen it firsthand. Keni wasn't the least bit intimidated by Mason. On the contrary, she made as many demands of him as he did her, and her tone let him know they weren't requests.

Mason's brother, Marcus, was also in the CIA, but had apparently gone rogue on an assignment in Colombia and was now missing. The agency had disavowed him and was not willing to go in to find him.

Kennedy snorted in derision. "Funny how they pick and choose who they're willing to just let disappear."

"Except he didn't go willingly. Intelligence suggests the Colombian cartel has him."

Her sister pursed her lips. "How long has he been missing?"

"Thirty-six hours."

"And you don't think he's dead yet?"

"No, not their style. They're going to ransom him."

"Why did he go rogue?"

Mason cocked his head and sighed. "Why do you think."

"Money? Drugs?" Her smirk suggested that wasn't really what she was thinking.

"What's your next guess."

Kennedy's face became serious. "Who is she?"

"Someone the cartel was trafficking. Marc went in undercover, but the agency pulled the plug on the assignment. He refused to leave without her. It appears his cover was blown, and since he didn't get out when he was ordered to, no one's going in to help him. Except me. And you. And possibly some members from his team."

"I'm assuming this isn't sanctioned, then."

"You would be correct."

"So who knows I'm alive, East Coast?"

"It's Mason. Agent Mason Hughes, and no one. Robinson said he shot you—on your instructions, I'm betting. The team had no reason to doubt it, and the agency signed off with no questions asked. Unfortunately for him, but fortunately for me, I watched your escape on the live surveillance camera feed."

Kennedy huffed out a mirthless chuckle. "I wondered if there were cameras, but didn't have time to worry about them. Does Robinson know you know?"

He shook his head. "Nope. I decided to hang onto this information to use as a bargaining chip, should the need ever arise. I guess you could say I'm calling it in—with you, at least."

"Why not with him, too?"

"Agent Jones, I wouldn't trust that idiot to save my neighbor's cat, let alone my brother's life."

Kennedy gave a genuine smile. "Probably a good idea." Her smile fell. "I'll help you, Hughes, but you have to let Reagan go first."

Mason tilted his head with his mouth turned down. "Come on, you've been around long enough to know I can't do that."

"Yeah, well, you were going to kill me, so—"

He interrupted her. "So you know I won't hesitate to kill your sister if you don't play ball."

Keni stared at him for a minute, as if assessing the validity of his threat, then sighed. Not a good sign for Reagan.

"Send me what you have, then call me back in an hour. We'll talk strategy after I've had a chance to look over everything. Now, let me talk to my sister."

Reagan peeked her face into the camera again. She'd long since stopped crying and had observed the whole exchange between her captor and her sibling, utterly fascinated with it all. No wonder Kennedy had loved her job so much—right up until they'd decided to kill her for falling in love with Dante, who, Reagan was guessing, was part of the cartel.

She was naïve, not stupid.

Chapter Four

Mason

At least his sassy hostage had calmed down and was being compliant. She seemed to have realized he had no intention of hurting her—unless Kennedy didn't cooperate. And fuck if he could hurt her regardless, but she didn't need to know that.

He took her soft hand, and surprisingly, she didn't pull away.

Leading her toward the living room, he teased, "Come on, sassy pants, let's get some real food in you. And you need to be drinking water."

She snorted as she plopped down on the couch. "Like I'm going to eat or drink anything you offer."

He couldn't say that he blamed her, although he acted like she was being silly.

"There's no need to drug you now; you're not going anywhere." *Except to my bed, and you're definitely not going to be drugged for that.*

Mason scolded himself as he walked onto the deck and fired up the grill. That thought should not be popping up in his head—but then again, his dick should not be popping up in his pants. Too bad neither was cooperating with him.

He brought a big tray into the living room with the salad he'd been preparing when she woke up, along with a bottle of unopened water, bowls, silverware, and dressing.

Setting the tray down on the coffee table, he handed her the water, which she reluctantly took but didn't open.

"You need to hydrate and get the drugs out of your system."

He then scooped a bowl of salad for her, but she didn't take it, so he set it down in front of her, then scooped a bowl for himself.

"The steaks are still marinating, but they won't take long to cook once I put them on the grill." He eyed her not eating and sighed. "Come on, Reagan, you've got to be hungry. You have my word I won't drug you again."

Wordlessly, she reached over and took the bowl of greens he'd dished for himself and switched them with the bowl he'd given her, then waited until he poured the dressing and used the same one.

He winked at her with a grin as he took a bite. She rolled her eyes, but a smile escaped her lips. He wished they weren't having to go full throttle to Colombia; it would have been nice to take the scenic route and get to know her. Every inch of her.

Too bad things weren't different. But if they had been, they'd never have met in the first place. He didn't spend his down time in Fargo, and he doubted she'd been anywhere he did spend his free days.

"So are you really a hockey fan or were you just making that up to throw me off guard?"

"Boston Bruins, baby," he said with a big grin.

She rolled her eyes—again, something that made him to want to kiss her.

"What? Who's your team?"

"The Fargo Force."

Now it was his turn to roll his eyes.

"I mean, a real team. A team in a league that could actually win the Stanley Cup."

"Oh, well, as far as NHL, the Wild, of course."

"Call me when they've won a championship."

"Pffft. Whatever. Because Boston's done so much since 2011."

The fact that she knew her hockey and was verbally sparring with him about his team was making his dick hard. Hell, everything about this woman made his cock ache. It was going to be a long fucking four nights, and yet he knew it wasn't going to be nearly long enough.

"Eat your salad," he growled with amusement.

"You're just mad because you know it's true."

"I've got two words—six championships. How many have the Wild won again?" He held his hand up to his ear. "What's that? Do I hear crickets?"

"Whatever," she huffed, but ate her salad, which he was happy to see. "Just you wait," Reagan told him confidently, emphasizing her words while waving her fork in small circles at him. "Our time's coming."

Oh, sassy pants, I wish our time was coming, too.

****

Reagan

They finished eating, and she helped him clean up before he locked her in the captain's quarters while he took food to the skeleton crew. Then, she knew, he was going to call Kennedy back.

"You need to rest. You're going to be groggy until the drugs are out of your system," he told her with a smile when she protested being made to return to her room.

Reagan was a little miffed when he closed the door behind him, but he was right—she was still tired. The soft pajamas she found in the drawers, along with the comfy bed, calmed her ire—although not for long, since having to pee every fifteen minutes from all the water he'd made her drink at dinner was not conducive to sleeping.

It was odd how concerned he was about her. Odd, yet charming, and kind. The man confused her. She was actually enjoying her time with him, and that felt like a betrayal to her sister. Then there was the matter of him threatening to kill her.

And he would have killed Kennedy, there was no doubt about that.

So, no—she couldn't *really* like him, she was just pretending to keep herself safe until he released her. That's all.

As tired as Reagan was, she still managed to put her ear to the door to try to catch his conversation with her sister. She was only able to make out bits and pieces, but could tell his tone was clipped and much harsher than it'd been when he talked to Kennedy earlier.

She heard him end the call and walk toward her door. She scrambled to get away from the door and into bed, but he never came back in.

Why was she disappointed he didn't come in?

She definitely needed to get some rest. It had to be the drugs still in her system making her want his company. Maybe more than just his company.

Okay, that's the lack of sex over the last year talking.

Reagan managed to sleep for several hours, but then was wide awake at two in the morning, thinking about Mason and wondering where he was sleeping. If she had been more of a brat, would he have slept in the captain's quarters with her? That might be in the cards for tomorrow. She wasn't feeling as fuzzy now and her spunk was coming back.

What had he called her? *Sassy pants.*

He was going to see how sassy she could get.

She crept to the door and tried turning the knob. Kennedy had always said, "You never know unless you try"— although even if she found the door unlocked, she wasn't sure how much good it would do her. She couldn't exactly escape in the middle of the Pacific, and sending an SOS would be fruitless. He was in the CIA; it wasn't as if anyone would come to her rescue—other than Kennedy. Besides, calling for help would mean having to explain why he'd taken her in the first place, and Reagan wouldn't blow her sister's new identity.

Still, she was feeling restless and felt like exploring.

Examining the lock, she determined she could pick it. Reagan had grown up hungry most of her young life. Back in Fargo, the Jones girls had become masters at opening doors without keys before they even hit their teens; breaking in somewhere had often meant the difference between eating that day or going hungry. She had been almost as good at it as Kennedy was, although she was probably a lot more out of practice than her sister now. It'd been a long time since she'd picked a lock, but it had to be like riding a bike, right?

She fished around for something to help her. Why did she have to wear her hair down today? When she had it up, there were always at least a few bobby pins in it, but not today. Reagan fished through all the drawers in the both the bedroom and the bathroom and came up empty-handed. She was about to give up and go back to bed when she noticed a brochure for the satellite TV onboard, and the salesman's card paper-clipped to it.

Jackpot.

She was out the door and tiptoeing through the yacht in a matter of minutes. It was eerily quiet at night; even the ocean seemed to be asleep. She explored the entire ship, except for the crew's quarters and the rooms near where she thought Mason was holed up. She didn't want to risk being caught and having to explain to him that she was out of her locked room just because she was bored. There was no malicious intent.

Reagan lay on a chaise lounge on the main deck, looking out at the dark skies and wondering what the hell was in store for her over the next few days. She felt guilty for getting kidnapped and forcing Kennedy back into a clandestine mission; her sister had a daughter and husband to think about now. She also felt ashamed for being attracted to Mason.

How was that even possible? Sure, he had a dimple that made him look like a charming grownup schoolboy when he smiled, and his muscles were drool-worthy. And he was funny, intelligent, and interesting, and dare she say kind? But still...

How could she consider him kind when he had threatened to kill her? And he'd planned on offing her only sister. She couldn't reconcile what he was on paper to how he was when she was with him.

He's an agent; they're trained to be the best actors there are. Her sister had told her as much the few times she'd talked about her life in the CIA.

Reagan just needed to keep her wits about her until they reached land, then pray that her sister would be able to help him rescue his brother, and that he'd keep his word and release her.

That was a lot of contingencies to her leaving the ship alive.

Chapter Five

Mason

He watched on the video cameras as she snuck out of her room in the white satin pajamas he'd left for her in the drawers. At first, he was going to storm after her, but became mesmerized by her image as she tried to stealthily maneuver her way around the ship. How she managed to look so damn sexy in a nightshirt and shorts, he had no idea, but she did, so he decided to just observe her for a while. The sight of her sneaking on deck was vaguely familiar yet different; it wasn't like she was going to jump overboard like her sister had.

He couldn't help but smile as he tracked her throughout the yacht, and he chuckled out loud when she paused in the kitchen to nibble on some Oreo cookies from the pantry. She then began opening drawers and doors to poke around, moving on to explore the unoccupied parts of the ship.

When she fell asleep on the lounger on deck, he came out to wrap a blanket around her, staring at her features a long time after tucking the corners around her shoulders and fighting the urge to kiss her cheek. He wondered what it would feel like to wake up with her in his arms after breathing in her scent all night. She had a sexy, unique smell that reminded him of the beach and summer.

She turned onto her side and snuggled further under the covers, making a little whimpering noise as she did, and once again, his dick moved.

I am so fucked. How is this possible?

His auto mechanic father's words echoed in his mind: *When it happens, it'll hit you like combustion. And there won't be a damn thing you can do about it.*

Like he said, he was so fucked.

Suddenly, her breathing changed and her eyes flew open, her face full of fear when she noticed him. He must have looked like a lurker—and technically, that's what he was. Reagan sat up like a shot, the blanket falling to her waist.

"I—I can explain."

Against his better judgment, he sat down next to her and put a hand on her shoulder. She stiffened under his touch, which shouldn't have bothered him as much as it did. He'd meant to calm her, but it seemed to have had the opposite reaction. Under normal circumstances, he would have welcomed that. Fear in a hostage was a good thing, but he was at war with himself over her being afraid of him.

"Hey, it's okay. I had a feeling that flimsy latch wasn't going to keep you in there for very long. I've seen what your sister can do with a lock—I should have known it ran in the family. Besides, where are you going to go?"

"I could have snuck in and killed you."

Well, shit.

Of course, if he was thinking with his brain instead of his damn dick—or worse, his heart—he would have considered that. He'd been trained for that to be his first assumption, yet the idea had never even crossed his mind with sweet Reagan Elizabeth Jones. Her drawing it to his attention reminded him she had sass too.

As if his fingers had a mind of their own, he swept the hair from the nape of her neck, then he leaned in and said softly, "That would have been a bad idea. Although I might have enjoyed the fight."

He couldn't help but notice her nipples stiffen under the white satin—she wasn't wearing a fucking bra, and he bit back a groan. *This is so bad.*

Standing abruptly, he ordered, "Get back to your room, Reagan. Try to stay put until breakfast, otherwise I'll put you over my knee."

Just the thought of her round ass in the air as his hand came down... *Fuck!*

His grip on her elbow was a little tighter than it probably needed to be as he unceremoniously yanked her toward the stairs, and she wrenched away from his grasp.

"Ow! Let go! I can do it without you manhandling me."

He was manhandling her when he just wanted to be holding her. He needed to get his shit together.

"Walk!" he boomed, ignoring her complaints.

"You're grouchy in the morning," she sassed, then tucked her tail and scurried forward like she was expecting a swat on her butt. Looking over her shoulder at him with a grin when she didn't receive it, she walked into the living area leading to the captain's quarters.

"I'll come get you for breakfast at eight. Don't come out until then."

"Such a grump," she muttered as she closed the door behind her. He locked the door again, although he didn't know why he was wasting his time; she'd proven it was useless. He'd have to see about finding a better way of keeping her confined. One that didn't involve him pinning her body underneath his.

****

Reagan

That man was infuriating. And sexy as hell with his messy bedhead, plaid blue and green pajama pants, and plain white t-shirt emphasizing his muscular arms and linebacker chest.

He'd started out sweet, then quickly turned pissy after she'd pointed out that she could have snuck in his room and killed him.

Fat chance of that happening. She couldn't even kill a spider, not to mention she couldn't just squash Mason Hughes with her shoe.

And 'Although I might have enjoyed the fight?' What the hell did he mean by that?

She hastily washed in the tiny standup shower off her bedroom. She would have loved a long, luxurious time under the hot water, but she wasn't sure how much fresh water was available on board, so she decided to make it quick.

As she stood naked in the cabin, going through the new clothes she'd found in the drawers last night, she suddenly felt like she was being watched. Covering her private parts with her hands, she looked around for any monitoring devices, then dressed quickly and waited for Mason to come retrieve her for breakfast.

She had barely sat down on her newly-made bed when there was a knock at the door. His appearance so soon after her being ready did not alleviate her worries about cameras in her stateroom.

Reagan marched to the door and flung it open, hand on her hip.

"Are there cameras in here?" she demanded.

He silently observed her, as if waiting for further outbursts. When there were no more forthcoming, he simply said, "No. Not in there."

"But there are on the ship?"

He tilted his head slightly, as if annoyed. "You know there are. You heard me telling Kennedy that I watched her escape."

"Oh my god, this is where you had her?"

Suddenly she felt sick to her stomach. She was probably sleeping in the same room they'd kept her sister while she waited for her impending execution, like who knew how many countless others. How many people had died on this yacht?

"So is this like your floating death ship?"

He'd started to guide her toward the kitchen and paused. "Huh?"

"This yacht. Murder in style or something?"

"I already told you, sassy pants, I'm not going to hurt you. Unless you give me reason to."

"But you were going to kill my sister. On this very boat."

"Yachts are ships, not boats," he corrected as he steered her forward.

"I think you're missing the point."

They reached the kitchen and she sat down, staring at him while silently willing him to reply.

He looked up at the ceiling with a sigh.

"I'm not sure what response you're looking for, Reagan."

Tell me you weren't going to assassinate my sister, you idiot.

"Would you have really killed Kennedy?" she whispered.

"Personally? Probably not. But I was the leader of the team that was sent to extract her. We did, and were ordered to wait for further instructions. Those orders came in to eliminate her."

She covered her mouth with her hand as she fought back a sob.

"You would have let her *die*," she hissed. "And now you want her help *saving* your brother?"

He sighed again, running his fingers through his now-combed hair.

"Look, Reagan. I didn't love the orders when they came through. I'd read Kennedy's file—she was an exemplary Marine and kick-ass agent as far as I could tell. But I just assumed she had decided to flip sides, and my allegiance is to the agency. But, at the same time, I also know what a numbskull Agent Robinson is—and I let him take her out of the servants' quarters alone. And I didn't stop her when I saw her traversing the hall by herself toward the deck. So maybe my subconscious was talking to me. But, at the end of the day, I would have followed orders."

"Yet now you're willing to disobey them."

"I'm not pretending to be holier-than-thou. I recognize that I'm the typical 'until-it-happens-to-me' guy. But it *has* happened to me, or at least someone I care about, and I'm fortunate enough to have the means to do something about it."

She scoffed. "And you had to kidnap me in the process. What if my sister hadn't accepted your *proposal*? Then what would you have done with me?"

Mason shrugged unapologetically. "I was betting on Kennedy caring as much about you as I do my little brother."

She persisted. "But what if she hadn't?"

He stepped into her personal space and looked down at her with a smirk that showed off his dimple, eyes twinkling. She could smell the soap from his shower and the mint from his toothpaste.

"Then I guess I would have had to find something else to do with you."

That should not have made her stomach get butterflies and her lady parts tingle, but here they were, fluttering and zinging.

"Like what?" she asked, way too breathlessly for her liking.

He stared at her mouth for a moment then stepped away, bringing a closed fist to his mouth and coughing.

"You know—cooking, cleaning, laundry."

She knew there was a ninety percent chance he was teasing her, yet her feelings were still hurt that he didn't say something like 'personal sex slave.'

What is wrong with me? I wouldn't sleep with him if he was the last man on the planet.

That was her story, and she was sticking to it.

Throughout her life, Reagan had been told she needed to work on her poker face. She was sure her disappointment was showing. To save her pride, she rolled her eyes and snarked, "I'd be sure to put extra starch in your underwear."

That made him laugh out loud and shake his head, muttering, "Sassy pants," as he took out royal blue ceramic mixing bowls from one of the cabinets to make breakfast.

"Can I help?"

He shook his head. "I actually enjoy cooking. It's kind of my stress reliever."

"You're going to make some woman very happy someday." The pang of jealousy that it wouldn't be her led her to add, "Or man. I guess I shouldn't just assume in this day and age."

It was obvious she was baiting him, but he dutifully took it while he whisked eggs in the bowl.

"I like women, sweetheart. A variety of them. Someday I'll settle down, but not anytime soon." He poured the contents into a heated frying pan, and they made a sizzling noise.

"Well, for your sake, I hope you get tested on a regular basis, Mr. Variety-Pack."

The corners of his mouth went up, even as he concentrated on making sure not to burn the eggs.

"I do. But I always wear a condom. Without fail."

"So no chance of little mini-Masons running around in the world, then?"

He looked away from his task to stare poignantly at her. "Not yet."

She drew a sharp breath in, but quickly caught herself and tried to sound nonchalant as she replied, "Oh. Well, I'm sure you've got plenty of time. But how will you choose from all your flavors of the month?"

"My dad assures me that I'll know when the right one comes along."

"So then what? You don't really expect me to believe you'd be content with one flavor for the rest of your life. What if you ended up with something like plain ol' vanilla?" *Like me?*

"I happen to like vanilla. It's delicious. And it's versatile, so you never get bored with it. You can add different sauces and whipped cream to keep it interesting. Maybe a banana every now and again. Then there's sprinkles... and don't forget the nuts and cherry."

"And you'd be happy with that? Even if the cookies and cream looked delicious?"

Were they really using ice cream as a metaphor for women?

"Nope. Once I decide to quit sampling and choose a flavor, I'm sticking with that. Forever."

He slid the eggs from the pan onto a plate, added two slices of toast he'd just buttered, and handed it to her.

"This looks delicious, thank you."

"If you're good today, I'll make you huevos rancheros tomorrow," he said with a wink. "If you're naughty, well..."

She cocked her head as she asked hopefully, "Yes?"

The CIA agent seemed to be caught off-guard at her asking him to continue that thought, but grinned when he replied, "I'll put you over my knee, and then make you eat cantaloupe for breakfast."

"I like cantaloupe," she challenged.

Mason's eyebrows went up in surprise, and his smile returned.

"Be careful what you wish for, sassy pants," he warned.

Chapter Six

Mason

Little Miss Reagan Jones was going to be a test of his willpower, he had no doubt. The desire to spank her or fuck her, or both, was strong.

As strong as the temptation to fall in love with her.

How could he not? She was spunky, interesting, smart, beautiful, and his dick seemed to have decided it'd found its soulmate, because it was standing at attention whenever she was around.

He'd dated a lot of beautiful, interesting women throughout his life, but something about Reagan Jones was electric.

Combustion.

AC/DC's song "Thunderstuck" began to play in his head. Yeah, that about summed it up.

And he needed to quash it. It'd help if she'd stop being so damn endearing. Because when she was, he became completely undone, letting his guard down, and wanting her to know the real him—to like him, even. Then he ended up doing stupid shit.

In his profession, he couldn't afford to make mistakes.

And certainly not now, when his brother's life was depending on him keeping his wits about him. He was just going to have to avoid spending time with her. Something she insisted on making difficult.

****

Watching her on his monitors, he knew it'd been a mistake to give her back her bag after he'd checked it for weapons or another cell phone, because there she was in her fucking white and yellow polka dot bikini that barely collectively covered an inch of skin. Her hair was piled high on her head as she rubbed suntan lotion on her body in the same lounger she'd fallen asleep in earlier.

This shit wasn't fair. At all.

She knew what she was doing to him, too, he was sure of it.

Mason adjusted himself—then, as if his feet had a mind of their own, he was making his way above deck.

This is not avoiding her, dumbass. He hadn't even made it two hours. *Pathetic.*

"Hey, you need to be careful. The sun is a lot stronger here in the Pacific than in Fargo."

"I made sure to put some sunscreen on, but I missed my back. Do you mind?"

She handed him the bottle, their fingers brushing, then turned her back toward him, not allowing him an opportunity to say no.

As his hands glided over her back and shoulders, he briefly closed his eyes. Her skin was like silk, and his large hands seemed even bigger against her tiny body. He felt her skin break out into tiny goosebumps at the same time as his cock began to push against his zipper. When he began rubbing the lotion just above her hips, he paused for a fraction of a second as he fought the urge to move his hands around her tiny waist and pull her against him.

"Wow, you're really good at this. Think I could talk you into giving me a massage sometime?"

She was fucking with him; she had to be, and he didn't like it one bit. He was hanging on by a thread as it was; she didn't need to taunt him.

He stood abruptly and told her, "All set," then tried to subtly adjust his dick before heading toward the stairs, calling over his shoulder, "Don't stay out all day, and make sure you drink lots of water. The salty air is drier than you realize."

Mason didn't give her a second glance and made his way to his office. He'd observe the monitors periodically to make sure she was behaving, but he was done fantasizing about her. It was unprofessional as fuck and would do a lot more harm than good. He needed to check his email to see if Agent Jones had sent the revisions to her plans that he'd suggested. Anything to keep his mind off the red-haired siren in the bikini.

And yet, there he was—watching her. Fantasizing about her. Sexually, sure—but there was more to it, and that's what had him so discombobulated. Because he was seeing her in a veil, or wearing his shirt when she came down to breakfast, or holding his hand as they walked along the streets of Paris. He was thinking about taking her to all his favorite places and showing her the world.

This was very bad, indeed.

****

Reagan

Could that man be any more hot and cold? The short answer was no. No, he could not.

One minute she thought he was attracted to her; the next he acted like she repulsed him.

Freaking pick one, man.

She preferred him being repulsed by her; when he acted interested he was far too tempting. Giving into temptation with him would be such a slap in the face to Kennedy; there's no way she'd be able to look at herself in the mirror if she did that to her sister. She didn't care how sexy his muscles were or adorable his dimple was. Or that when he rubbed suntan lotion on her back, she wanted to crawl into his lap and purr like a cat while begging him to touch her all over.

Damn, she really needed to find a man once she got back to Fargo. She hadn't been touched all over in—well, forever.

Pulling the Renee Rose and Lee Savino book from her bag, she became lost in the sexy world of bad-boy alphas. Forget Mason Hughes; she had werewolf shifters to fantasize about. Maybe they'd come to her rescue.

She dozed off under the afternoon sun, dreaming of the CIA Agent. They'd had amazing sex in her dream—although it wasn't detailed; it was one of those things she just *knew*—and now they were dressed for a cocktail party that they were late to, but they were in a rowboat in the middle of Pelican Lake with no oars.

The Fargo version of *up a creek without a paddle*?

She opened her eyes to a big shadow blocking the sunlight.

"You've had enough sun today, Reagan. Get dressed and make yourself some lunch."

She leisurely extended her limbs out in a full-body stretch, moaning out loud as she did, then slowly sat up with a welcoming smile. *This hostage gig wasn't so bad so far.* Mason frowned back at her, shoving the cover-up he was holding in his hand at her.

"Put this on. You're going to get sunburned."

"I used plenty of sunblock; I think I'm okay."

Reagan gathered her things and stood. She took the terrycloth garment from him, but instead of putting it on, she stuffed it in her bag, then followed him below deck.

"Can I make you something, too?" she asked, glancing backward at him as she opened the pantry, holding the doors wide with both hands while she contemplated the selection.

"No," he replied curtly. "I have work I need to do; I'll eat later."

Without another word he was gone.

She shrugged, looking back at the contents while trying not to take his aloofness personally.

"Whatever, dude," she mumbled out loud, and pulled a blue box of Kraft Mac n' Cheese from the shelf.

Chapter Seven

Mason

She didn't even have the courtesy to put a damn cover-up on when she entered the kitchen. No, she had to stand there looking sexy as fuck with her freckled, sun-kissed skin, and that body that was made for him to do all sorts of naughty things to. Right down to her goddamn adorable pink toes. Her tits in that halter bikini top had his fingers itching to *oops!* untie it and let them spill into his waiting palms. Then she had to turn around at the pantry and show him her luscious ass...

He'd had to get the hell out of the kitchen before he stripped her naked and fucked her senseless on the granite island counter.

His cock was screaming, *Go back!*—along with his heart—but his head was commending him. Just two and half more days and they'd be in Colombia; he'd rescue his brother and then send her on her way with her big sister. He'd never have to see her again.

That thought shouldn't make his chest ache, but it did— to the point that he was physically rubbing it when she knocked quietly on his open door, then walked in with a bowl of macaroni and cheese and a turkey sandwich on a wooden tray. She'd had enough consideration for him to put on a pair of shorts, but she was still killing him softly in that yellow bikini top with white polka dots.

"Hey, I brought you some lunch."

When he didn't respond right away, she teased, "I promise I didn't drug it or even spit in it. See?" then made a show of taking a bite of the macaroni. Her lips wrapped around the fork only added to his torture.

Looking away quickly before he sprouted full wood, he grunted, "Thanks," then resumed looking at the documents Kennedy sent him, pretending to be completely absorbed in them instead of noticing her scent filling his office.

Mason expected her to take the hint and leave; he should have known better. He hadn't nicknamed her 'sassy pants' for nothing.

"So, what are you working on?" she asked, invading his personal space and leaning over him to try and catch a glimpse at his computer screen. All he had to do was turn his head and his mouth would be on her tits.

"Just looking at your sister's plan," he said, switching off the monitor and spinning around in his chair in the opposite direction with his arms crossed, forcing her to step back to avoid the corner of his chair hitting her knees when he came the full one hundred eighty degrees. "Do you need something?"

"Oh, um, no. I just brought you lunch."

"I know. You told me that."

"Well, um, aren't you going to eat it?"

Now he was suspicious, and he narrowed his eyes at her.

"Why? I thought you said you didn't drug it. Did you poison it instead?"

It was her turn to narrow her eyes.

"What? No, of course not!"

"So what's so important that I try it?"

"Because I wanted to know if you liked it, asshole," she said with disdain, then stormed out of the room.

Now he *felt* like the asshole she just accused him of being.

Following her out the door, he yelled after her, "Reagan, wait."

Of course she ignored him, as he had expected. He followed her through the yacht toward the kitchen and found her with her back to him at the kitchen sink, plugging it and adding dish soap when he walked in.

"Hey, Reagan. I'm sorry. Thanks for bringing me lunch. That was really thoughtful of you. I'm sorry if I was a jerk."

She shrugged but didn't say anything, just began washing dishes.

Mason wanted to pin her against the sink, take that damn top off her, and kiss her neck as he pleaded for forgiveness. Caress her curves, whisper in her ear, press his stiff cock against her ass so she knew how much he wanted her.

Bad idea, dude. She's your fucking hostage.

Although *hostage* didn't feel like an accurate descriptor of the situation anymore. She was more like *a guest against her will.*

Still, he needed to turn the fuck around, or he was going to do something he'd regret.

"I am sorry. Thank you again," he said quietly, then retreated back to his office.

****

Reagan

What a jerk.

She didn't know why she'd tried to do anything nice for him. It wasn't like it was even a big deal—it was a turkey sandwich and macaroni and cheese, for Chrissake—but she was trying to offer a gesture of goodwill, and he was rude. She was blaming the dream for her wanting him to like her. And her time on the yacht had been much more pleasant when he'd been kind to her. His being cold really bothered her, which was stupid. Who cared if he didn't want to be around her? Not her.

This was a good thing. No more conflicted or guilty feelings about being attracted to him. He had solved that.

Reagan finished cleaning up and went to the living room, where she'd seen an entertainment system with a big screen television and Blu-ray player. Maybe there were movies she could watch.

She was curled up under a tan cashmere throw watching *This Means War*, a rom-com starring Reese Witherspoon, yummy Tom Hardy, and Chris Pine about two CIA agents who were best friends and discovered that they were dating the same woman. About a quarter way through the movie, Mason set down a bowl of chips on the coffee table, as well as boxes of movie theater candy and sodas, then sat on the end of other end of the couch and silently began to watch with her, laughing in the appropriate places and taking handfuls of chips to munch on.

He had a nice laugh, deep and contagious, and she found herself laughing in parts that would have normally elicited only a smile, simply because Mason was laughing. At one point, she shifted, and he tugged on her feet until they were in his lap, rearranging the blanket so it was once again covering her. Then he began to knead her ankles and the balls of her feet, and Reagan had to fight to keep from moaning audibly.

"That feels really good. My massage therapist doesn't even do that good of a job," she praised him, then instantly regretted speaking out loud, afraid to break whatever spell was between them. To her relief, he continued massaging, not replying other than to glance at her with a knowing smile, then resumed watching the movie.

Reagan kept stealing glances at his profile. If circumstances were different, she could definitely see herself getting serious with him. Or rather, someone *like* him. Not him. Definitely not him.

He disrupted her thoughts when he stood and offered her his hand, his expression sober.

"I'm sorry to have to do this, Reagan."

She gulped and tried to withdraw her hand from his grasp.

"Do what? Are you going to kill me?"

"What? No—of course not."

She quickly glanced around, looking for something to use as a weapon or a way to escape.

"Oh, because you'd tell me if you were going to kill me, right?" Her voice sounded shaky, even to her own ears.

He pulled her closer to him, wrapping his arm around her waist and whispering in her ear, "I'm not going to hurt you. I promise."

She felt his hard cock under his jeans against her bare stomach, and her nipples became equally as stiff. Her body was a fucking traitor.

"But I have to tie you up and gag you before I call your sister. It seems she needs to be reminded that I mean business."

"You just said you wouldn't hurt me."

He winked at her.

"She doesn't need to know that, now does she?"

It wasn't like Reagan was a willing participant in deceiving Kennedy, but it didn't matter—it still felt like it.

Maybe she should have put up more of a fight when he tied her arms behind her back, her boobs thrust forward on display in her bikini top. Or kicked at him as he tied her feet together, or moved her head side to side when he put the rag around her mouth. But no, she just complacently let him bind and gag her.

Tears of guilt began to stream down her cheeks when Kennedy's beautiful face appeared on the phone screen.

"Oh, baby sister, I'm so sorry." Keni's voice was calm but Reagan knew by her tone she was in distress.

Mason turned the screen to face him. "Good evening, Agent Jones. I just wanted to remind you what's at stake."

"You harm a hair on her head—" Kennedy started, and Mason began to demonstratively caress Reagan's shoulders, trailing down between her breasts. She closed her eyes, willing herself not to melt into his touch. What this man was doing to her wasn't fair.

"I'm not planning on hurting her. Not yet, anyway." Mason's chuckle was sinister. "Not when there's so many other things I'd rather do."

"Reagan. Listen to me. I promise, I will get you out of there."

"It'll be easy to do, Agent Jones. Just pretend your sister's well-being is dependent on my brother's well-being."

"Fine, Mason. You've made your point. I'll be in Colombia in the morning. Dante will be flying down with me in the event that we can use his contacts."

The memory of how her sister met Dante came to the forefront. She'd been on assignment—with Dante being part of the assignment. Then Kennedy fell in love with him and threw everything off kilter. Some of the guilt Reagan was feeling because of her attraction to Mason dissipated. Besides, she needed to keep Mason attracted to her, right? He'd be less apt to really hurt her that way.

He removed his hands from Reagan's chest, and she instantly wished he hadn't.

"I'm glad you see things my way. I'll be in touch. Don't worry—your sister is safe, for now. I won't touch her again, unless you give me a reason to."

How fucked up was it that part of her was willing her sister to do just that?

"I love you, Reagan. Just hang in there, baby sister."

She wanted to alleviate her sister's worry, and the only thing she could think to do in her predicament was wink at her.

A slow smile formed on Kennedy's lips.

"Talk to you tomorrow, Agent Hughes."

Chapter Eight

Mason

After he untied her, he set her on her feet and assured her again, "I would never touch you, Reagan. That was just for show."

You could have knocked him over with a feather when she squeaked out, "Why not? What's wrong with me?"

He held her by the shoulders and looked down into her green eyes.

"Not a damn thing, sweetheart. You're perfect."

"Then why do you act like touching me would be catastrophic?"

The corners of his mouth turned up in a slight smile.

"Because you're way too good for me, sassy pants."

"It's because you think of me as boring ol' vanilla, isn't it?"

He nodded. "Yeah, you are vanilla. But I told you before, vanilla happens to be my favorite flavor."

"So, why?"

Was she really asking why he wasn't making a move on her?

He sat down on the bed, and tugged her onto his lap. *Bad fucking idea.* She fit perfectly against his chest, he couldn't help but imagine how she'd fit underneath him—naked.

"Oh, my tiny little sprite..." He let out a deep sigh. "You are my dream woman. If I had you in my bed, I don't think I'd be willing or able to let you go."

She appeared to bite back a smile and looked down. "You're just saying that to make me feel better."

He tipped her chin with his knuckle so she was looking at him.

"Do you know how hard it's been these last thirty-six hours to keep my hands to myself? Especially with you wearing this fucking bikini?"

She reached behind her and untied the strings, exposing her firm tits.

"Is that better?"

Dear God, she was even more beautiful than he'd imagined.

"Reagan..." he growled in warning, gripping her hip to keep himself from touching her breasts. Fuuuuck, how he wanted to dip his head and suck on her pink nipples.

She reached between them and began to stroke his hard cock over his pants.

"Yes?" she asked innocently.

He pulled her hand away from his crotch.

"This is a bad idea, sweetheart."

Her face fell and, just like earlier, Mason felt like an asshole.

Now he was smack dab in a dilemma. She was obviously willing, and his dick was more than ready to take things further, but his head was telling him *absolutely not*, while his heart was saying, *maybe things could work out.*

But he knew damn well things could never work out between them.

Then you'd at least have the memories of being with her, which is better than nothing.

He knew deep down that was bullshit logic, but at the moment, he didn't care. The justification worked for the time being. Regret could come tomorrow, or in a few days—whenever his brother was safe and he had to let her go.

And he was going to let her go. That much he knew.

Mason leaned down and captured her lips with his. Her soft mouth was warm with a hint of the Junior Mints candy she'd nibbled on during the movie. Their tongues tangled as she pressed her chest against him. Breaking the kiss, he caressed her cheek with the back of his index finger, searching her jade eyes.

"Are you sure about this?" he whispered.

She stared back at him, and her voice didn't waver when she replied, "Positive."

"I have something in my room. Wait here."

He went to his cabin, scolding himself the entire time about what a bad idea this was while he searched his bag until he found the box of condoms he was looking for. His cock was essentially giving his brain the middle finger. There was no doubt which organ was in charge. Should he bring the whole pack or just grab a couple? He opted to bring the box and leave them in the nightstand in her stateroom. For next time.

There will be no next time, his brain reprimanded. His cock and his heart laughed, *Yeah, sure.*

As he hurried back to her quarters, the thought entered his head that she might have changed her mind while he was gone. A sense of relief came over him when he walked in and found her sitting up in bed with the covers tucked around her chest.

"Last chance," he advised.

The little minx looked up at him through her lashes and smiled seductively while pulling back the covers in invitation, revealing her beautiful, naked body.

He stared at her for a moment, mesmerized.

"Fuck, you're gorgeous."

She shyly looked down and bit her bottom lip, trying to disguise her grin.

He kicked off his shoes but didn't bother getting undressed before lying down beside her and pulling her body into his. She felt... perfect. Like she was made just for him.

Reagan tugged on his shirt, and Mason sat up to let her slip it over his head. She wrapped her arms around his back and pulled him down on top of her. He caught himself on his forearms, but his torso enveloped her petite frame. She traced the rough scars on his back then moved her fingernails softly down his spine.

"I've wanted to feel you underneath me since the moment I first laid eyes on you," he confided, staring at her lips while brushing her hair from her shoulder.

"Me too," she replied breathlessly as she lifted her hips upward to press against his throbbing cock.

"You have no idea what you've done to me, do you?"

She moved her pelvis in small circles on his dick with a devilish smile.

"I sort of have an idea."

"You've put a spell on me, Reagan Elizabeth Jones. There's no other explanation. You're a witch, a temptress, and I'm helpless to do anything but obey."

"Then you should stop talking and take your pants off."

"As you wish," he said with a smirk and pulled his pants down his thighs.

"Underwear, too."

"So demanding for such a little thing," he chuckled but did as she requested.

He pulled her on top of him as he settled back down on the bed. They lay there naked, neither in a hurry to move. While she let him hold her, he relished how perfectly content he was in that moment. His sassy sprite was in bed with him; he could die a happy man.

Well, not quite yet. There were still some things he needed to attend to. Like her pussy.

Mason flipped her onto her back and took her mouth with his. His lips tenderly kissed hers, then she gently bit down on his bottom lip and darted her tongue in his mouth, seeking out his to tangle with. He took a deep breath before tilting his head and deepening the kiss, and she let out a soft moan that went straight to his already rock-hard cock.

He was dying to be inside her, but he also wanted to take his time and savor her. Moving his mouth down her neck, he wrapped his arms around her core and hugged her tight when she arched her back. Fuck, he loved how soft and curvy she felt under him.

He slid down her body and traced his tongue along one taut nipple, biting softly then suckling. Reagan gasped quietly when he licked the underside of her tit then drew his tongue across her chest to her other boob, where he worked in reverse, suckling, biting, and tracing.

She ran her fingers through his hair, clutching a handful to draw his head closer to her body as she bowed off the bed and groaned.

Mason began to kiss and gently suck her skin down to her stomach, dropping his hand between her thighs. He could feel the heat generating from her and had to purposefully will himself to slow down and not dive head first into her pussy.

Painstakingly, he moved his mouth over her mons, breathing in her delicious aroma, his mouth watering in anticipation. Pulling her lips apart with both hands, he peered at her beautiful wetness before darting his tongue up and down her labia then circling her knot until it was fat and peeking out from the hood.

Mason slid a finger inside her wetness and began to fuck her in rhythm with his mouth working her clit. Reagan whimpered as she moved her hips in harmony, spreading her legs farther to welcome him in deeper.

"Mmm, fuuuuck, you taste so good, sassy pants," he mouthed against her pussy.

He began to flick her clit faster with his tongue while increasing the tempo of his hand moving in and out of her cunt. Feeling her body heat rise and her breathing quicken while she tightened around his finger, he could tell she was close and increased his efforts. His redheaded sprite began to pant, "Don't stop." *Like that was going to happen.*

Mason's frantic pace soon paid off, and she began to quiver under his touch. Her body lurched forward, and he kept going until she pushed at the top of his head while trying to close her thighs.

He chuckled when he emerged from between her legs and saw the euphoric look on her face. Wiping his mouth with the top sheet, he moved up her body and wrapped her in his arms while she caught her breath.

"That was—" She gulped for air. "That was flipping amazing."

Even if she was exaggerating, he felt his ego inflate to twice its size—and it was already pretty big to begin with.

"Mmm, baby, I'm just getting started."

He ripped the black foil package and slipped the condom on, lining up at her entrance and pushing balls deep inside.

"Fuuuck, Reagan," was all he could mutter as he buried his face in her neck. Her tight pussy felt so damn good, he was afraid to move—worried he'd bust a nut right then. That would not be good for his ego, and probably not for his status as her lover either.

Slowly, he began to thrust in and out of her, developing a rhythm that had her whimpering and moaning. Mason was determined to make her come again before he did, and sat up on his knees in order to play with her sensitive clit while continuing to drive into her pussy.

He really wished he had some of that duration spray he'd seen advertised, especially when she started cooing about how good his cock felt inside her pussy. Sweet and sassy Reagan Jones talking dirty was so fucking hot, and he increased the pressure on her knot. She started to pant and thrust up against him, her cunt pulsating around his cock as she came undone. She was a beautiful sight to behold as she gasped and thrashed about, and he followed her climax with a roar of his own release. Gripping her hips, he spurted rope after rope inside the latex barrier, pausing briefly to treasure the moment before reluctantly pulling out of her.

He got out of bed and disposed of the condom before grabbing a hand towel for her. With a wink, he handed it to her and slid in beside her under the covers.

As she tended to herself, she looked over at him and gave him a shy smile.

"So now what?"

He tugged on her elbow to bring her back down next to him and wrapped his arm around her middle.

"Now, we nap."

He couldn't think of anything better—wiped out from sex and falling asleep next to the beautiful little nymph who'd worn him out. Then she sighed and softly kissed his chest, and he was pretty sure he'd just died and gone to heaven.

Chapter Nine

Reagan

It was dusk when she woke up in the king-sized bed alone. Taking a full body stretch, she couldn't help but smile broadly. She knew she should feel guilty or be filled with regret or something negative, but there was none of it. Just contented bliss and a satisfied feeling that she'd never felt after sex.

It had been freaking amazing.

Ah-*maze*-ing.

Wow, had it ever.

She hoped they'd get to do that again, and soon.

Reagan got dressed in black yoga pants and a gray t-shirt she'd found in the drawers, as well as the bra she'd worn onboard yesterday. She was happy to find her door unlocked so she could venture out to try and find Mason.

He was sitting behind a desk in the office with his phone to his ear. She knocked softly, and he looked up with a smile, winking at her and gesturing for her to sit in the chair opposite him while he continued talking.

"The captain says we're on schedule to get there in about thirty-six hours."

Pause.

"The arrangements should be in place for your arrival tomorrow."

Another pause, but he quickly glanced up at her.

"She's fine, Agent Jones. I assure you."

Pause.

He sighed then muttered, "I'll call you back."

Mason hung up and tossed his phone on the desk.

"Well, that was obviously your sister. We're going to call her back, and you're going to assure her you're unharmed and being treated well. I think it'd be in our best interest to not share *how* well, don't you?"

Part of her wanted to be honest with Kennedy. She wasn't ashamed of what she'd done, although maybe she should be. It *was* pretty slutty of her to sleep with a man she'd known less than forty-eight hours—particularly the man who kidnapped her and was forcing Keni out of retirement. Oh, and the same man who just happened to be the leader of the team that had also kidnapped her sister and been assigned to kill her.

Okay, he might be right about not telling Kennedy, but it still didn't sit well with her. Although technically, if she didn't say anything, she wouldn't be lying.

"You know, maybe you shouldn't let me really talk. Just let her see I'm okay but that's it. I hate the idea of being dishonest with my sister."

That made one corner of his mouth turn up, his blue eyes twinkling while his sexy dimple was on display.

"Come here."

She dutifully went to stand in front of him, and he snaked his arm around her waist and drew her into his lap. Kissing her hair, he murmured, "Just tell her you're okay and that I haven't hurt you. But try to act scared, or at least nervous. I'm sorry you're in this position. I'm sorry about the whole damn thing—but Marcus needs me. I hope you understand."

The funny thing was, she *did* understand. She'd do anything to help Kennedy if her sister were in trouble—including kidnapping and blackmail. And yet, Reagan felt like she was letting Keni put her life in danger because she thought her little sister had been kidnapped—which was technically true, but Reagan didn't believe for a second her own life was in danger—not at Mason's hands, anyway. Shouldn't Kennedy have all the facts before doing something so risky? She had baby Madison to think about now.

"You ready?" he asked as he squeezed her knee.

"Yep."

He patted the side of her thigh, indicating she should stand, and he followed.

"Let's call from the couch," he suggested.

She sat on the end of the sofa and turned to face him with a nervous smile.

"Ready?"

She nodded and he dialed, then turned the phone so the screen and camera were on her. Kennedy's anxious face appeared.

"Reagan! Oh God, honey. How are you holding up? Has he hurt you?"

"I'm fine, Keni. He's been nothing but kind—really."

Her sister narrowed her eyes.

"You were bound and gagged the last time I saw you."

She took a deep breath. Kennedy needed to know all the facts before making her decision to help Marcus.

"It was just for show. He cares about me—if you decide not to go through with this, he's not going to hurt me."

Kennedy closed her eyes and hung her head as she shook it.

"Oh, Reagan... Baby sister... He's a spy, honey. He's been trained to—"

Mason turned the phone to face him. Reagan didn't know if he was mad that she had revealed he wouldn't hurt her, but she needed her sister not to worry or feel obligated.

His grin was sinister and the hairs on her neck stood up when he told Kennedy, "Didn't you hear her, big sis? I *care* about her. She's in good hands," then clicked to end the call.

Had she really been played like that?

****

Mason

Goddammit.

He knew he should have just gagged her again when calling Kennedy back. But damn Agent Jones was being obstinate about ensuring he *hadn't harmed a hair on her sister's head* before moving forward.

What the fuck was he supposed to do? She couldn't know she was holding the trump card—that he'd never hurt Reagan.

Well, now his redheaded little cherry sprite thought he'd tricked her. The look on her face hurt his soul. *Fuck. Fuck. Fuck.* Why couldn't things ever just go as planned?

He dropped to his knees in front of where she sat on the couch and grabbed her hands. She didn't respond as he gripped her fingers, just left her wrists loose in his grasp like wet noodles.

"I *do* care about you, Reagan. And you're right—I would never hurt you, but you kind of put me in a bind with Kennedy. If I don't have any leverage with her, this isn't going to work." She didn't reply, and he abruptly let go of her hands and sat back on his heels, letting out an exasperated, "Dammit!"

She flinched at his outburst, only making him feel worse. Shaking his head, he said in a low voice, "This is my fault. I shouldn't have let you talk. I should have known better."

And he should have. But everything about this woman had taken his instincts and training and thrown them out the window.

"What happened between us earlier was real for me. Every second. I know you felt it, too, so you know I'm not lying about that."

"I don't know what to believe," she whispered as a lone tear escaped down her cheek. He brushed it away with his thumb and rested his forehead against hers.

"You know in your heart what's true."

"The problem is, I've never been a very good judge when it comes to men. Lack of a role model and all the things that come with having daddy issues, I guess. My sister could always point out the snakes. It took me a long time and many lessons learned to trust her judgment. She's never been wrong—not once."

Maybe this was a blessing in disguise. They were going to go their separate ways in, hopefully, less than two days. This would make it less messy.

Fuck that. He had two more days with her—he was going to cherish it, and it wasn't going to be spent with her thinking he was going to hurt her in the end. Not physically, anyway.

"Well, there's a first time for everything. She's wrong— I'm not going to hurt you, and you know it. You even said so yourself, with conviction, I might add."

She sat watching him without saying anything.

"What can I do to convince you?"

He wasn't expecting her response.

"Include me in the plan. I have a right to know what danger you're putting my sister in because of me."

Mason furrowed his brows.

"Explain what you mean by *include you.*"

"I don't mean putting me to work or anything like that. Just let me sit in on the strategy calls so I know what's going on. Let me look at what plans have been drawn up. Tell me who the players are."

He stared at her a long time before replying. She put her hand on her hip and raised her eyebrows as if daring him to say no. *So goddamn sassy.*

He shook his head wryly and let out a long sigh as he agreed. All his instincts and training went out the window when it came to Reagan Elizabeth Jones.

Chapter Ten

Reagan

Well, so much for doing *that* again. *Dang it.* She'd been looking forward to maybe sucking his cock next time.

She took a deep sigh as she lay fully clothed on top of the comforter on her bed and stared up at the ceiling. She hadn't expected him to acquiesce and let her be involved with his brother's rescue, so that had been an unexpected surprise. Now her head was swimming with all the intricate details he'd shared about how they expected things to occur, and the backup plan, and the backup plan to the backup plan.

Good grief, how did they keep it all straight?

There were a lot more players than she'd thought. In addition to Mason and Reagan, there were three members from Marcus' team who were willing to risk their jobs to get their work brother home safe, as well as someone named Jacob who was what they called a *fixer*, whatever the hell that was. He didn't seem to have an allegiance to anybody in particular but one could secure his services for the right price. And he could be trusted to know Kennedy was alive—the other three from Marcus' team were going to be kept in the dark about that.

She sat up like a shot and quickly made her way to Mason's office, where she'd left him after they'd eaten dinner in there.

"I have an idea," she said excitedly as she burst through his door.

He looked up from his computer monitor with a grin.

"What's your idea, sassy pants?"

"Use me instead of Kennedy for the bait. That way her cover doesn't get blown with Marcus or his teammates."

He was shaking his head before she'd even finished her thought.

"Not a chance. You're not trained for this work, Reagan. It was one thing to let you in on the plan, it's something completely different to let you be a part of the mission. There's no way in hell your sister would agree to it—let alone me. I appreciate your enthusiasm and willingness to help, baby, but you'd be a liability, not an asset out there."

"Number one—you don't get to call me baby. Number two—I'm more skilled than you think I am. I would certainly not be a liability."

Mason leaned back in his chair and folded his arms across his chest as he surveyed her standing her ground in front of his desk. His blue eyes twinkled when he asked, "Have you ever killed someone, tough stuff? With a knife? Or, hell, even a gun? How about strangled them with your bare hands?"

She glanced down briefly. "No, of course not."

"Well, sweetheart, that's probably what's going to be required. What did you think *neutralize* meant when I explained that part of the plan to you?"

She tried to hide her shock.

"I don't know... knock them unconscious? Tie them up?"

"So you think you could do that part?"

"Well, sure."

Mason shook his head, trying to disguise the smile on his face by pretending to rub his jaw.

"You're a jerk," she spit out before turning to leave. He quickly reached across the desk and grabbed her elbow to keep her from escaping, not letting go as he came around to where she stood.

"I'm not trying to be a jerk, but my little sprite, you're not qualified for this assignment. I'll bet you couldn't kill a mouse, let alone a man."

She didn't respond, just looked down at her bare feet to avoid thinking about what he was saying. She decided she liked the pink color of her toenail polish.

He sat down and pulled her into his lap while she offered a token resistance.

With his chin on her shoulder, he traced circles on her arm as he told her, "That's not a criticism. Your kind heart is something I admire and adore about you. I wouldn't want you to change a thing."

She leaned back to look him in the eye.

"So how is Keni qualified for this assignment? Has she killed someone before?"

Reagan could tell by the look on his face that she had. The corners of his mouth turned down in a frown, his eyes thoughtful.

"Your sister's file isn't my business to discuss."

Wow. Kennedy really is a badass.

"I'm not asking you to gossip about the details; I just want to know—how qualified is she?"

With a poker face, he tucked her hair behind her ear, simply offering, "Sufficiently."

Reagan was just now beginning to realize the extent of her sister's badassery.

"I had no idea," she whispered as she stared at the stapler on his desk. Looking back at him, she sat up straighter. "I mean, I guess I must have known, deep down. She'd go away for months at a time, and there'd be no way we could contact her. But it was that way when she was in the Marines, too, so it didn't seem strange. I just thought she was in locations where it wouldn't be feasible to communicate with her family. I never realized her missions were so dangerous—until we were told she'd drowned. I thought it must have been really bad for her to drown—she was always an amazing swimmer. She could swim to the island in Pelican Lake in practically one breath."

A slow smile formed on his lips.

"What?" Reagan asked.

He shook his head. "Nothing. That just explains some things; it's not in her file how strong a swimmer she is."

"Probably not. The swim coach practically begged her to join the team in high school, but she wanted to play basketball instead." She wrinkled her nose and giggled. "She turned out to be not very good."

"What about you? Did you play any sports?"

She shrugged. "No, sports cost money. Money we didn't have, and I wasn't athletically inclined enough for coaches to take a chance and offer me a scholarship like they did Keni. Luckily, the art teacher at my school took me under her wing and made sure I had enough art supplies to do my homework. When I won my first competition, she told me the supplies were part of the prize. It wasn't until after I'd graduated that I learned she'd paid for them out of her own pocket." Her eyes welled with tears at the memory, and she brushed them away with her fingertips. "What about you? You had to have played sports."

Mason grinned. "Football and baseball, although I was a better baseball player. I ended up playing catcher at a D2 school close to home."

"What school?"

"University of New Haven."

"Oh, that's cool."

She knew he could tell by her face she'd never heard of it but didn't want to be rude and say as much.

"It's okay, I'd never heard of it either until their recruiters came calling," he said with a chuckle and wink.

"Still, that's really impressive, Mason."

He shrugged humbly. "It's just throwing a ball; definitely nothing that requires talent like an art scholarship."

Reagan cocked her head. "Why would you say that? Playing a sport takes a lot of talent."

"But you were able to parlay your talent into a career."

"True, but you were able to use yours to pay for an education that translated into a career, so, I don't really see the difference."

"I guess. I just think you're über-talented, and I'm in awe."

She made a face.

"How do you know I'm *über-talented*?" She put air quotes around the phrase.

"I have Google, sweetheart. I saw your work in the Etherton Gallery."

She gulped, feeling her cheeks turn pink.

"You—you did? Why would you do that?"

He shrugged. "I was curious about you."

"When did you do that?"

"When you were napping."

After they'd had sex, he meant.

"I wasn't lying. You have bewitched me. I want to know everything about you, Reagan Elizabeth Jones."

"Don't you think that'll ruin the mystery? Then I'll just be plain ol' vanilla Reagan Jones, part-time graphic arts instructor from Fargo, North Dakota, whose idea of a wild, exciting night is bowling and margaritas with girlfriends at

Bowl-o-Rama. I lead a very dull life, Mason. The shine will wear off quickly once you get to know me."

He dropped a kiss on her forehead.

"I doubt that, sassy pants. I think you're beautiful, intelligent, spunky, and sexy as hell. That translates to anywhere you are—Fargo, North Dakota, Ensenada, Mexico, Paris, France, or somewhere in between. *You* fascinate me, not your geography."

"My point is I'm not very interesting. You would be bored with me in a month."

"I find that hard to believe."

She patted his cheek dismissively. "Believe it. Vanilla—no sprinkles."

He was tracing his fingers up and down her spine, watching her face carefully as he pulled her back into his web.

"I'll bring the sprinkles," he said softly.

Damn that man and his dimple. And blue eyes. And six-pack abs. And the wicked tongue that had done amazing things to her body earlier. Unspeakable, dirty things.

He leaned down and captured her mouth with his, and she let out a whimper. She was helpless against his charms. His lips were tender as he caressed her mouth with his. It wasn't exactly a chaste kiss, but it wasn't slam-her-against-the-wall passionate—it was loving.

When he broke the kiss and leaned his forehead against hers with his eyes closed, she whispered, "Are you going to kill me?"

"It guts me that you're afraid of me."

"Answer the question."

He tilted her chin so she was looking into his crystal blue eyes.

"I would die rather than hurt you, Reagan. I swear on my grandmother's grave—you have nothing to fear from me."

She believed him in her soul, but her head was screaming at her that she was an idiot.

****

Mason

He'd considered leaving her alone tonight, then realized he only had two more nights with her, so fuck that. He didn't even care if they had sex, as long as he could hold her all night. Wake up next to her. Touch her.

Mason patted her thigh. "Come on, sassy, let's go to bed."

Reagan leaned back, her eyebrows raised. "Sassy? What happened to sassy pants?"

He grinned as he lifted her off his lap. "It's a nickname for your nickname."

They walked to her cabin, and he followed her in, tugging his t-shirt over his head and kicking off his shoes as he walked toward the bed.

She looked at him, obviously startled. "Wait, you're sleeping here tonight?"

"Yeah, I am. We don't have to mess around, I just want to have you next to me so I know you're safe. But, for the record, I'm not opposed to messing around."

"Fat chance," she huffed as she walked into the bathroom with her pajamas—to change, he assumed.

"I've already seen you naked," he called through the door. "You can change in front of me, you know."

After a beat, the door opened, and she reappeared in the white satin pajama set. He hadn't noticed the heart-shaped buttons when he bought it. She looked so sweet and innocent; knowing she wasn't—just with him, in his mind, at least—he immediately sprung wood. Since he was only wearing white boxer briefs, it was kind of hard to disguise, and she pointedly looked down at his dick then at his face with a look that suggested, *Really?*

"Sorry, sassy, you look so pure in those white PJs—it makes me want to do dirty things to you."

They moved to either side of the bed, pulling back the covers at the same time.

"Well, there will be no more of that," she mumbled as she slid into bed, then reached up to switch the lamp on the nightstand off.

Mason covered the distance in the king-sized bed and pulled her into his body. He noticed she didn't put up a fuss.

"No can do, sweetheart. I only have two more nights with you. I wasted last night without you in my arms. Not making that mistake again."

"Fine." Her tone suggested she was annoyed, yet she turned over and snuggled into his side, wrapping her arm around his middle.

Was it possible to be in love with someone after only knowing them two days?

His father's words echoed in his ear.

Combustion.

How was he going to let her go in a few days?

He really had no idea, but he had no idea how he could possibly keep her either.

As pissed off as he'd been at his brother for pissing away his career over a woman, and possibly losing his life, Mason finally began to understand what had driven Marcus to such extremes. Because he knew without a doubt that he'd be willing to do the same for Reagan.

He tightened his grip on her hip. He was so fucked.

Chapter Eleven

Mason

Falling asleep with a rock-hard dick proved easier than he'd thought. He had some kick-ass sex dreams though—and she was anything but vanilla in them.

He wondered if he was still dreaming when he was roused from his slumber and found her between his legs, his cock out and in her hand as she studied it carefully. Mason wasn't sure if she knew that he was awake and watching her. She seemed enthralled with his member, subtly stroking the shaft then tentatively snaking her tongue out, licking around his helmet. He decided to pretend he was still asleep—he thought that would embolden her and help her continue. And he definitely wanted her to keep going.

She sucked his tip into her mouth, and he groaned out loud, keeping his eyes shut while he tried to pass it off that he was dreaming. The little minx took him deeper and deeper in her mouth until he heard her gag and slurp off him. Her grip became firmer as she stroked his slippery cock from the base while bobbing her head up and down. Her tongue skimmed along the vein on the underside of his dick, pressing hard, and he moaned again while lifting his hips slightly. She took him deep in her mouth again and held him there, not gagging this time. When she moaned around his shaft, he felt his cock flex in her throat and almost came right then.

She slowly pulled him from her mouth and resumed jerking him—faster this time—and her other hand cupped his balls. Mason warred with himself about letting her know he was awake. He worried she'd lose her brazenness, and that boldness was turning him the fuck on. He didn't want it to stop.

She returned her mouth to his cock while she continued stroking his shaft with one hand and manipulating his sac in her other hand like her own personal Baoding balls. He felt his climax start in his stomach, and began to pant heavier. She must have known he was close to coming because she squeezed him a little firmer, pulled faster on his cock, and sucked harder as she increased her tempo with her mouth.

Mason began to grunt, hoping to warn her he was about to come. To his surprise, Miss Self-Proclaimed Vanilla sucked him until he came, taking every drop of his cum in her mouth and swallowing. He would have loved to have seen that.

Next time.

Then a sad thought entered his brain. *Will there be a next time?* There had to be.

She gently pulled his underwear back up around him, making sure the waistband was straight, then nestled in against his side. He felt her smile against his chest, like she'd just completed a covert mission with him being none the wiser.

He was about to return the favor; then he heard soft snoring coming from his little sexy sprite.

In the morning.

****

Reagan

Oh my god, I totally gave Mason a blowjob in the middle of the night.

He had a really nice cock. Just the right size, straight, a little veiny, and the tip was perfectly shaped. The coloring was a nice contrast to his skin tone.

It was the graphic designer in her; what could she say? She noticed things like that.

When he saw she was awake, he rolled over and put his head to her chest, murmuring, "Good morning."

"Good morning."

She looked up at the ceiling and bit the corner of her bottom lip.

"Was it really slutty to wake you in the middle of the night like that?"

Reagan felt him chuckle.

"I didn't know if I was supposed to pretend it was all a dream."

Lifting her head slightly, she looked down at him.

"What? No, of course not. Is that why you barely responded? I thought maybe I was doing it wrong."

Plunking her head back on the pillow, she heard him mutter, "Definitely nothing wrong with your technique."

Well, that was a relief. She'd given head before—more times than a nice girl should be willing to admit—but she wasn't exactly confident in her abilities.

His fingers began to trace up her side to her breast until he was palming it and lightly massaging her flesh.

"One thing you need to know about me, sweetheart, is I'm all about reciprocation."

He moved to kneel beside her and pushed her nipple up between his lips. She decided she liked reciprocation—she liked it a lot.

He took his time swirling his tongue and biting down on her puckered flesh, alternating between each boob while kneading the opposite one. Was it possible to have an orgasm just from having your breasts played with? Because she was on the cusp.

She arched her back off the bed as she ran her fingers through his hair, moaning her approval of his attention.

One of his hands reached between her legs, and she knew he found her soaked; she was so turned on. He slid a finger inside her as his thumb circled her clit. Good grief, he knew exactly how to touch her. But she wanted more.

Stroking his leaking cock over his underwear, she begged, "Please fuck me, Mason. Please," before tugging on the waistband.

His cock sprang free, and he awkwardly pulled the boxer briefs down his thighs while she got onto all fours. Wiggling her behind at him, Reagan giggled, "Hurry!" and was rewarded with a slap to her ass as Mason leaned over and opened the nightstand drawer.

She heard the tearing of the package, followed by the sound of latex being slipped onto his dick, and she raised her hips higher in anticipation. Reagan was expecting his cock, which he satisfyingly thrust inside her, but she was not expecting him to wrap his arm around her waist and polish her clit as he fucked her.

"Oh yes. Fuck, that feels so good," she purred, widening her knees to encourage him to fuck her deeper.

He softly bit her back as he continued manhandling her clit while rhythmically pumping his cock into her pussy. Her body flushed hot, and Mason increased the pressure on her knot while quickening the pace. Soon, she was dropping her hips as the most delicious orgasm racked her body, making her shudder and spasm beneath him. He never let up on his ministrations until her pussy began to milk his cock, then he leaned back, gripped her hips and started to pound her from behind. The sound of their flesh slapping was erotic, and his balls hitting her sensitive clit had her falling over the edge just as he roared his release. His rumble as he came was so fucking sexy—and the fact that she'd caused him to do it made her feel like a goddess.

His hands came around her body to palm her tits and tug her tighter into him, his face burrowing into her neck.

"Fuuuuck," he growled right below her ear—the spot that always made her break out in goosebumps.

Mason chuckled when he felt the dots on her flesh and began to kiss down her spine as he gently pulled out of her.

"Hold that thought," he whispered, then disappeared into the bathroom. She collapsed on the bed with a thud, and rolled over when he returned moments later with a towel for her. This time, instead of handing it to her, he tended to cleaning her up himself.

He threw the towel on the ground and wrapped his arms around her as they lay on the bed, neither saying anything.

She wasn't sure what to say. She didn't think "Oh, hey, I think I might be falling in love with you, but I know that's a disaster waiting to happen since I'm outta here tomorrow, but thanks for the amazing sex in the meantime" was very appropriate. Even if it perfectly described how she was feeling.

He spoke first.

"What did you want to be when you were little?"

She wasn't expecting the question, which seemed to come from out of the blue, but answered without much thought.

"A school nurse, until I realized needles made me queasy. Our school nurse, Mrs. Feutz, always made sure Keni and I had eaten breakfast, and would bring us clothes when she'd notice one of our three outfits getting threadbare. She was the one who taught me how to use a washing machine and microwave and would slip food in my backpack on Fridays so I had something to eat on the weekends. She was my version of Mother Teresa. I don't know if I would have survived childhood without her. I owe her a debt of gratitude that I hope to be able to repay someday. I try to pay it forward whenever I can, you know? But I could never hope to make as big an impact on someone's life as she did mine."

She looked up at his somber face as he digested what she'd just shared. "What about you? What did you want to be?"

"Nothing as altruistic as that; wow. You were insightful and thoughtful even as a child."

"No," she corrected. "I was just neglected, and appreciative when people showed me and my sister any kindness."

"Is that why you and Kennedy are so close?"

"I don't know, maybe? We were a lot closer as kids. She grew up, joined the Marines, then the CIA—she was gone, well, all the time. I hadn't seen her in almost a year when I got the knock on the door that she'd drowned. It took her another six months to let me know she was alive."

She felt him nod against her hair.

"I don't mean to sound bitter, because I'm not. I understand why she couldn't let us know she was alive and had to stay hidden. And I don't begrudge her leaving Fargo and making a better life for herself... I just miss her. And I wonder if she misses me as much."

"I'm sure she does," he said in a low voice as he stroked her back with his fingertips.

"Anyway, you never answered my question. What about you? What did you want to be when you grew up?"

"A chef."

She sat up in order to have a better look at his face to see if he was teasing her.

"Nuh-uh. Shut up."

"I'm serious. Then as I got older, it morphed into owning a restaurant. Except there aren't a lot of culinary schools with baseball teams offering scholarships. My dad was a mechanic and my mom was a homemaker, so I went where I could get a free education."

"What did you major in?"

"Business administration. In case the restaurant thing panned out someday."

"So how on earth did you end up in the CIA?"

"You know... they were hiring," he said with a laugh.

"Seriously?"

"Yeah. Pretty much. I mean, there's also the patriotism factor and the feeling that you're doing something for your country, so I was an easy sell for the recruiters on campus when they were signing seniors up for the employment test. I passed the physical fitness portion with flying colors, and scored high enough on the written that they moved me through the interview process. Six months' worth of background checks and two polygraphs later, after a government doctor gave me a clean bill of health, I was hired."

"Wow."

The smile on his face didn't reach his eyes when he let out a small sigh.

"I should've opened the restaurant."

Chapter Twelve

Mason

He sat at his desk, thinking about this morning in bed with Reagan and their pillow talk after. He hadn't thought about owning a restaurant in probably ten years; now he couldn't help wondering what his life would be like if he'd chosen that path. Would he have a wife? Kids? A house with a big backyard for the German shepherds he'd always wanted, instead of the sparsely-decorated condo outside of Boston where he'd crash when he had more than two days off in a row so he could visit his parents? A girlfriend was practically impossible, and a wife seemed out of the question. And kids, or even a dog? No fucking way.

He'd once thought this was the life. Traveling, money, excitement, protecting the greater good... he'd loved every minute of it. So much so that he had recruited his little brother into the agency. Now, here Mason was—saving his brother's life because their employer had washed its hands of him, and he wasn't so sure anymore.

Could he somehow fit into Reagan's life? He didn't know. The fantasy was there, but how reality reconciled with the daydream remained to be seen.

The little voice in his head began to chastise him. *Get your head in the game!* What he needed to focus on right now was rescuing his baby brother, not this white-picket-fence shit.

She walked into his office in her black yoga pants and tight pink t-shirt, with her hair piled high on her head in a messy bun, carrying a yogurt cup and plastic spoon, and flashed him a big smile.

But the white-picket-fence shit is so damn appealing.

****

The plan was in place; they'd made it through the locks of the Panama Canal with no problem and were scheduled to arrive in the marina at approximately six in the morning. Kennedy and Dante had landed in Cartagena, and she'd already met up with Jacob. There were eyes on where they thought Marcus was being held. There was nothing left for him to do other than one more phone call to Jacob.

Mason decided to make her a candlelight dinner on the deck, along with some wine, and maybe even slow dancing before he took her back to the stateroom and made love to her all night.

"I think that sounds like the perfect plan," she whispered breathlessly when he took her in his arms and suggested it after he hung up the phone with Jacob.

"Good," he smiled. "Me, too."

"Can I help with dinner?"

"No. Why don't you go lie down and relax for a while. Meet me on deck at six thirty?"

She nodded with a shy smile.

Mason leaned down slowly until their lips met in a sensual kiss. He was about to break away when she moaned, drew her arms around his neck, and pressed against him. Instead of pulling apart, their kiss deepened, and soon she was straddling him in his office chair, grinding her hips against his.

God, he wanted to fuck her right there on the desk, but he had been looking forward to their last night together being filled with romance.

"Reagan," he murmured against her mouth even as his hands continued exploring her curves. "We need to stop so I can go make dinner."

Her pout was fucking adorable.

Rubbing her mons over her yoga pants with his thumb, he teased, "I promise, I'll make it worth the wait, sweetheart."

She giggled and slid off his lap.

"You better," she said, then picked up her yogurt cup, spun on her heel, and disappeared out the office door.

"Sassy pants," he murmured, shaking his head with a grin.

****

Reagan

Mason had told her to take a nap—yeah, like she was really gonna be able to sleep. She was brimming with excitement about her *date* tonight. Reagan didn't care what anyone would have said; she was calling it a date.

Still, she lay down and stared up at the ceiling, lost in thought about the blond-haired, blue-eyed man she was pretty sure she was in love with.

Gorgeous, smart, interesting, funny, sexy, amazing in bed... and that dimple and those abs—seriously? Like she stood a chance.

Still, Reagan knew this couldn't last beyond tomorrow. He was a spy; he traveled the world on a regular basis. He didn't do relationships. She was a teacher, and before this trip, the farthest she'd ever been from Fargo was when she went to see Kennedy graduate Marine boot camp in San Diego—and that was for only three days. Other than that, she'd never been farther than Minneapolis. And her biological clock had started ticking—she was ready for a relationship and babies. Unfortunately, she hadn't met Mr. Right, only Mr. I'll-Fuck-You-Until-Mr.-Right-Comes-Along.

It appeared her streak was still intact. Except the thought of not seeing Mason again hurt way more than she'd ever hurt over a man. He was going to be her 'one that got away,' she just knew it. But what other option was there?

None.

Reagan would have to settle for her one epic love affair. She liked that spin so much better.

Glancing at the clock on the nightstand, she decided to start getting ready. She took her time showering, shaving, and lotioning. Realizing it was a losing battle with her hair and the equatorial humidity, she piled it on her head and strategically placed ringlets to frame her heart-shaped face, then painstakingly applied her makeup. When she was satisfied, she slipped on the dress and heels she had been going to wear to the baptism rehearsal—until she got kidnapped.

Was that really only a few days ago? It seemed like a lifetime.

Sixty twenty-five; right on time.

Giving herself a onceover in the mirror, she took a deep breath and headed toward the deck.

She couldn't have scripted a better reaction from Mason when he saw her.

He'd been lighting a candle when she appeared, and he stood frozen, staring as if he'd never seen anything like her until the match burned his fingers and brought him out of his trance.

When she reached the table, he pulled her chair out—still not taking his eyes off her.

"Wow, sweetheart, you look..." He shook his head and widened his eyes like he was looking for words before continuing, "...beautiful. I'm glad we're alone and not out somewhere, because I'd probably want to kill every man who stared at you if we were."

That made her chuckle.

"I never pegged you for the jealous type."

"I'm not, usually, but I've never considered a woman *mine* until I met you."

His words sent the butterflies to her stomach and zinging to her lady parts. She'd never wanted a man to feel like he owned her, but that was exactly what she wanted from Mason Hughes. She wanted him to never want to let her go.

She sat down, and he helped her move her chair forward.

"I'll be right back with the appetizers. Have some champagne," he said, gesturing to the flute he'd already filled.

Reagan went to grab her glass and hesitated, eyeing his full one then quickly glanced around before switching them. With a satisfied smile like she was brilliant, she took a drink. Looking out at the ocean as she sipped the tiny bubbles, feeling the salty breeze blow across her face, she thought, "What a perfect night." Then she was immediately filled with anxiety, wondering what was going to go wrong. In her experience, there was no such thing as a perfect anything.

He reappeared with crabcakes and a side sauce.

"Did you make those?" she asked with suspicion in her voice as she inspected one with her fork. They smelled delicious.

He grinned and puffed out his chest a little.

"I did."

She took one bite and her eyes got big.

"Wow. These are amazing!"

He winked, murmuring, "Thanks," before taking a bite of his own.

The CIA agent looked dashing tonight. The cobalt blue button-down made his eyes appear bluer than the ocean surrounding them. He had a slight tan that was also highlighted by the color of his shirt. Blue was definitely his color. And his linebacker physique made her fingers itch with wanting to run her hands all over his body. Then there was that dimple. *Sigh*. That was her favorite thing about his body. *Wellllll, second favorite.*

They laughed and drank all through dinner, telling each other stories of their lives: their childhood, college years, jobs—at least, as much as Mason could tell her about his. After they'd cleared the dinner dishes and were back on deck with another glass of champagne, he stood, turned up the music on his phone and opened his arms.

"Care to dance?"

With her eyes locked on his, she rose from her chair and walked toward him. He was so handsome, and it seemed the more she got to know him, the more attractive he became. And that dimple was going to be the death of her.

There was a sense of sadness in the air, both of them realizing tonight was probably their last night together, but neither voicing it out loud.

Reagan almost whispered *I love you* as he slowly moved her around the deck, swaying to the beat in his arms, but stopped herself. How could she love him after such a short period of time? This was just a crush, that's all. What would be the point of saying something like that? Besides, she'd be devastated when he didn't say it back. He made her *feel* like he loved her, and that was going to have to be enough. She couldn't expect anything more from him, no matter how hard she wished for it.

She looked up to find him watching her face intently.

"Awful lot going on up there," he murmured with a knowing smile.

"I was just thinking about how perfect tonight has been, and how I wish it didn't have to end."

His expression became more somber, his mouth turning downward slightly.

"I wish that too. How about if tonight we pretend it's just beginning—that we have a long future ahead of us? Just for tonight. No talk about tomorrow."

Reagan couldn't think of anything she'd like more. She pulled him to the table where their half-full champagne flutes sat. She handed him his glass then picked up hers, raising it in a toast.

"To our long future," she said with a smile.

"To sitting on our front porch, holding hands in our rocking chairs, watching our great-grandchildren play," he winked as he clinked his glass against hers.

What a beautiful thought.

She almost became sad again at the realization that wasn't in the cards for them, but remembered their deal. *Just for tonight.* She was going to savor the hell out of this fantasy; at least she'd have the memory of her perfect night with Mason Hughes to cherish forever. She'd worry about her love hangover tomorrow.

Chapter Thirteen

Mason

He was so fucking gone over this woman. G-O-N-E.

Playing pretend with her tonight was the easiest thing he'd ever done, because he'd never wanted anything more in his life. The idea of growing old with her? *Hell yeah.* Mason wasn't going to let a little thing like reality ruin their night together. He refused to even let the thought *last night together* enter his head again. Tonight, they were going to be together forever.

"Where should we live?"

Reagan didn't hesitate in playing along. She tilted her head as she contemplated her answer.

"I don't know—you've seen more of the world than I have, where do you suggest?"

"I'm partial to Key West."

She scrunched up her nose. "Too many hurricanes."

"How about San Diego then?"

"I've only been once, but I thought it was beautiful."

"San Diego it is." He spun her around the deck. "How many babies should we have?"

"Hmm. We're getting kind of old; I don't think we should have any more than three."

"Boys? Girls?"

She tilted her head back to look at him and smiled. "I'm not sure? What would you prefer?"

"Two boys and a girl."

He felt her stroking the hair along his neckline and was suddenly more attuned to her tits mashed against his chest.

"You know we don't really get to decide that, right? We'll have to take what we get."

"As long as they're healthy, I'll be happy," he said with a grin, then dipped her.

Staring down at her, he really could see their unborn babies in her eyes. He knew she felt it too, because she was staring back at him like she was dumbstruck.

Mason slowly brought her upright, and they stood still, neither of them averting their gaze. Nothing had ever felt more right in his life, and he lowered his lips to hers. It began gently, but she softly whimpered against his mouth, and he wrapped his arms around her while he deepened the kiss— then it got heated fast.

Their make out session was erotic and sensual, and he was enjoying the hell out of just kissing her while they grinded together on their makeshift dancefloor like two horny teenagers at prom.

Finally she palmed his hard cock over his pants, slowly rubbing his shaft while he squeezed her ass over her dress as their tongues continued to tangle.

He broke the kiss and softly asked in her ear, "Should we take things back to your cabin?"

"Oh god, I thought you'd never ask," she groaned as she pressed against him.

Taking her hand in his, he led her to the table and picked up the bottle of bubbly and their glasses before gesturing to the doorway that would lead them to her stateroom.

As she walked in front of him, Mason didn't take his eyes off her ass. He couldn't wait to have it naked in his hands squeezing it. Maybe spanking it a little too. A vision flashed in his mind of her flesh jiggling as he brought his hand down on her butt while he pounded her from behind. They couldn't get to her room fast enough.

He set the bottle and glasses down on the small end table in the sitting area of the room and turned just as her green dress dropped to the floor. His eyes were glued to her tight body while she stepped out of the material, heels still on, in nothing but her white lace bra and panties. The redheaded goddess looked at him shyly, biting her bottom lip with a small smile as he slowly walked to where she stood.

Taking her in his arms, he knew—tonight would never be enough. Mason wanted forever.

The scent of her shampoo filled his senses as his hands glided up and down her bare back. He paused at the center of her back and undid the clasp of her bra, pulling the straps down her arms until she was exposed to him.

Groaning at how beautiful she was, he dipped his head and pushed one nipple up into his mouth, suckling while his left hand teased and pinched her other nipple. Reagan tugged at his short hair, drawing him closer to her chest as she gasped and moaned at his ministrations. He was going to learn every inch of her body tonight—commit it to memory to replay over and over in the his lonely future.

He turned her around, gripping her tits in his palms as he kissed one shoulder, then across her neck to the other. Her body erupted in goosebumps when he started at the base of her neck and began to lay soft kisses down her spine to the hollow at the base of her back. Dropping to his knees, he tugged on her panties until they were at her ankles, and he slid his hands up one calf, past her knee, then up her thigh. Mason took his time caressing her inner thigh; he could feel the heat generating from her pussy, and knew that when he touched her, he was going to find her soaked.

She lifted on her toes and bowed her legs, encouraging him to touch her cunt, but the tease was too delicious, and instead of tracing his fingers through her folds like he knew she wanted, he began to reverently rub her ass instead. His cock was so hard, he was sure there was going to be a zipper imprint on it when he took his pants off.

Mason gently bit down on her creamy flesh, and she drew in a sharp breath of surprise, then softly moaned when he kissed her skin. Pulling her cheeks apart, he flicked his tongue along her crack and down to her wet center, where he dove his tongue inside her heat and began to tongue-fuck her.

"Ohhhh goooooodddd." She shuddered and reached behind her to pull his head closer.

He smiled and pressed on the small of her back, bending her forward onto the bed and pulling her legs farther apart once her chest hit the mattress.

His fingers began to explore her wetness, searching for her magic button as he resumed darting his tongue in and out of her.

"God, I love how you taste," he groaned while he lapped up her juices and rubbed her clit.

Her little legs tensed around his shoulders and began to shake when he increased the tempo.

"Come on my tongue, sweetheart. Let me taste it."

She began to moan louder and gasped, "Yessssss. Oh fuck, don't stop! Don't stop!"

Mason began to use two hands—one to rub her clit, the other to fingerfuck her. He bit down on her butt when he felt her pussy clench around his finger, and she cried out as her orgasm shook her body.

Replacing his fingers with his mouth, he licked her clean until she yipped and jumped at his touch, temporarily too sensitive to let him continue.

"You are the fucking sexiest woman on the planet," he growled against her skin as he kissed up her spine while she lay panting on the bed. "I'm never going to get sick of this."

Mason enveloped her body with his, pressing his hard-on against her ass and kissing her neck.

Reagan blindly reached behind her, fumbling with the buttons on his slacks until he slid to her side so she could better tend to undressing him.

His cock was leaking; he wanted her so damn badly.

"Ohhh," she whispered when his dick sprang free from his underwear and pants, and she quickly tugged them off, along with his socks and shoes. There he lay, naked from the waist down, so he began to unbutton his shirt cuffs while she ran her hands up his thighs, seemingly mesmerized by his cock and paying no attention to his upper half.

His sassy girl must have realized her fixation with his cock, because she finally looked up and noticed he was working on his front buttons and seemed embarrassed she hadn't done that for him.

Giggling, she whispered, "Oops, sorry. Let me help you with that," and moved to straddle his hips while she finished the task. His cock flexed against her heat, like it was egging him to put it where it belonged. She felt it, and looked down at him, one side of her mouth turning up. He didn't give a shit; he wanted her—now—and he wasn't ashamed of it.

Reagan wagged her finger at him, smirking.

"One good tease deserves another, baby."

She took her time with his buttons, softly rocking against him as she did.

"Be careful, sassy pants," he warned. "I'll fuck you bareback right here."

Without warning, she sank down on his shaft.

"I like you bareback," she cooed as she began to ride him.

It was nirvana—there was no other way to describe the feeling of being sheathed only by her warm, wet pussy. He was never leaving it.

Finally his brain began to operate again, and his hands found her hips, tugging down to still her movement.

"Sweetheart, are you sure? I mean, I'm clean—I know that for a fact, but I'm not snipped."

"I've had the birth control implant. I'm good for another two years. And I'm clean too."

His hands moved up her waist to cup her tits, as if to say, *Carry on then.*

She leaned down, and he captured her nipple between his lips, sucking gently before biting down. Her whimpers drove him crazy. Switching to her other tit, he felt her getting wetter, and she began to buck her hips faster.

Being bareback inside her wet pussy while she fucked him faster was not conducive to long-lasting sex, but he wasn't about to slow her down—he could tell she was going to come soon.

The problem was, so was he. He just needed to last until she started, and that was proving to be more difficult than he'd like.

"Fuuuck, Reagan," he moaned, closing his eyes and trying to think of Bruins stats, but they were no match for her tiny gasps and mewls.

She sat up and the sight of her tits bouncing made him grit his teeth. He reached between them, finding her clit and rubbing hard with his thumb. That was the trick, because he felt her walls grip his cock hard as she climaxed.

With a roar, he thrust up into her, jackhammering her pussy until he released rope after rope of cum deep inside her.

It was the most amazing orgasm he'd ever experienced.

"Holy fuuuck," he panted, placing his hand on his forehead. "I think I'm seeing stars."

That made her giggle and nuzzle his neck.

"Mmm, me too. We definitely need to do that again."

Again?

"You're insatiable, sweetheart," he chided.

He felt her shrug. "Your fault. Stop being so sexy if you don't like it."

Mason rolled over on top of her, kissing her neck down to her chest.

"Oh, I never said anything about not liking it. On the contrary…"

Again, she giggled. "Good."

Yeah, he had no idea how he was supposed to let her go tomorrow.

Chapter Fourteen

Reagan

Best. Sex. Ever.

Actually, best night of her life—period.

She lay staring at his face bathed in moonlight, absent-mindedly stroking his hair while listening to his steady breathing. She couldn't help but smile as she studied his face. The tiny scar along his cheekbone seemed to be the only flaw, and she would hardly call it a flaw, since it seemed to enhance his appeal.

Reagan couldn't help herself; she leaned over and softly kissed it. His grasp around her waist tightened while his other hand slid across his core to her breast on his chest and kneaded it.

"You need to sleep, sweetheart," he murmured, his voice coarse from slumber.

"I know," she sighed as moved down and snuggled against his side.

How was she supposed to sleep? She'd finally found Mr. Right, except everything about their circumstances couldn't be more wrong.

It isn't fair.

Reagan hadn't realized she'd uttered it out loud until she felt his fingertips run up and down her spine as he whispered, "It never is, baby."

She knew his words were supposed to offer some sort of comfort, but all they did was remind her that he'd been here before—in some woman's arms the night before he never saw her again. This was business as usual for him.

He might be an old pro at this, but she definitely was not.

It was okay. If there was one thing she was, it was a fast learner.

****

Mason

He was up before the summer sun. There was a lot to do today—not least of which was saving his brother's life. The captain told him they'd be in the marina in less than an hour; he headed to his office to go over the plan one last time, looking for any flaws.

It had been heavenly waking up next to Reagan for the second morning in a row, and he would have given his left nut to have stayed in bed with her all day. She was so fucking adorable when she whimpered, rolled over, and hugged a pillow in his place when he slipped out of bed.

Unfortunately, he didn't have that luxury.

His phone rang, indicating it was Jacob.

"Everything all set?" he asked the fixer.

"Agent Jones has been pacing back and forth for the last fifteen minutes. When are you scheduled to dock?"

His hackles went up. He'd given consideration to the idea of Kennedy rescuing her sister instead of his brother and leaving him high and dry, but thought they'd reached an agreement—now he wasn't so sure.

"Soon," Mason offered noncommittally.

There was a commotion on the other end, with Jacob telling him, "Hold on," before coming back on and saying, "I'm going to put you on video."

No sooner had he said that than Kennedy's face appeared, barking at him, "Hughes, let me talk to my sister."

He fought not to roll his eyes.

"Do you even know your sister, Agent Jones? She's not going to be up willingly for at least two more hours."

That caused Keni to chuckle.

"I guess you've gotten to know her pretty well."

"Yeah, you could say that," he replied, his tone wistful.

Kennedy stared at him silently, cocking her head as if trying to figure something out.

"We're all set for you. Once you get to the marina, Jacob will be waiting to take you to where Marcus' team is expecting to meet you. He will be orchestrating things between us, so this will be our last direct contact until I collect my sister. Agent Hughes, let me reiterate, if there is a single hair on her head that is out of place, I will kill you."

"I'm fine, Keni," a little voice squeaked from the door.

He looked up and saw Reagan in the threshold in her pajamas, her face free of any makeup. Her hair was smoother than it had been when he'd left her, but was still a little messy, like she'd run her fingers through it but not a brush.

"Little sister, is that you?" Kennedy called.

Reagan came around his desk and stood behind his chair, one hand on either of his shoulders. Keni narrowed her eyes as she observed Reagan's comfort with him. His first instinct was to draw away from her touch under Kennedy's scrutiny. *Fuck that*, he decided.

"Hi Ken," Reagan said softly. "Are you okay?"

The older sister pffted. "I'm peachy. I need to be sure you're the one who is okay."

His little red-haired nymph subtly squeezed his shoulders. "I'm fine. Mason has been nothing but kind."

"So you keep saying. The question is, *how* kind?"

"He's been a perfect gentleman, if that's what you're implying."

I wouldn't exactly say that, he mused, forcing his face to remain neutral instead of smirking at his little joke.

"Just a little while longer, honey. You'll be on a plane back to Mexico by dinnertime, I promise."

Mason gripped the armrests with both hands. He wanted to possessively pull her into his lap, wrap his arms around her, and snarl at Agent Jones, "The hell she will."

"I'm sorry I ruined Madison's baptism," Reagan whispered.

"Are you serious right now? First of all, *you* didn't ruin anything." Kennedy pointedly glared at Mason before turning her attention back to her sister. "And secondly, do you think any of us care that we had to reschedule that? All we care about is getting you back safe and sound. *I'm* the one who's sorry for getting you caught up in my mess."

He interjected, "For what it's worth, Agent Jones, thank you. I do appreciate you helping me rescue my little brother."

"Like I had a choice," she scoffed. "And I didn't do it for you, Hughes, I did it for my sister."

"So I guess I played my cards right."

"We'll see by tonight. Good luck."

"You too," he muttered before disconnecting the call.

Mason glanced at his watch as he spun around in his chair, drawing her into his lap like he'd wanted to moments earlier.

Resting his chin on her shoulder, he said, "We should be at the dock in thirty minutes. Are you hungry?"

She shook her head, her hands fidgeting in her lap. "I'm too nervous to eat. What's going to happen next? You're not really going to handcuff me to the bed while you're gone like you said, are you?"

"Nah."

Her shoulders sagged in relief. "Oh, good. That would have sucked. I'm sure my arm would have fallen asleep. I promise, I'll stay in my cabin until you return. You have my word."

"Um, I don't think so."

She jerked back to look at his face. "What do you mean, *you don't think so*? I don't understand. How can you not trust me?"

He ran his hand up and down her arm. "Oh, I trust you. It's your big sister I don't trust. You're coming with me."

"What? No. Are you crazy? You said so yourself, I'd be a liability. I can't kill anyone."

"Not crazy, just cautious. And I'm not going to ask you to kill anyone, sweetheart."

"I would hardly call dragging me along with you cautious. As a matter of fact, I'd call it the opposite of cautious. More like reckless. I have no training. I'm out of shape—I barely go to the gym twice a month. My Spanish is rusty. What could I possibly be, other than in the way?"

The corner of his mouth lifted.

"Insurance."

Chapter Fifteen

Reagan

As she got dressed under Mason's watchful eye, all she could do was fume. *Insurance? This is bullshit.* Is that all she was to him? A goddamn insurance policy to make sure Kennedy would help him? Is that all she'd ever been to him—from the get-go?

"I thought you cared about me." Her accusatory tone seemed to surprise him.

"Of course I do. How does taking you with me negate that?"

She crossed her arms over her chest.

"I don't know—it just does. It's like you think I'm going to betray you and leave. I would never want anything bad to happen to someone you care about. If Kennedy can help your brother, she will—she gave you her word. She's a good person. You don't have to drag me along as a guarantee."

"Reagan, I betrayed your sister—she wouldn't help me if it weren't for the fact that I'm holding you hostage. And the truth is, I don't blame her—not one bit. And I also wouldn't blame her if she attempted to rescue you and set me up to get killed in the process; if I were in her position, I'd consider it. So I'm taking you with me. You're not going to be in harm's way—I promise. You're probably safer with me than here alone with the crew, anyway. I mean, not that they would hurt you; they just wouldn't offer much protection if you needed it."

"I'm still mad," she pouted.

With a smirk, he drew her into his arms and kissed her hair.

"I'm sorry, sweetheart. I'll make it up to you."

"When?" she challenged, pulling back to look at him. She didn't believe him for a second. Once they rescued his brother, he was sending her on her way, and he'd be free to move on to the next woman stupid enough to fall for him.

He smiled as he ignored her question. "Are you ready? You sure you don't want to grab something to eat?"

"Positive. Let's go."

Five minutes later, they were off the boat and into a waiting car. It was nothing like the black luxury car in Mexico with tinted windows. Instead they were going to be driven around in a royal blue Chevy Camaro.

"Jacob—you sexy beast, how the fuck are you?" Mason said with a grin when he opened the car door.

He moved the seat forward and gestured for her to climb into the backseat, then Mason fit his six-foot-one body in the front passenger seat. Jacob was not at all what she imagined a 'fixer' would look like. Apparently, movies didn't do them justice because every character she'd ever seen on the screen that called himself a fixer looked like a weasel. The man in the driver's seat—with his brown hair, green eyes, and cheekbones a model would be jealous of—was anything but weasel-looking.

Jacob neither grinned back at Mason nor answered his question about how he was doing. Instead, he grunted, "Why did you bring her?" after barely glancing at Reagan.

"Call it a gut feeling, but I think she needs to be with me today."

Jacob put the car into drive, muttering, "You better hope Kennedy doesn't catch wind of this."

"If Agent Jones is as good as I think she is, she already knows."

Just then a phone started ringing through the car's Bluetooth system. Jacob looked at the screen on the dash and cursed under his breath at the number that was displayed.

"Speak of the devil," he mumbled before answering it.

Kennedy's voice echoed in stereo throughout the sports car before Jacob even said hello.

"What. In. The. *Fuck* do you think you're doing? You're going to get Reagan killed. Jesus Christ, it's one thing to use her as bait for me, but it's something completely different to use her as bait for the Colombian cartel. You fucking bastard—take her back to the yacht now or the deal's off."

Mason's voice was as calm as Kennedy's was excited.

"She's not going back to the yacht. She's not going to be in any danger." With a grin, he glanced over at the brown-haired man in the driver's seat, then continued talking into the air. "Jacob has agreed to keep her with him—kind of like escrow. He'll release her once Marcus is out safe."

Jacob shot Mason a look and asked "I have?" In a louder voice, he called out, "I didn't agree to this, Keni. Don't get pissed off at me."

Kennedy let out a string of curse words. "If anything happens to her, Jake, you're number two on my list to kill. I'm not fucking kidding. I will hunt you down—right after I slice Mason into fish food."

Their driver sighed. "I have no doubt about that. Your sister will be safe with me as long as she does what she's told."

"I will," Reagan squeaked out from the backseat. "You won't have to worry about me. I'd like to go home in one piece and breathing."

"Stay close to Jakey, Rea. For all his bluster, he's really a teddy bear."

Reagan knew her sister was egging on the grumpy but handsome man. Surprisingly, he didn't appear riled as he drove through the city, but he did throw in a parting shot before hanging up.

"Talk to you soon, *Bella*," Jacob said with a smirk.

Bella was Kennedy's new identity, which no one was supposed to know about. There was a reason the man was considered to be the best in the business.

Barely taking his eyes off the road, Jacob handed Mason a bag. "Burner phone with everyone's numbers programmed in, ear piece with me on the other end, Colombian pesos, gum, map, and safehouse location—should shit go south, meet there after five. The team has a vest for you."

Mason wasted no time sticking the ear piece in his ear then counted the money before slipping it into his front shirt pocket, along with the gum. The map and phone he put in his pants pocket. He stared at the scrap of paper with the location of the safehouse then tore it in three pieces and left it on the console.

They went over the plan once more. Not much had changed from when she'd sat in on his strategy session—she liked that. It felt like she was still included in things, not just the dumb hostage.

They pulled up to the curb next to a café on one of the busy streets of Cartagena, and Mason grabbed the door handle with one hand, then paused before getting out. He turned toward Jacob, pointing his finger at the man.

"Take care of her. Kennedy isn't the only one you'll have to worry about if anything happens to her," he warned then looked back at her with a grin and a wink. That wink made her feel way more special than it should have.

Without another word, he was out the door and Jacob was driving away before the door even shut completely, grumbling, "Then maybe you shouldn't have asked me to babysit, asshole." She saw Mason duck into the café just as the Camaro turned the corner and sped off down the street.

This was going to be a long day—she wished she had grabbed breakfast. Jacob didn't seem like the type who was going to be very hospitable and feed her.

Just then, her stomach growled, and he smirked at her through the rearview mirror.

"You hungry?"

Maybe he wasn't going to be as inhospitable as she'd thought.

****

Mason

For all Jacob's bluster, he was a good guy. Well, a good guy for a mercenary, and Mason knew he wouldn't let anything happen to Reagan—if for no other reason than he didn't want to tangle with Kennedy Jones. If he was smart anyway. Obviously, *Mason* wasn't smart. But desperate times called for desperate measures, and Marcus' life being in jeopardy definitely constituted desperate times.

In the café, he rendezvoused with Eddie Landon, one of the three rebels from his brother's team who had disobeyed orders and come back to Colombia to get Marcus home safely.

The other two, Erik Yu and Raul Garcia, were doing more surveillance.

"The agency got a ransom demand last night," Eddie told him once Mason got his coffee and sat down at one of the bistro tables. They were made of wrought iron with colorful tiles adorning the top.

"Jesus, it took them long enough," he muttered, blowing on the hot beverage before taking a sip.

Eddie sighed, moving his bottom jaw side to side—probably a nervous tic he didn't even realize he had.

"I'm sure Marcus didn't give up anything easily."

They were both quiet as they contemplated what his brother had probably endured, and what it must have taken to get him to offer enough information to put out a ransom demand.

"I hope this chick is worth it," Eddie muttered bitterly, shaking his head. "He just pissed away his career for a woman after knowing her—what? A week? But hopefully not his life."

Mason suddenly understood why his brother might go to this length to save someone he'd just met. He would do the same for Reagan without hesitation.

"What about us? Don't you think we're pissing our careers away to save Marcus?"

Eddie shook his head confidently. "Nah. Marcus is going to reappear, having *single-handedly* escaped his captors. The agency will do their hero pomp and circumstance, then allow him to quietly retire. They may have their suspicions of our involvement, but unless one of us gets killed today, they'll never be able to prove it."

"Maybe for you. I borrowed a yacht for this little excursion.

"Oh fuck! Why the hell did you do that?"

"I thought it'd be the easiest way to transport twelve or so women out of Cartagena undetected."

"Wait—what? We're transporting them?"

Mason furrowed his brow. "Yeah. What the fuck did you think we were going to do?"

Eddie shrugged. "I dunno. Free them and send them on their way."

"Well, we'll do that eventually. But we need to be sure they're released somewhere safe where they aren't going to fall into the same predicament to be sold again."

Eddie's phone beeped with a text.

"They're out front," he said as he grabbed his coffee and stood up. Mason followed the man out the door and down the street to a waiting maroon minivan that had seen better days. It was in stark contrast to his ride from the marina.

After getting in the middle seat and reacquainting himself with the men he'd met only a handful of times before, he looked around the vehicle and smiled. They made quite the diverse crew. There was him with his blond hair and Irish/Italian heritage. Eddie was an African American, about five foot ten and two hundred pounds of muscle; his bald head made him look tough as hell. Erik was of Korean descent, also about five foot ten, with jet black hair; he was leaner than Eddie but still with an athletic build. Raul was first-generation American by birthright—his parents escaped from Cuba in the seventies and were welcomed into the US as political refugees. From what Marcus had told Mason, Raul definitely fit the Latin lover stereotype to a T.

Erik handed Mason a bulletproof vest, and as he slipped it over his head, Eddie asked suspiciously, "Where'd you get your female contact? She seems to be pretty badass."

Mason only grinned and offered, "That's what I hear." He had made a deal with Kennedy; he wasn't revealing who she was. He was glad to learn Jacob hadn't disclosed her identity either.

"Let's roll," Raul said, starting the engine.

He took a deep breath. "Let's do this."

****

They were in position on the warehouse roof, waiting for the go-ahead from Jacob.

The fixer was definitely earning his money this week. He had orchestrated a meeting for Kennedy with some of the cartel yesterday. She was posing as a woman from LA setting up an underground brothel and needing 'labor,' which the Colombians seemed eager to provide for the price she was offering. Flanked by Dante—who refused to leave her side and was posing as one of her bodyguards—and one of Dante's actual bodyguards, they were able to get a feel for the layout of the building and plant seven CIA-grade cameras and bugs in the process.

Marcus' teammates had spent the night watching the feed of the warehouse from their hotel room, with Kennedy and Dante viewing the footage from their suite, and Jacob observing from his.

After surveying the building and being shown the dozen captive women, Kennedy thought Marcus was being held in a room on the second floor. Their mole affirmed her assessment.

Kennedy had called another meeting this morning with the cartel leaders—off-site this time—to discuss shipment dates. Fortunately, once the boss-men left the warehouse, security was minimal. They probably thought women held in a cage and a man who'd more than likely been beaten severely weren't too difficult to guard—although Mason thought it was pretty arrogant on the cartel's part to think no one would be coming for his brother. They should pay their people better, because according to Jacob, it had been pretty easy to flip the first one he'd approached.

Jacob's art of persuasion probably played a role. The man could sell ice to an Eskimo. There was a reason he knew everything about everyone—and it wasn't just because he threw dollar bills around, although Mason was sure that helped. No, Jacob was cunning. He could get people to tell secrets without them even realizing they were doing it. Women adored him, and men admired him—but Mason knew it was all a façade. He was certain no one knew the real

Jacob Smith, and he could almost guarantee *Smith* wasn't the man's real last name.

Jacob's voice came in Mason's ear, and judging by the team's expressions, he was speaking to them simultaneously.

"My inside man says the rest of the guards are getting blowjobs. Try not to kill him when you get inside—navy polo, jeans. He should give up without a fight. Maybe tie him up to make it look good or knock him out, rough him up a little."

"We can definitely do that," Eddie said with a chuckle as he got into a crouching position.

Mason silently gestured toward the window they had been avoiding, then the four men were on the move. They had decided to wait and see if an opportunity to covertly breach the building presented itself, but if it didn't, they were prepared to go in with guns blazing. Stealth mode felt safer for the captives, though, and he was relieved they were going in this way.

Horny assholes.

A horny asshole was how Kennedy had escaped his custody—one of his men had fallen for her ruse that she wanted him. It was the oldest trick in the book, yet it had still worked. Probably because men were so predictable when it came to thinking with their dicks.

Normally he sat in condescending judgment of horny assholes, but given his last few days with Reagan Jones, Mason felt like he was now no better than the rest of them. And that bothered him.

But Reagan was so much more to him than just wanting to get his dick wet. Should he have messed around with her? *Fuck no.* Would he do it again? *In a damn heartbeat.*

The plan was to neutralize the threat, find Marcus, rescue the women, and make a discreet exit in as short a time as possible, but there were a lot of unknowns at play—the biggest being what condition they were going to find Marcus in.

They rappelled down from the window at the roofline to the first floor. They really did look like badasses straight out of an action movie, and Mason wasn't ashamed to admit he lived for this shit. The thrill, the danger, saving people's lives—he was an adrenaline junkie.

Navy polo guy had his hands up the minute he saw them. It was probably a cheap shot when Eddie knocked him out with one punch, then zip-tied his hands and feet, but the guy would appreciate the bruises when he was trying to explain to his bosses how he was still alive. It remained to be seen if the man's colleagues would be as lucky.

"You've got three other guards—two in the room to the left and one in the room to the right. The women are being housed in the middle room," came the voice in his ear.

Eddie and Raul took the room on the left; Erik and Mason took the room on the right.

The door wasn't even locked when they tried it. As expected, the overweight guard was in a chair with his pants around his ankles while a petite, topless, dark-haired woman was on her knees between his legs, timidly bobbing her head up and down on his cock. The dumbass' gun was five feet away on a table as he grunted and gripped both hands on the armrests. The young beauty's tits swayed before him as she awkwardly worked his dick over.

Mason opted not to put a bullet in the man's brain. He did get some satisfaction though from the look on the fucker's face when he opened his eyes to find the two CIA agents standing there, guns drawn, smirks on their faces. To the woman's credit, she'd looked up as they quietly entered the room, but hadn't screamed at the sight of them. They'd put a finger to their lips, and she had followed their orders and kept sucking the man's cock until they told the guard not to move. Then she scrambled out of the way, covering her bare breasts. The guard's eyes grew wide while his cock went flaccid like a sad, deflated balloon.

Squatting so he was eye-level with the woman, Erik picked up her blouse, which was laying on the floor, and handed it to her, telling her in Spanish, "You're safe now." Then he looked away when she lifted her arms to slip it over her head.

Her terrified look let them know she wasn't a believer.

Erik seemed to take her lack of faith personally and gripped her forearm as they stood, looking her in the eye. "I promise. We're here to help you and the other women."

A single tear rolled down her cheek and the Korean-American hugged her. To Mason's surprise, she let him.

Mason had just zip-tied the asshole to the chair, leaving his pants around his ankles and his tiny dick on display, when Raul and Eddie appeared with two skinny, young brunette women who looked as terrified as the one being comforted by Erik.

Eddie immediately threw his arms up to his face, as if to block the sight from his eyes.

"Whoa! I've seen enough little dicks today to last a lifetime."

The man in the chair took offense at the insult and started to curse at them. Mason happily put a gag in the asshole's mouth.

"What about the other two?"

"Knocked the fuck out. One of them is going to have a black and blue dick when he wakes up. Bruce Lee here"—Raul gestured to the woman whose elbow he was holding—"kicked the shit out of his crotch after he went down."

The tiny spitfire obviously didn't understand English, but she could tell they were talking about her and started sputtering in Spanish about cutting the guard's genitals off with a rusty knife.

"Where is the American?" Mason asked her in her native language.

She looked at him, obviously confused, and shook her head.

"No sé." *I don't know.*

"We haven't been allowed out of the room, except to be used by the men they bring here and by the guards when the boss-men leave us alone with them," the woman still holding onto Erik explained in Spanish.

"How long have you been here?" Raul asked the woman whose arm he was still holding.

"I don't know," she whispered. "A month? Two months? You lose track of time in here."

"Susana knows. She's been keeping track," Erik's new charge offered.

Before Mason could ask who or where Susana was, Jacob's voice resonated in his ear. "You guys need to move it. Kennedy says they're on their way back."

"Shit. You guys deal with the women; I'm going to go find Marcus."

Mason was out the door and running up the steel stairs, gun in hand as his footsteps echoed off the warehouse walls. He tried the first door he came to and, finding it locked, kicked it open to discover it empty.

Same with the second room. And the third. And fourth.

Marcus was not here.

"He's not fucking here, Jacob!" Mason roared as he came out of the last room.

"He's gotta be."

Mason didn't even bother going back to the stairs. Instead he leapt over the railing and landed on a desk, then jumped onto the main floor. The only cartel man not unconscious was the guard whose blowjob Mason and Erik had interrupted.

As his fellow operatives ushered the women out and piled them into the maroon minivan, he stormed into the office where the man remained tied to the office chair— shriveled cock still out for all to see.

Putting his gun in his waistband, Mason grabbed the man by the front of his shirt and demanded, "Where is he? Where is the American?"

The guard just smiled, which infuriated Mason.

Shoving him down back into the chair, he took his gun from his waistband and pointed it at the man's head, then changed his mind and directed his aim at the Colombian's cock.

That wiped the smile from the guard's face.

Mason pulled the hammer on the gun. "Where. Is. The. American."

Chapter Sixteen

Reagan

Jacob was barking into his headset, "Mason, he's gotta be there. You need to check the upstairs rooms again."

After dropping Mason at the café, they'd taken position in an office across from the warehouse and had been watching an iPad screen with different feeds from the cameras Kennedy and Dante had planted yesterday. Some of the angles were skewed so she had to cock her head to see what was really taking place.

Reagan could see three large, handsome men who looked straight out of a commercial for a cop show—bulletproof vests with weapons holstered at the side, earpieces in their ears—ushering scantily-clad young Hispanic women out the door.

She looked out the window into the alley and saw them being hustled into an older model maroon minivan, its paint fading from years in the elements and two of the hubcaps missing.

Mason was nowhere to be seen—he was not helping the women into the vehicle, and she couldn't see him on the iPad screen when she peeked over Jacob's shoulder. Jacob could hear him though, judging by the instructions he was barking into his microphone.

"What the fuck are you doing? You need to go check the offices closer. Don't listen to that asshole. He's sending you on a wild goose chase, man." Jacob was silent for a moment, then slumped back in his chair, sighed, and muttered, "Okay, but you're making a mistake," as he reached into his front pocket and pulled out his car keys.

"I'll take them to him," Reagan eagerly volunteered, extending her hand.

Eyeing her suspiciously, Jacob held the keys in his fist before reluctantly releasing them into her outstretched palm.

"Come right back here," he ordered as she raced out the door.

She ran down the stairs at breakneck speed and burst into the alley through the nondescript metal door. Mason was coming through the warehouse door just as the minivan turned the corner.

He saw her and jogged across the pavement to where she stood. "What are you doing?"

"Bringing you the car keys," she whispered breathlessly. He was sexy as hell in his tactical gear.

Without hesitation, he leaned down and kissed her tenderly. She could hear Jacob's voice from Mason's earpiece.

"I think you should check the offices again, Mason."

Pulling away from her mouth, he said into the air, "No time."

Leaning down again, he whispered in her ear, "I love you, sassy pants. Get back inside," then turned to jog down the alley to where the Camaro was parked, leaving her standing there, stunned, as he drove away.

Jacob's voice echoed in her head—*I think you should check the offices again*—and she darted across the street without a second thought.

Tiptoeing past the groaning man in the blue polo laying on the floor with his hands and feet bound, she then took the metal stairs two at a time and tentatively entered through the first door she came to. The jamb was splintered from where Mason had kicked it open.

She flipped on the fluorescent light and stood in the doorway. The room was empty except for an industrial metal desk, old office chair, and computer. Her initial thought was to move on to the next room, but Reagan kept hearing Jacob's instructions to Mason: *Check the offices closer.*

She moved inside the room and looked around, noticing a closet door that she hurried to open. It was full of bankers' boxes and computer paper. She quickly walked the perimeter of the room, but found nothing unusual.

She ran to the next office, which was laid out exactly the same as the first, right down to the identical industrial desk and chair. As she approached the closet door this time, the hair on her neck stood up, and she slowly opened the door, standing to the side when she did.

Lying in a heap on the floor was a bloodied, semi-conscious man, bound and gagged. His face was swollen and purple, his blond hair matted in dried blood.

Reagan dropped to her knees and cradled his head in her lap as she gingerly removed the gag, then realized she had nothing to help her remove the zip ties around his wrists and ankles. The man let out a soft moan.

How the hell am I going to get him out of here? There was no way she could carry him.

Just then she heard hurried footsteps bounding up the stairs. *Oh god!*

She tried scooching him over so she could get in the closet next to him then heard Mason's voice bellow out, "Reagan!"

"In here!"

He burst through the doorway, rocking back on his heels while both hands gripped the doorjamb as if to slow himself down.

Mason quickly scanned the room and his eyes found hers while she held his brother's head and gently stroked his hair.

"Fuck," he sputtered and rushed to them, wasting no time in pulling his knife and cutting the ties binding Marcus. He held his brother's face gently in his hands as he examined him.

"You dumb bastard. Was she worth it?" he sighed quietly.

To Reagan's surprise—and Mason's, judging by the look on his face—Marcus mumbled, "Absolutely."

That brought a grin to the older brother's face. "You're hopeless. Come on, can you walk? We gotta get out of here." Mason hoisted the bloodied man to his feet, bringing Marcus' arm around his shoulder. Reagan slipped under Marcus' other arm to help steady him on the opposite side, and they began their way toward the exit.

"I'm not leaving without Susana," the youngest Hughes brother stubbornly mumbled. He shifted his body and dropped to dead weight, no longer helping Reagan and Mason move him toward the door.

"She's already out," Mason grunted, and was instantly rewarded with Marcus' cooperation again.

They'd just gotten to the bottom of the stairs when the sound of tires screeching to a halt echoed in the alley.

Mason slammed the car keys into her hand and kicked the back door open.

"The car is at the end of the street. If I'm not there in two minutes, go to the marina; Jacob—and probably Kennedy— will meet you there."

"Where are you going?"

"To buy you guys some time. Go!"

He pecked her on the lips, then shoved them out the door.

Reagan shuffled down the street as quickly as she could with Marcus leaning most of his body weight on her shoulders. Her stomach dropped to her toes when she heard men shouting, followed by gunfire. She tried to hurry the injured man along.

More gunfire.

"Come on, Marcus, you have to help me out here."

"I'm pretty sure I've got internal bleeding and cracked ribs, lady. I'm moving as fast as I can."

Pretty snarky for someone who'd been held captive for six days, but he did seem to perk up and move faster.

Only when she got the car started did she allow herself to wonder if Mason was okay. How long had it been? Had it been two minutes? How was Jacob going to get out of there if they left him?

"Can you drive?" Marcus' faint voice asked from the passenger seat where she had unceremoniously deposited him. He was slumped against the door but looking at her through his swollen eyes.

"Yeah, but... shouldn't we wait? It hasn't been two minutes."

"It's been more than two minutes. You heard Mason. Get us to the marina."

"But—"

"No buts," he interrupted, then asked in an annoyed tone, "Do you need me to drive?"

"Listen, pal. If it weren't for me, you'd still be stuffed in that closet, so you might want to lose the attitude."

Surprisingly, he acquiesced. "You're right. But you should know better—you follow your team leader's orders, and your leader said to go to the marina after waiting two minutes."

"Mason's not my leader. I'm not part of his team. My sister is helping him, but she's definitely not taking orders from him."

"Who's your sister?"

"That's not important. All you need to know is she helped save your life."

She didn't miss the skeptical look on Marcus' bruised face, and he snarled, "Well, *you* still need to follow Mason's orders and get us the hell out of here."

"You seem awfully eager to just abandon your brother."

"*Abandon him*?" he growled. "Lady, we're a fucking liability to him. I don't have a weapon, and even if I did, I'd be shooting blind since I can barely see. And I sure as fuck can't fight in my condition. So unless you've got a gun stashed somewhere in those yoga pants or have some ninja skills you're hiding, I'll say it again. We're. A. Fucking. Burden. We'd just be one more responsibility he'd have to deal with if we got caught."

She hadn't thought of it like that. Still, they were in a car down the street. She could drive away anytime if they felt threatened. Staring intently up the street for any sign of Mason, she decided, they should wait a few more minutes.

Then came a knock on her window, and she screamed, hitting the gas but only revving the engine because she hadn't put the Camaro in drive.

"Reagan." She recognized that voice and looked out of the corner of her eye to see her sister.

She flung open the door and hugged Kennedy.

"Oh my god—are you okay? How did you know we were here?"

Keni wasted no time exchanging pleasantries, other than hugging her back briefly before ushering her into the back seat. "Mason told me," she said, then hopped in and floored it the hundred yards to the back of the warehouse.

She roared up to the door Reagan and Marcus had just escaped from, and Jacob came out, fireman-carrying a bleeding Mason. Reagan felt nauseous. Marcus jumped out so Jacob could deposit Mason in the passenger seat. Kennedy got out of the driver's seat, leaning in to tell her younger sister, "I'll find you at the hospital," and Jacob took her place behind the wheel and took off.

"Reagan, I need you to apply pressure to his neck," Jacob calmly ordered her as he maneuvered the Cartagena streets like they were the autobahn.

That's when she noticed the ripped bloody rag crudely wrapped around Mason's neck, and another part of the same rag tied around his left thigh.

Holding the cloth in place at his neck, she cried, "Oh my god, how many times was he shot?"

Jacob glanced at her as he drove. "I don't know. Two for sure."

Mason's hand came up to her wrist holding the ripped cloth and gently squeezed. His face was ashen but he offered her a small smile and wink.

"You can't be fucking charming right now—you've been shot, for fuck's sake, and I'm not used to life or death crises," she half-sobbed, half-yelled at him.

"Reagan, listen to me," Jacob said. "When we get to the hospital, you're going to say his name is Connor Jacobson. His identification was in his wallet that was stolen when you two were robbed. That's when he got shot. You don't know me—I'm just someone who happened to come across you and dropped you off at the hospital."

"Um, what about his vest?"

Jacob made a face and spat out, "Fuck!" Then looked over at Mason and grimaced. "Sorry, buddy. She's gonna have to take that off you. Can you apply the pressure for just a minute?"

Mason nodded, and Reagan gingerly ripped the Velcro straps holding the vest in place on his core, then gently lifted it off him as best she could. She wasn't expecting it to be as heavy as it was and had some difficulty given her awkward position in the backseat.

"Oooh, sorry," she winced when she hit Mason in the head as she tried to pull it over his head and into the back seat.

She scrutinized the vest now sitting next to her and panicked. "Oh my god!" She came over the console and ripped his shirt open so buttons flew everywhere in the front seat. Running her hands over his chest and stomach, she found no bullet holes, but there were already three terrible bruises—one directly over his heart—from where he had been shot and the vest absorbed the impact.

"Oh my sweet Mason. Thank god you were wearing your vest."

She swallowed a sob, and he grabbed one of her hands and brought it to his lips.

Tears streamed down her cheeks at the thought of losing him; then she took a deep breath and regained her composure, wiping the tears with the back of her hand. Taking over applying pressure to his neck, she whispered, "Hang in there, baby." He winked at her again. *Damn him.*

"How the hell are we going to explain *that*?" she asked Jacob, nodding at the welted red and purple spots on Mason's core.

"Well, we probably could have avoided it for a while if you hadn't gone Hulk Hogan and ripped his damn shirt open." He drove for a few seconds before suggesting, "I guess you guys were playing paintball earlier."

She snorted. "No one is going to believe that."

"It doesn't matter. They just need to treat him and get him stabilized, then by the time they start asking more questions, he'll be out of there."

Reagan nodded. "Okay."

They could see the hospital in the distance.

"Okay, recap. What's his name?"

"Connor Jacobson."

"And who are you?"

"Um…. his wife?" The idea had its merits.

Jacob nodded. "His wife. And how did he get shot?"

"We got lost while out sight-seeing and were approached by three men. They demanded my purse, his wallet, our phones, everything. I guess we must not have had enough money or something because after opening Connor's wallet and seeing how much was in there, they shot him for no reason, then took off in a car. I'm not sure what kind—it all happened so fast. Some man heard me screaming and offered to help, but I have no idea who he was or why he drove away after dropping us off."

Jacob looked at her out of the corner of his eye and smirked. "Damn, girl. You sure you haven't done this before?"

"God, no. I don't know how I'm doing it now."

"Fight or flight—it's amazing what a person is capable of when flight isn't an option."

She looked over at the man bleeding profusely in the passenger seat. Flight was definitely not an option.

They pulled up to the emergency room bay, and Jacob jumped out to flag down a young man in scrubs pushing an empty wheelchair. They loaded Mason in the chair and rushed him inside, Reagan at his side, while Jacob quietly disappeared.

A team quickly surrounded them and went to work on Mason while Reagan quietly observed from the corner of the room.

"Mr. Jacobson, can you hear me?" one doctor asked as he shined a small flashlight in Mason's eyes.

Mason responded with a thumbs-up.

"We're going to have to take you into surgery to repair the damage to your neck and leg."

The American subtly nodded in understanding, then urgently waved Reagan to his side. She was next to him in seconds, tears in her eyes, squeezing his hand and murmuring, "You're going to be okay, babe."

He kissed her knuckles and winked at her. *Goddamn him.*

"Your wife will be here waiting for you when you get out," the doctor said authoritatively, and began to push the gurney out the door. Mason didn't let go of her fingers until the distance forced him to, mouthing, *I love you* as they wheeled him away.

The adrenaline finally began to wear off, and she found herself feeling like she was ready to collapse. Locking herself in the nearest bathroom, she began to ugly-cry instead.

Chapter Seventeen

Mason

Being shot while wearing a bulletproof vest still hurt like a bitch. Being shot in the neck and thigh? He would definitely not recommend it.

"You're a lucky man, Mr. Jacobson. The bullet in your neck missed both the carotid artery and your windpipe. The bullet in your thigh missed the femoral artery by millimeters," the doctor told him once he woke up from surgery.

Funny, Mason wasn't feeling very lucky.

Mr. Jacobson? Who the fuck is Jacobson? Oh, probably me.

"I'll go update your wife and then send her in," the young doctor said before leaving the recovery room.

My wife?

Reagan appeared a few minutes later. Her eyes were puffy and her skin splotchy, but she put on a brave face and smiled when she approached his bedside and squeezed his hand.

Ah, my wife.

"Hello, Mrs. Hughes," he said weakly, his voice barely above a whisper.

Her eyes widened. "Mrs. *Jacobson*," she hissed as she looked around to see who'd overheard him.

"I like the sound of Mrs. Hughes better," he teased.

"*Connor*," she warned through gritted teeth and raised eyebrows.

He brought her fingers to his lips.

"I'm glad you're here. Thank you."

Brushing his hair at his forehead, she looked into his eyes and leaned in, inches from his lips. "Baby, wild horses couldn't have kept me away."

She seemed like she was about to kiss him when they were interrupted by the nurse appearing.

"Let's get you into your own room, Mr. Jacobson," the older woman in scrubs said in broken but cheery English.

Reagan thanked the woman in Spanish and proceeded to politely chat with her while they transported him. His 'wife' never left his side.

"Connor? Jacobson?" he asked when they were alone.

It was one of his many aliases, and one that he had a US passport for. Of course she wasn't going to tell a Cartagena hospital his real name—especially with him coming in shot— but how did Reagan know about Connor Jacobson?

"Jacob picked it out on the drive here."

Mason's memory after pushing Reagan and Marcus out the door was hazy; he had lost a lot of blood after getting shot, even without any arteries being hit. He remembered shooting some cartel members, then Kennedy, Dante, and Dante's man arriving. He knew he'd been carried out to a car and seemed to recall Jacob's voice, but it was Reagan's fearful face that kept resurfacing. And the distinct feeling of wanting to comfort and assure her.

Mason figured he had until morning, tops, before he needed to get out of the hospital. Fortunately, the cartel men who survived the firefight were two-bit players, like blue polo guy, and would have no interest in hunting him down. Anyone who had a vested reason in finding him right away was now dead. Unfortunately, his body was laughing at the idea of moving any time soon and waving the middle finger at him for even thinking it.

He knew he needed to sleep.

****

"Hey, how are you feeling?" Jacob's voice came the side of his bed when he opened his eyes.

"Like I've been shot." His voice was raspy, but at least it worked.

That made Jacob chuckle. "Yeah, you look like it, too."

"How's Marcus?"

"Beat the fuck up, but Erik says his own private nursemaid is helping him heal. Or at least forget that he's hurting."

"And the women?"

"All safe on the yacht, which is en route to Panama as we speak. We're going to transport you to Ensenada in the morning."

"Ensenada? Why Ensenada?"

"Because that's where I'll be," came the soft voice of his beautiful sassy pants. He hadn't noticed her curled up in the chair in the corner.

"Dante has assured me he can have a nurse to tend to you without rousing suspicion," the dark-haired man added.

"So I'm supposed to stay at his estate?" They had to be shitting him.

"Yeah, and I hope you have a wad of cash stashed somewhere, because I'm guessing you're not exactly going to file a workman's comp claim for this, and you still owe me a shitload of money."

"Don't worry about it," came a woman's voice from the doorway. "We'll cover it."

There stood the woman Mason had been ordered to kill not more than a year ago. The one who had helped save him and his brother's life today. Why the hell was she was agreeing to help him any further?

He knew he was about to find out when Kennedy said with a smile, "I need to debrief with Mason. Can you two give me a minute?"

Reagan and Jacob looked at each other, as if silently asking, *What's this all about?* But they both stood at the same time and walked toward the door.

The two sisters hugged briefly, then Reagan said, "We'll be in the cafeteria if you need us," before following Jacob outside the room.

Mason looked at Kennedy. He knew damn well she wasn't there to simply debrief with him.

"How are you feeling?" she asked as she approached his bed and sat down in the chair next to him and patted his hand, careful to avoid the IV that was taped to his skin.

He gave a wry smile. "I've been better."

With her hand still on top of his, the woman—who was now brown-haired—nodded absent-mindedly, as if she wasn't really listening to his answer and was thinking about something else.

She removed her hand. "So apparently you and my sister are in love." Her pursed lips indicated she didn't approve—not that he blamed her.

"I didn't mean for that to happen. It just did."

Her grin was empathetic. "I understand how that goes."

"So does my brother, apparently. Thank you for that, by the way. And for showing up today when you did. I definitely owe you."

"You probably think keeping my secret will be a way to repay me, but you'd be wrong. I know you're going to keep your end of the bargain with that."

He had a feeling he knew where this conversation was going. "So what would be a good way to repay you?"

"You really need to consider ending things with Reagan."

He frowned at the older Jones sister without replying.

"You can't be with her, and you know it. What kind of life would she have? For fuck's sake, she could have been killed today."

Mason knew what Kennedy was saying was true. Hell, he'd been at war with himself over the same thing. Except his heart was imploring him, *Find a way*.

"Is that why you're willing to help me? To ensure I end things with your sister?"

Kennedy shrugged in response.

"I can't make that promise right now," he told her quietly.

"I understand. But if you really love her, you'll think about what's best for her. She's supposed to be back at work in two weeks, yet she's willing to take a leave of absence next semester, give up her only source of income—for you. Think about that. You're going to heal and be on your way, and she's going to be left without a job until the beginning of next year."

"I would make sure she was financially supported."

"You know perfectly well I would never let her want for anything. What concerns me is her giving up her life for you— her job, her friends... but what happens to her life once you up and disappear for months—a year?"

He nodded solemnly. "I get where you're coming from, I do. But I love her. You of all people should understand I can't just let her go."

"And I gave up my life, my role in the agency, my whole identity to be with the man I love. Are you willing to do that for Reagan?"

Mason remained silent. He didn't have an answer for that. He hadn't had enough time to process what being with her long-term would mean.

"Until you can definitely say yes, you need to tread lightly with her heart, Agent Hughes."

Once again, he knew she was right.

Chapter Eighteen

Reagan

To her surprise, Jacob hadn't been a jerk about her running across the street instead of going back to where he was observing in the office building. Quite the opposite actually, and she wasn't sure what to think about it.

"You saved Marcus' life—you realize that, right? Not me, not your sister, not your boyfriend—*you*," he told her once they'd sat down in the hospital cafeteria. He took a sip of his coffee as he gauged her reaction to what he'd said.

"I wouldn't exactly say that. I think everybody played a part; I just came in at the end and happened to be the one who found him stuffed in a closet."

"What possessed you to go in there alone?"

"I just kept hearing your words *look closer* and knew I had to do something." Reagan smiled around the straw in her mouth as she took a drink of soda. "Besides, I knew you'd see me and Mason would come back for me. That's what made me brave."

"You were brave indeed."

"Do you think Mason's going to be okay?"

"I think with some time and physical therapy he'll be as good as new. He's been through worse than this."

"He's been worse than *this*?"

"Yeah. We almost lost him a few years ago in an explosion—got hit by a lot of shrapnel."

That explained the scars she'd felt on his back.

Reagan cocked her head.

"I was under the impression you didn't work together very often. You're someone he called as a last resort to fix things when nobody else could. But you come at a hefty price."

He smiled. "I'm not cheap. And you're right—we don't work together often. But, I'm not called in on the easy jobs, so when we do, it's usually dangerous."

"Are you married? Have a girlfriend?"

His smile turned sad at her question. "No. I almost was once, but I realized I was asking too much of her. This profession isn't for people with wives and families."

Jacob's words made her sad, which was probably why she confessed, "Well Mason and I fell in love and we're going to figure this out."

The sympathetic smile on his face suggested he didn't believe Mason loved her. She'd dare say it looked like he thought she was pathetic and making things up.

"What? You don't think Mason fell in love with me?"

He sighed. "You're beautiful and smart, and would obviously make someone very happy, but Mason knows what's at stake. He doesn't fall in love—not for real anyway. I'm not trying to hurt you, but you need to know the score. I'd hate for you to get hurt worse because of false expectations.

Once he no longer needs you, he's going to send you on your way."

Ouch. I think I would have preferred not knowing the score.

****

Her heart was a little heavier when they returned to Mason's room, but her spirits lifted at his smile when he saw her walk in the room.

"Hi baby," she murmured in his ear as he gripped her hand. "Did my sister leave?"

He nodded and blinked, his eyes slow to reopen.

"You need to sleep. We're busting you out in the morning."

Mason scooted over, lifting his wires and tubes to indicate she should lie down next to him, which she did happily, if gingerly, tentatively slipping her arm around his waist while he stroked her hair.

Reagan glanced over at Jacob watching them closely and tried not to appear smug.

You're wrong—he is in love with me.

"I'll see you two in morning," he murmured as he walked toward the door.

"Hey Jake." Mason's raspy voice caused the man to pause and look at them. "Thanks."

A small smile formed on the fixer's lips. "Try to get some rest."

****

Mason

The doctors weren't thrilled with the idea of him leaving the hospital but acquiesced when he explained he was traveling on a private jet with a private nurse Jacob had hired. Once they learned that, they presented him with his discharge papers and bill, which they asked him to pay before leaving.

The amount was almost laughable. He paid it from the money in his wallet and still would have had some left over if he hadn't given it to them.

"For the patients who need help paying," he explained when the woman looked at him confused.

"You realize you have no way of knowing if she's going to just pocket that money," Reagan whispered once the woman left, and she started to gently help him get dressed in the sweats and t-shirt she'd bought him in the gift shop. The yacht had left with his clothes, and he needed something loose-fitting for stitches and bruises.

He shrugged. "You're right. But that's on her conscience if she does. Maybe it will help them feel less inclined to call the police about me being here."

"Um, I believe Jacob already took care of that bribe."

He closed his eyes and sighed. His bill for the fixer's services this time was going to be astronomical. But he was grateful.

The orderly arrived with a wheelchair, and he was transported to the front of the building where the car Kennedy had sent was waiting for them.

Once they were situated inside, he held her hand and took a deep breath.

"Sweetheart, we need to talk about you going back to Fargo."

Chapter Nineteen

Reagan

Her back stiffened and Jacob's words echoed in her mind.

Mason doesn't fall in love.

He'll send you on your way when he no longer needs you.

This was it. He no longer needed her.

"What about it?" she asked curtly as she tried to withdraw her hand from his, refusing to look at him. He didn't let go, and instead began to stroke her knuckles.

"I know a new semester is starting soon where you work..."

She raised her shoulders. "I'm taking a leave of absence and staying in Ensenada to be with you."

"What if I went back to Fargo with you? So you wouldn't have to take a leave."

Well, that's not what I was expecting.

She turned to look at him.

"I would love that. How long would you stay?"

"As long as I could."

It was the vaguest, most non-committal answer in the history of answers, and still she was ecstatic. Mason was coming to Fargo with her!

"Should we stay in Ensenada at least until you no longer need a nurse? Bullet wounds might be easier to overlook there than in North Dakota."

"Speaking of… do you know exactly where Kennedy plans on us staying?"

"I think at the villa where you kidna—er, picked me up."

One corner of his mouth went up when she corrected herself.

They pulled onto the tarmac where Dante's private jet was waiting. She was surprised to find Jacob waiting at the bottom of the stairs leading up to the plane.

"You made it," the handsome fixer said as he opened the car door. Helping Mason out and toward the portable staircase, he asked, "Any trouble at the hospital?"

"Not a bit," Mason replied as he gripped the rails and began his slow ascent to the plane's interior.

They found Dante and Kennedy situated on one of the couches. Dante's scary, brawny bodyguard was in a seat with a magazine in one of the corners of the luxury aircraft. Jacob helped Mason down the aisle, which was three times wider than any she'd seen the few times she'd been on commercial jets. Jacob sat down next to Kennedy; Reagan and Mason took a seat on the couch opposite them. He was slightly winded from the exertion of getting from the car to his seat on the plane.

"Thanks for taking care of the police questioning," Mason said to the brown-haired American man when he'd caught his breath.

"It's why you pay me the big bucks."

Reagan was curious just how big those bucks were. She heard a baby's cry from the back bedroom and raised her eyebrows at Kennedy.

"You brought Madison with you?"

"Of course. I'm still nursing," she answered as she stood.

Reagan looked at her, smirking.

"What? I brought Rosa," Kennedy said, returning the smirk. Then she made her way to the back of the plane where the baby was fussing. Dante was close behind.

She would say this about her new brother-in-law; he obviously loved his wife and daughter.

The pilot's voice came from the overhead speakers as the jet started to move. "Please fasten your seatbelts. We've been cleared for takeoff and are currently number five in line for the runway."

A gray-haired Hispanic woman appeared from the bedroom, sat down in the seat next to Reagan, and fastened her seatbelt. The younger Jones sister recognized her as one of the housekeepers at Dante's estate.

"Rosa! So good to see you. What are you doing here?"

"I'm helping with la bebé."

"Oh. Did Quinn go back to California?"

"No, no. She's still in Ensenada."

"I don't understand."

The woman gave a kind smile that reached her eyes while gently explaining. "Quinn is Bella's assistant, not her nanny. Mr. Dante and Mrs. Bella aren't hiring someone for that yet, so I'm helping out when needed."

"Bella and Dante are lucky to have you. It's important to have someone they can trust with Madison."

Mason entwined his fingers in hers.

"Are you going to want a nanny for our kids?"

Huh? Our what?

Jacob must have heard his question because his eyes were wide with surprise when Reagan glanced at him.

"Um. I don't know? I've never really thought about it. I mean, I've always assumed I'd have to keep working, so it seemed like daycare or a babysitter was a given."

"Not your mother?"

Just the thought made her both cringe and chuckle. "Yeaaaah, no. Maybe for a Friday night date, but nothing regular or for a long period of time. My mother wasn't exactly mother-of-the-year, although she has said she wants to be better for her grandchildren. She was always far more interested in whatever man she was dating at the time. Keni and I were lucky if she remembered to feed us regularly."

He drew her hand toward his lips and kissed her knuckles.

"Maybe my parents will follow us to San Diego."

She held her breath for a second before slowly releasing it.

"You mean Fargo. She might not be the best mom, but she's the only one I have. With my sister being so far away, she kind of relies on me to help her. I can't just abandon her."

"No, of course not. We'll put her in a condo nearby."

"San Diego, huh?"

"Well, you said Key West has too many hurricanes, remember?"

She did remember that night. It was a wonderful night, pretending they had a long future ahead of them. Was he just continuing their game of make-believe, or did he really mean it?

Glancing over at Jacob's face, still in disbelief, she wasn't sure what to think.

Chapter Twenty

Mason

Reagan sat down in the seat next to him with the baby facing her in her lap. The little girl was adorable with her big brown eyes and toothless smile—a smile that she seemed to give without discrimination to anyone who happened to look at her. Mason couldn't help but smile back.

But what caused his heart to skip a beat was watching the redheaded woman holding the baby. Her smile and animated expressions while she talked to the little girl stirred something inside him, and he couldn't help but imagine what it would be like if it were their child she was holding.

What kind of father will I be like?

He'd always known he wanted to be one, but until their night of make-believe future on the yacht, he had just put it into the *someday* category.

Maybe someday was closer than he realized.

They were nearing the Ensenada airport; Kennedy was sitting on the couch with one leg tucked underneath her, clicking away on her iPad. She made a dramatic press of a button, saying, "Done," then pointedly looked across the aisle where Jacob was sitting.

"I just transferred Mason's remaining payment to you. I trust I will never hear from you again after today."

"I appreciate that," was the fixer's only response, then he turned to look out the window. Kennedy demonstratively glowered at him, folding her arms at her chest.

"Jacob?" She posed it as a question, but Mason knew it was really more of a warning.

The dark-haired American looked away from the window and smiled sweetly at the former CIA agent.

"Yeah?"

"You are *not* to contact me again—ever. Do you understand?"

He shook his head solemnly. "I can't promise you'll never hear from me again. You know how small this world is."

Kennedy's eyebrows went up. "Let me rephrase then. It would be in your best interest if I never hear from you again."

Jacob stubbornly refused to agree.

Dante moved closer to his wife and began to rub tiny circles on her back. To Mason's surprise, instead of roaring out demands they never be contacted again *or else*, Dante remained quiet, a look of slight amusement on his face while his wife stewed.

They touched down on the runway and taxied to a private hanger where they were greeted by two black cars with tinted windows. Mason found descending the stairs to be much easier than ascending them, but Jacob went ahead of him, just in case he needed someone to break his fall.

Before sliding into the back of one of the waiting cars, Jacob turned to Mason. "Let me know when you're back in business." He cast a quick glance at Reagan and broke out into a grin, adding, "Or out of it," then sat down in the seat and closed the car door before Mason could reply.

Out of the spy business? There was a time when the mere idea would have been unfathomable, but as he entwined his fingers with Reagan's, Mason realized it was something to consider.

Kennedy had been watching him carefully. Her expression was hard to decipher, but he'd be willing to bet she wasn't happy. Still, she remained quiet as they loaded into Dante's limo. Madison smiled brightly at the bandaged-up man while her father strapped her into her carseat.

The car began to move but the only sounds in the backseat were the baby's giggling. Mason leaned forward and offered Madison one of his fingers to play with.

"Thank you again for letting me stay in Ensenada," he awkwardly offered in the too-quiet car.

Dante, who hadn't said much to him on the plane, replied, "You'll be safe here for as long as you're my guest," but then threw in a jab: "Unless your government decides to pay us another visit." He was referring to when Mason and his team had landed a helicopter on Dante's estate and extracted Kennedy against her will.

Madison let go of his index finger, and he sat back. Reagan leaned her head against his shoulder and enveloped his hand in both of hers. Kennedy continued to silently observe them.

Dante and Kennedy—*er, Bella*—had their driver drop Mason and Reagan at the villa where Reagan had been staying with her mother, Delilah Jones: the same location he had originally picked her up from—and had been smitten before they even reached the marina.

Once Reagan had been kidnapped, the Guzmans had moved Delilah to the pool house on their property to keep her safe. With the new threat from the Colombian cartel, they decided she'd remain at Bella's, leaving Reagan alone with Mason in the Santa Fe style house with nine-foot walls and meticulous grounds. Well, 'alone' save for the security team of nine men.

"I really wish you'd reconsider staying at the house with us," Bella sighed at Reagan as they moved to get out of the car.

"She'll be fine here," Dante interjected. "I've added cameras that will be monitored by personnel at the estate, plus the extra security. Besides, Mason isn't going to let anything happen to her."

That was true.

"They'll have to get through me."

Bella snorted in derision as Mason staggered out of the car. "That wouldn't be too hard right now."

"True. But I'm still perfectly capable of shooting a gun."

He felt Reagan's hand firmly on his back. "Let's hope we won't have to test that," she said with a placating smile while ushering him toward the big wooden gates.

"I'll see you tomorrow," she called as she ducked down to wave goodbye to the passengers in the car.

"Call if you need anything," Dante said before the door closed.

The grounds of the villa were lush and beautiful, filled with plants and trees. The lighted walkway leading to the house was lined with vegetation and flowers, and Mason felt like he was in the rainforest as he hobbled along the path with Reagan's assistance.

"Tomorrow I need to get crutches," he mumbled. He did not like it one bit that he had to rely on anyone for mobility.

There was a grand, curved stone staircase with a decorative wrought iron and wooden railing in the burnt-orange entryway of the house when they walked in, and he took a deep breath at the thought of maneuvering up them. To his relief, she pointed down a short hall.

"You're going to stay in the bedroom on the first floor. It's not as big as the upstairs rooms, but it has a connecting bathroom, so I think you'll be fine."

"You mean *we*. *We'll* be staying in the bedroom on the first floor."

A small smile escaped her lips.

"I didn't want to assume anything."

He reached out to pull her closer.

"Sweetheart, when it comes to you and me—assume away. I fucking adore you."

Her arms came around his middle. "It won't hurt my feelings if you decide you want to sleep alone. I'll completely understand. Actually, now that I think about it, that would probably be for the best."

He fought the growl that was coming from his throat at the idea of her in the same house and not in his bed.

"Not gonna happen."

"But you need to rest," she protested.

"*Not gonna happen*," he reiterated.

The corners of her mouth lifted, but she kept up the façade when she grumbled, "Fine," even as she squeezed him a little tighter.

They stood in the foyer, and she pointed in various directions to show him where different rooms were located throughout the house. Then they shuffled down the Saltillo-tiled hall to the bedroom.

He hopped inside and sat down on the purple velvet chaise lounge, relieved to be seated again. The room continued the theme of the house he had seen so far: brightly colored, ornate décor, large furniture. It was not at all his minimalistic style, but he felt comfortable here. Probably because of the company.

He sat back and stretched out, gesturing for her to join him, but she shook her head.

"I'm going to go check on things and see about dinner," she said as she handed him the television remote. "Just lie back and take it easy. You should still be in the hospital, for goodness sake."

****

"I need to go see my mom tomorrow. I think I'll go when the nurse comes," Reagan announced when she brought in a dinner tray for him as he lay on the bed in his boxers and a white t-shirt, the covers folded to the footboard. He wasn't wild about not eating at the table, but he'd exerted a lot of energy today. Just the thought of hopping to the kitchen and back made him tired, so he didn't put up a fuss when she suggested she bring him dinner. Dante's other housekeeper, Maria, had sent over food for them; all they had to do was put it in the oven. "I'll be right back."

She returned a minute later with her own tray, and sat down next to him on the bed.

"Thanks for bringing me dinner, sweetheart."

"Of course. That's why you came here, isn't it? So I could help take care of you while you heal."

He hadn't had someone take care of him since he had lived at home with his parents. He kind of liked the idea.

"Well, I appreciate it."

Her smile in return made his heart happy.

They chatted about innocuous things throughout dinner. It felt as if they had both been purposefully avoiding talking about the events that had taken place the day before, but knew at some point they were going to have to. Just not tonight.

Tonight they were simply going to enjoy each other's company. Something that was easy for Mason to do with the beautiful redheaded woman.

She disappeared with their dirty dishes. While he liked the idea of her taking care of him, he wasn't fond of just lying in bed while she did everything. He stood to hobble to the kitchen and help her clean up.

"Do you need help getting to the bathroom?" came her voice from the doorway.

"No, I was coming to help you."

Even her scowl was adorable. "Get your ass back in bed."

"Yes, ma'am. But only if you join me."

He leaned back against the pillows and winked. She sighed and walked over to tuck the covers around him.

"You need your rest, Agent Hughes," she murmured as she smoothed the blanket.

Mason threw the sheet and blanket back on the other side of the bed and patted the mattress with a grin.

"I know, but I'd rest so much better if you were next to me."

A tiny smile escaped her lips, and she walked to the foot of the four-poster bed.

"You're impossibly charming for someone who was shot multiple times just yesterday."

"It's my superpower."

She leaned against the footboard, standing on her tiptoes as she looked at him with an eyebrow raised.

"What is? Charming women into your bed?" She dramatically dropped her heels.

"No, sassy pants, just being charming in general. There's only one woman I want in my bed, and she's being cheeky because she knows I'm too weak to put her over my knee."

Reagan smirked. "Aw, that's a shame," she said, then walked out.

She walked out.

"Hey!" he called after her. "Where are you going?"

No response.

"I will limp my ass all over this house looking for you, Reagan Elizabeth!" he shouted.

Still no response.

Well fuck. Now what? Mason really didn't want to make good on his threat, but he wasn't one to make an ultimatum and not follow through on it. Sighing heavily, he threw the covers off and swung his legs to the edge of the bed.

"You really are the worst patient on the planet."

She was standing in the doorway again with her Kindle in her hand, now wearing a black satin camisole and matching boy shorts. She was stunning. *Be still, my heart— and my dick.*

"Wow," was all he could get out.

He didn't take his eyes off her as she came through the threshold and sauntered toward the bed. He might have imagined it, but there seemed to be a little extra sway in her hips as he gawked at her. *Is my mouth open?* He clamped his jaw shut.

"I'll sleep in here. But no funny business. You need to rest."

Yeah, sure. No funny business with you looking like that.

"Uh huh," was his gruff reply.

She narrowed her eyes as she got situated next to him. "I mean it. You were shot yesterday. In the neck and leg, in case you forgot."

He wrapped his arms around her and pulled her on top of his bruised core. Her face was inches from his, and he smirked, "Yeah, but not in my cock." He flexed his hips up against hers. "That's still working just fine."

****

Reagan

"So I can feel." She tried to suppress a giggle but it didn't work. *Since when do I giggle?* Rolling off him, she continued. "But seriously, Mason, you're not exactly in any condition to be messing around. I mean, look at you. You're the very definition of *walking wounded*."

He glanced down at his core. Although he was wearing a t-shirt, they both knew about the bruises underneath from where he'd been shot in the vest. His gaze traveled down to his heavily bandaged leg as he felt for the dressing on his neck.

"So what are you saying? I don't turn you on, all beat up like this?" he said with a chuckle.

The sad thing was, he still did. His abs and chest were still sexy, even if they were bruised to hell, and his muscular thighs made her heart skip a beat—bandages and all. And while the dressing around his neck was concerning, it didn't take away from his handsome face or that damn dimple that seemed to make her powerless against his charms.

"I don't have an injured-soldier fetish," she teased. *Just a Mason Hughes one.*

"Okay, okay. Point taken." He tugged the t-shirt at the back of his neck and gingerly pulled it over his head. "Just let me feel your body against mine. You calm me."

That might have been the most romantic thing anyone had ever said to her.

"I feel the same way," she said softly as she nestled against his side. "Actually, I think it's more like you make me feel safe."

"I'd never let anything happen to you, sweetheart," he murmured against her hair as his fingertips moved up and down her back.

"I know."

And she did. If there was anything she was sure of, it was that he'd always protect her. That was what made her brave enough to run into the warehouse yesterday—she knew he'd come back for her.

Reagan softly kissed his chest.

"Thank you for going back to the warehouse."

She felt his soft laughter in his chest against her cheek.

"The second Jacob started cussing, I knew what you'd done. At the time I wanted to tan your ass; now I just want to kiss it. Thank *you* for finding Marcus. I hate to think what would have happened to him when the Colombians returned to the warehouse and found the women gone."

"They might not have had made the connection if just the women were missing, but not Marcus."

"Maybe not, but they might have taken it out on him."

She winced to think of Mason's brother having to endure anything worse than he already had over the last several days.

"Speaking of, have you heard how he's doing?"

"From what Eddie tells me, Susana hasn't left his side."

"I'm assuming Susana is the girl he refused to leave without?"

"Yeah."

"Well, I hope everything works out for them. I hope she's not with him because she feels guilty he sacrificed so much for her."

She wondered if that might be why Mason was insisting she return to Fargo in a few weeks—so she wouldn't sacrifice her semester, and he wouldn't feel guilty leaving her.

"I hope not, too. He's giving everything up for her. It would really suck if the feelings turned out to be one-sided."

Indeed.

Chapter Twenty-One

Mason

He wasn't lying when he told Reagan she calmed him. She did. There was just something about her: her touch, her scent, the sound of her voice... it soothed his soul.

But lying so close to her without making love to her was torture on his cock.

As he watched her breasts rise and fall under the moonlight coming in through the window, he had to remind himself not to touch her and rouse her from her slumber. The creamy mounds of tantalizing flesh peeking out from the black satin were making that difficult, and Mason found himself tracing her nipple over the material.

He was instantly rewarded with the hardening bud and her soft, sleepy moan. Feeling brave, he pulled the top down to fully expose her tits, briefly closing his eyes and smiling with satisfaction at the sight.

Mason dipped his head and circled his tongue along the outline of one rosy peak, then closed his lips around it and began to suck gently. He felt her back arch and heard her coo with pleasure as her fingers twined in his hair.

"Baby," she whispered hoarsely. "We can't."

"Like hell we can't," he growled as he cupped her other breast. She didn't protest further as he lavished her tits with attention.

Reagan pushed lightly on his shoulder and sat up, moving to straddle his rigid cock, bulging beneath his boxer briefs.

"Take your shorts off," he demanded.

She quickly complied, then tugged on his underwear until it was lying next to her pajama bottoms on the floor. At his urging, her top quickly joined the pile, and she sat back on top of him, seeming to be mindful of the black and blue spots on his core as she positioned her hands on his chest.

"Are you sure?" she whispered.

He answered by pulling her pussy down on his cock until he was fully seated inside her.

"Oooh," she whimpered as she began to rock on him.

"Fuck, you feel good," he moaned as he thrust up.

Their bodies began to move in rhythm. She was sexy as fuck riding him with her head thrown back, and he reached between them to fondle her clit, causing her to gasp then moan softly.

Mason shifted his weight slightly when his thigh began to throb.

Not now, he pleaded with his aching leg. He knew she was on the cusp of climaxing and there was no way he was going to stop until she did.

Except.

His leg went from a throbbing pain to a stabbing one. His cock reacted accordingly, which Reagan quickly noticed, and she stopped abruptly.

"Oh god, I've hurt you!" she cried out as she moved off him to the side and switched on the bedside lamp.

He reached up and stroked her arm.

"No, sweetheart, *you* didn't hurt me. I just moved wrong and tweaked my leg."

"You should have let me do all the work," she teased, then began to examine his bandages. "It doesn't seem to be bleeding." Tucking one pillow under his thigh and another under his calf, she murmured, "We should probably keep it elevated though."

"My own naked Florence Nightingale," he said with a smirk.

"Let me grab your pain pills."

She went to walk to the kitchen buck-naked, and he shouted, "Whoa, whoa! Nuh-uh. Put a robe on. You don't need to be flashing any of the security guys."

"Oh, whoops. I never thought of that." She giggled and pulled a robe on, then added, "Probably nothing they haven't already seen then. I sunbathed topless here last week." She was out the door before he could respond.

Mason suspected she was purposefully tormenting him and wasn't really serious. But the thought of any other man seeing her topless made his blood boil.

"That's not fucking funny!" he called after her.

She reappeared with a glass of water and his prescription bottle of pain medication.

"I thought it was hilarious," she murmured as she handed him the water.

"Not even a little."

He swallowed the pills with a drink, then set the glass on the nightstand and grabbed her by the belt of her robe. Tugging her closer, he untied it and pulled the gown apart to openly leer at her naked body.

"Fuck, you're beautiful. I'm sorry I didn't make you come before we stopped."

She leaned over and pecked his lips, then stood up straight and tugged on the fabric, closing it in the middle by bunching the material in her hand before walking around to her side of the bed. Bending over, she picked up their discarded clothes and acted like she was going to put them back on.

"Aw, don't. Please? I promise I'll behave."

Reagan eyed him suspiciously. They both knew he was lying.

"I'll go upstairs and sleep if you don't," she warned.

He didn't want that.

"Scout's honor," he said, giving the three-fingers salute. She didn't need to know he was never a Boy Scout.

She slid under the covers next to him and nestled her bare chest against his side. The pain in his leg had dulled so his dick was quick to stand up again.

"Glad to see it's not broken," she murmured with a grin, gesturing to the growing tent under the covers. "But I'm not kidding. I learned my lesson—what would we have done if your stitches ripped open? I'd have had to call my sister. Do you want to be the one to explain to Bella at two in the morning why you're bleeding and need a doctor immediately?"

Mason had to concede she had a point.

"Okay, okay. I already promised I'd behave, what more do you want?"

"Um, you to mean it."

He looked her solemnly in the eye. "I wouldn't have sex with you again tonight even if you begged me."

Please don't test me. Please don't test me.

****

Reagan

She was feeling guilty for being such a dirty girl. What kind of woman fucked her boyfriend the day after he'd been shot multiple times? A slutty one, that's what kind.

The younger Jones sister had had her share of one-night stands in her thirty-two years, so she wasn't exactly innocent, but she never would have classified herself as slutty before. But given how easily she had hopped on Mason at the slightest provocation, and considering he was freaking *injured,* she was labeling herself now.

But he made it so damn difficult not to be.

She was standing her ground, though. Just the thought of having to make that phone call to her sister put the brakes on her hormones. She imagined the conversation going something like this:

Hey, it's me. We need the doctor to come right away, Mason's sutures came apart.

Bella: It's two o'clock in the damn morning. How in the hell did his stitches break open?

Well, um. He must have moved wrong while he was sleeping or something.

Bella: Ugh. That's such bullshit, and I can't believe you're trying to sell me that crap. I know perfectly well what you two were doing to cause his stitches to pop. Jesus Christ, Reagan, he was fucking shot yesterday, and you can't go two days without humping him? What are you two—goddamn rabbits? I certainly hope you're using protection.

Annnnd, she was no longer horny.

Then his dick pitched a tent under the covers. *Damn him.*

Her sister's voice popped in her head. *You can't go two days without humping him?*

"Do you want to be the one to explain to Bella at two in the morning why you're bleeding and need a doctor immediately?"

Mason vowed, "I wouldn't have sex with you again tonight even if you begged me."

She raised an eyebrow at him.

"Okay, maybe if you *begged* me."

That made her burst out laughing. "I promise, I won't beg."

"Tonight, anyway," he clarified with a wink.

Reagan smiled and kissed his cheek, then leaned across him and turned off the light, her bare breasts skimming his chest as she did.

"It's late. Go to sleep."

His hand squeezed her ass but he did as she directed, and she quickly followed suit.

Chapter Twenty-Two

Mason

Waking up naked and finding himself spooning an equally nude Reagan Jones had to be the best feeling in the world.

The scent of her shampoo filled his senses as her long, shiny red hair tickled his chest and chin; the feel of her silky skin while his hands wrapped around her soft middle and his cock nestled between her ass; her ankle wrapped around his calf... it was fucking heaven.

His hand glided up her body from her tummy to cup her tits. Mason loved how perfectly her boobs fit in his hands. He squeezed gently, and as if on reflex, she pressed her ass against his morning wood and lifted her hands above her head to stretch.

Reagan rolled over and curled against him with her eyes closed.

"It's too early," she whined.

This would normally be the point where he'd slip out of bed so he didn't disturb her while he started going through texts and emails; then, if it was early enough, he'd try to get in a quick workout before going to the kitchen to start making breakfast. This invalid crap was for the birds. And he had to piss.

Mason sat up and gently swung his legs to the edge of the bed, and using his good leg, scooted himself to the foot of the bed. He stood and hopped to the bathroom, only having to pause once to steady himself before reaching it.

I'm definitely getting crutches today.

When he came back out, the bed was empty and made, except his side was neatly turned down, as if waiting for him to get back in.

Fuck that. He wasn't spending his day in bed.

"Hey, babe..." he called down the hall from the doorway.

Wiping her hands with a paper towel, she appeared from where she had told him the kitchen was last night.

"Good morning," she smiled cheerfully.

Damn, she was good for his soul. Just the sight of her fresh, morning face—free of makeup and eyes still puffy from sleep—made his heart happy.

"I hate to ask, but would you mind helping me to the kitchen?"

"Oh! Of course I don't mind."

They carefully made their way to the kitchen where she helped sit him down at the table, then she went back to making breakfast.

It was fucking mesmerizing.

Either the effects of last night's drugs were hitting him, or he was madly, head over heels in love with this woman.

When his dick moved after she smiled at him once she noticed him watching her, he decided it was the latter.

The million-dollar-question now was, how were they going to make it work?

"I think the nurse is scheduled to arrive at ten. I'm going to go see my mom then and will probably have lunch with her, Bella and the baby. I'll try to be back around one. Do you think you'll be okay until then?"

"I'll be fine. Hopefully the nurse will have crutches for me so I should be fine getting around until you get back. Besides, I've got some work I need to catch up on."

She shot him a disapproving look.

"Can't you just take a few days off and let your body heal without the added work stress?"

"Trust me, sweetheart, I'm not going to be doing a lot. Just answering emails and texts, and I'll probably try to touch base with Marcus or at least try to get a hold of one of the guys from his team just to make sure everyone is doing okay. I'll work for ninety minutes—tops."

"And then you're going to take it easy? Watch TV or maybe read a book? Nap?"

"I'll wait until you get back to nap," he said with a wink.

He could see her fighting her smile, but she wasn't successful.

"You're impossible," she said shaking her head as she flipped pancakes onto a plate and brought it to him, returning a moment later with butter, syrup, and utensils.

"What would you like to drink? Orange juice, coffee, milk, or water?"

"Coffee, please."

Mason was pouring syrup on his pancakes when she set his mug in front of him.

"Aren't you going to eat?"

"Yes, but don't wait for me. Eat it while it's hot."

He looked down and noticed she'd already put cream and sugar in his coffee and tentatively took a sip. It was perfect.

"How did you know how I like my coffee?"

The question seemed to surprise her.

"We've had breakfast together several times already."

"And you paid attention to how I took my coffee?"

"Of course. Didn't you pay attention to how I took mine?"

He knew that was a trick question.

"You don't drink coffee. You like juice in the morning."

She was smiling when she set her plate down on the table and took the seat kitty-corner from his.

"See? It's not hard."

Still, the fact that she cared enough to pay attention to what he liked made him feel special. She had a way of always making him feel important.

He'd never experienced that with a woman before, but he liked it.

****

Reagan

Her mother ran to hug her the minute Reagan walked through Bella's front door.

"I'm so glad you're okay. We were so worried!"

"I'm fine, Mama. I'm sorry to worry you. Bella and Dante were amazing." Reagan decided not to offer any more details than that, and her mom seemed content not knowing anything more.

Her sister walked into the foyer carrying the baby, who smiled when Reagan started making funny faces at her.

"I love being the favorite auntie," she said as she took Madison in her arms and began to bounce around the entryway to entertain her niece.

"Everything okay at the villa last night?"

"Yeah. The nurse arrived this morning to change his bandages, and if he has his way, get him some crutches. He's taking his medicine, although he's only had to take his pain pills once." Reagan didn't volunteer the reason *why* he had to take his pain medication, but a small smile escaped at the thought.

Of course Bella didn't miss it, but she simply narrowed her eyes without saying anything.

"Let's go in the family room," her mother suggested.

She carried Madison into the family room and set her down on the blanket already spread out with her toys, then sat down beside her to continue playing with her.

"Mama is going back to Fargo on Monday, so we're going to do the baptism this Sunday," Bella said as she sat down next to their mother on the couch.

"Oh, good. Are you heading back to San Diego next week?"

"No, we're going to stay in Ensenada for a while. John is going to go back instead."

"I hope you're not staying because of me. We're going to head back to Fargo next week."

"*We?*" Bella asked with eyebrows raised.

"Mason is coming back with me."

"Oh, that's wonderful!" Delilah exclaimed, clapping her hands. "When do I get to meet your young man?"

"Mama… first of all, he's not that young, and secondly, I don't think that's a good idea just yet," Bella interposed.

"Why not, for heaven's sake?"

"He's recovering from an accident," her sister said without missing a beat. "He's pretty self-conscious about it."

"Oh, was he burned?"

"No, but he was hurt pretty badly and needs time to recover."

"You'll meet him soon enough, Mama," Reagan told her.

"But don't count on it anytime soon," Bella quickly added, and Reagan cocked her head.

What the hell is that all about?

Her sister noticed Reagan looking at her.

"What? I don't think he's going to want to meet anyone you know, given his *circumstances*."

Not ever?

That's not at all what she was envisioning. She certainly didn't want to have to hide her boyfriend from everyone she knew in Fargo. But now that she paused to think about it, that was precisely what she was going to have to do.

Well, this sucks.

The disappointment must have shown on her face because Bella offered a sympathetic smile and sat down beside her.

"I'm sorry, honey. I wouldn't have wished this for you. It's almost impossible to have a lasting relationship with a spy. Between the secrecy, the worry, and the time apart..."

"Then I guess I better enjoy my time with him while I can."

"That's what I'd suggest. Don't think too much about the future and just enjoy your time with him."

Good advice that she was going to follow.

Chapter Twenty-Three

Reagan

She came back to the villa and found Mason in black basketball shorts and a white t-shirt, tapping away on his laptop while sitting on the couch in the living room. His injured leg was elevated on the cushions, a pair of crutches within his reach. It was obvious that he had new bandages around his neck.

"Hi baby," she said as she leaned over the back of the sofa and kissed his cheek.

"I'm so glad you're back," he replied without looking at her.

She went to move away, but he grasped her wrist with one hand and brought it his lips, not letting her go while he finished typing with the other hand. He closed the computer and moved it to the floor then tugged her over the couch onto his body. She tried to land as gracefully and gently as she could so as not to hurt him. His arms came around her, and she burrowed her face against his chest.

"Did you take a shower?"

"Yeah, the nurse wanted to give me a sponge bath before changing the bandages and I wasn't having that shit."

"You smell good. Very clean."

"You always smell like coconut. I like it."

"It's my shampoo. Or my lotion."

He nuzzled her hair and took a deep breath in.

"I think it's both."

"How did your appointment go? When is she coming back?"

"She said the wounds look good; they're starting to heal like they should but she wants to change the bandages and check on things daily. She thinks I'll be ready for physical therapy by the time we head to Fargo next week."

"I know a good physical therapist I can introduce you to," she offered, and looked up at his face to gauge his response.

"I think it'd be better if I use someone you don't know."

Her sister's words came back to her.

"I'm not going to be able to introduce you to anyone I know, am I?" she asked softly.

"Yes and no. Yes, I'll meet people you know, and you can introduce me as your boyfriend. But we're going to have to use an alias. So you're essentially going to be lying to everyone. And I mean *everyone*. You can't share my secret with your best girlfriend or your mom. That's for their safety as well as mine."

"I have a sister who was in the CIA, remember? I understand how it works."

"I know you do. But are you going to be okay with having a boyfriend in the CIA?"

"Mason, I don't care what we have to do to be together, as long as we are."

"It's not going to be easy," he warned.

"No, but it'll be worth it," she countered.

He kissed her hair and whispered, "I promise it will be."

****

Mason

He'd attempted to seduce her after she came back from seeing her mom but she insisted on simply snuggling with their clothes on—which was bullshit, if you asked him.

But as he closed his eyes with her in his arms, he admitted it was a pretty great consolation.

"I love you, sassy pants," he murmured against her hair.

"I love you, too, James."

He stiffened and pulled away from her. *Did she really just call me by the wrong name?*

She lifted her head and looked up at him. "What's wrong?"

"You called me James. Who's James?"

She started giggling and snuggled back against him, patting his stomach in reassurance.

"Bond, silly. You're like my own secret agent."

Mason chuckled as brought his arms back around her.

"Does that make you Pussy Galore? Or Holly Goodhead? I know—Strawberry Fields."

"You sure know a lot about Bond Girls."

"Those are Bond Girls?" he asked in feigned confusion.

He felt her shake her head against his chest and imagined her rolling her eyes.

"You're impossible."

"I've always been partial to Holly Goodhead myself."

"Oh my god, you've just been downgraded to Austin Powers. Go to sleep."

In his worst British accent, he asked, "Do I make you horny, baby?"

Her shoulders shook with laughter. "I have no idea how."

Cupping her mons over her shorts, he whispered, "I can show you how."

Her hips subtly moved against his hand then she let out a long, frustrated groan and moved away from his hand.

"You have to let your body heal."

He began rubbing between her legs. "I think you riding my cock would help that."

She spread her legs ever so slightly, and he snaked his fingers under her shorts, tracing circles over where her panties were getting wet.

"Come on, sweetheart. Let me finish what I started last night."

As if to remind her, he moved her panties aside and slid his index finger inside her soaked pussy and began to slowly fuck her.

Her breathing quickened, and she let out a little whimper. He was so fucking hard. What he wouldn't give to be able to strip her naked and drive himself deep inside her.

"Please, baby? Sit on my cock," he urged.

He withdrew his hand and began to unbutton her shorts. She didn't protest, even lifting her hips and tugging at the hem to help when he began to push them down her thighs. She pulled them the rest of the way off, then tucked her fingers under the elastic waistbands of his shorts and boxer briefs. Instead of pulling them down as he anticipated, she reached underneath and palmed his rock-hard dick.

"Mmm," she moaned as she began to rub his length. "I love how warm and soft your skin is."

Her hands felt so good on his shaft; he closed his eyes and relished the sensation. She curled her fingers around him, smearing the pre-cum around the tip with her thumb, then began to awkwardly jerk him off under his underwear. The restrictiveness of his clothing was driving him crazy, and he frantically began tugging them down his thighs to give her better access.

Reagan let out a small gasp when his cock finally sprang free, and immediately leaned down to take him in her mouth.

All of him.

"Holy fuck," he groaned as he felt his dick pulse up and down against her throat. She slowly slurped off him, leaving his shaft nice and slippery, then she began to bob her head up and down on him.

He tugged on her hair until she stopped and looked up at him, his dick still between her lips.

"Sit on my cock, sweetheart. I want to come in your pussy."

She smiled and popped him out of her mouth, then moved her body so she was straddling him. Her drenched pussy lips wrapped around his shaft but she didn't move to slide him inside her.

He tugged on her shirt, and she immediately complied by taking it off, along with her bra, and tossing them aside. He raised up and pulled his t-shirt over his head.

"You let me do the work this time. If I feel you doing anything, I'm going to stop. Just lie there and let me fuck you," she warned.

"Yes, ma'am."

It probably wasn't possible, but his cock might have gotten a little harder with her bossy demands.

She sank down on his cock, and they moaned in unison at the sensation.

"Fuck, you feel good," he growled as he gripped her hips, holding her still while he remained deep inside her.

Her hips began to rock, and soon she was riding him like a cowgirl rides a bull—starting at the waist and rolling her hips through to her thighs. She closed her eyes and piled her hair on top of her head, lost in ecstasy. Her tits bounced with her movement, nipples hard as diamonds.

It was the most erotic thing he'd ever seen.

Reaching between them, he began to play with her puffy clit. She leaned her left hand back on his left thigh—his uninjured one—and widened her legs while she continued riding his dick. He could feel her getting wetter and starting to clench her cunt around his cock.

"Mmm, yes, sweetheart. Come all over my dick."

She started to gasp and buck, and Mason rubbed her nub frantically while fighting his own impending release.

"That's it, you dirty girl. Come while you fuck me like a naughty slut."

Those were the magic words. She went still and threw her head back, and he felt her pussy begin to milk his cock. His self-control dissipated.

"Oh my god, oh my god, oh my god," she chanted, then shuddered forward, jerking uncontrollably.

He pulled her hips down tight against his as he began to spurt rope after rope inside her.

Goddamn, bareback with this woman is the shit.

She lay on top of his chest with his arms wrapped around her, both of them trying to catch their breath. Beads of sweat at her hairline made her face stick to his skin when she tried to move. He could feel his cum leaking out of her onto his leg. He fucking loved it.

Finally, she rolled off him and scurried to the bathroom while he enjoyed the view of her backside. She returned a few minutes later with a towel and washcloth and carefully cleaned him up, even lifting his balls and wiping underneath before drying him off.

When she was satisfied, she tossed the linens in a hamper in the corner of the room and climbed back in bed with him.

They lay there silently, bodies touching, until she asked in a quiet voice, "Weren't we supposed to just snuggle?"

"Sorry, not sorry," he murmured as he ran his fingers through her hair.

As a matter of fact, he was just the opposite.

Chapter Twenty-Four

Mason

The next couple of days could only be described as wonderful, with the exception of the healing bullet wounds in his body that prohibited him from leaving the villa or taking the lead when it came to having sex. But being holed up with the woman he loved more than made up for it. He couldn't wait to get snowed in with her this winter in Fargo when he was healthy. He imagined that would be as close to perfect as it got.

Other than the few short hours she spent at her sister's every day when the nurse came, they'd been with each other every waking moment—which only served to help him fall deeper in love with her.

He'd declined an agency assignment, saying he had injured himself without going into specifics of when or where.

Marcus had gotten the hero's welcome that Eddie had said he would—especially given how the rescue had 'somehow' been leaked to the media. That was convenient since he'd brought the thirteen rescued women to the States for asylum—it helped the powers that be overlook the borrowing of the yacht. The agency interviewed them and decided to reopen their investigation—probably more as a PR stunt then anything, but at least his brother had been allowed to retire quietly.

The idea of retirement was a lot more appealing to Mason these days.

He allowed himself to consider what it would be like to live a semi-normal life with Reagan and decided he liked it. He had been daydreaming about marrying her and having babies, which was probably why he agreed when she asked if he would go to Madison's baptism with her and meet her mother, along with Dante and Bella's guests.

Sitting on the bed and looking at the suit she'd laid out for him, he wondered out loud, "What the fuck have I done?"

This was such a bad idea—of epic proportions.

The alarm bells should have been going off when they were creating his cover story. Mason and Reagan had just recently started dating after meeting online, and he was a chef exploring opening his own restaurant. That would alleviate the risk of him saying he was employed somewhere and having one of the guests be familiar with the restaurant he named. He knew the hard way what a small world it was. But as they fabricated the story, he found himself wanting it to be true and wondering what it would take to make it happen.

Hopefully nothing as drastic as Agent Jones had had to do.

A dose of reality set in that morning as he went about the task of getting ready. He should not have agreed to this. He needed to tell her he couldn't go.

"Hey, I forgot—I bought you an ascot; it should help hide the bandages on your neck, and you won't have to button the top button on your shirt," she said as she walked in the room with a teal tie that matched the new silk dress she was wearing.

She looked stunning. Her dress was pleated and draped, showing off her tight figure; the color made her hair, which was curled and flowing around her shoulders, look even more fiery red than usual and the green in her eyes sparkle a little brighter. The matching peep-toe, four-inch pumps made her legs look a mile long. Her skin still was sun-kissed from the day she'd spent on deck on the yacht, and the soft pink lipstick on her lips made him want to grab her and kiss it off her.

Her bright smile forced him to swallow any talk of not going with her. There was no way he was doing anything to ruin her happiness.

"Wow, you look amazing," he said, letting out a low whistle.

She grinned and smoothed invisible wrinkles along the front of her dress.

"What? This old thing?"

He grasped for her hand to pull her between his legs where he sat on the bed.

"That might have worked if I hadn't watched you cut the price tags off it last night," he murmured with a wink and stroked her hipbone over the silky material. "You really do look beautiful, sweetheart."

Reagan cupped his face in her hand as she looked down into his eyes.

"Thank you, baby. And thank you for going with me today. It really does mean a lot to me."

Score one for me keeping my mouth shut.

"I'm honored to be your date."

She leaned down and softly kissed his lips, pulling away just as he became hungry for more of her and his cock started to tent his boxer briefs.

"You need to get dressed. The driver is going to be here in fifteen minutes."

He sighed, and she pecked his lips again.

"We have two more full days here," she offered in consolation as she stepped away from him.

"Two more days of having you all to myself," he murmured.

"Then it's back to reality."

Well, reality for her; not exactly for him. He was going to be a guest in her home in Fargo, starting physical therapy and increasing his presence with the agency—online, at least, while trying to meld into her everyday life. He had no idea what was in store for him, but decided as long as he was with her, he didn't care what it was.

He began the task of getting dressed, careful of his bandaged leg as he changed out of his loose shorts and put the suit pants on.

"Did you make an appointment with the physical therapist?" she asked while putting her earrings in.

"Yeah, actually I was able to do it online. I'm scheduled to start on Friday. I hope it's okay that I used your address?"

She furrowed her brow slightly.

"Well, yeah, it's okay. That's where you're going to be living, isn't it?"

Holy shit, we're going to be living together.

He hadn't thought of it like that. He'd never lived with a woman other than his mom when he was growing up. He had never even shared a bedroom before, unless you counted his dorm room his freshman year in college.

"What's wrong?" she asked while looking at him in the mirror.

He realized he'd been scowling and quickly tried to neutralize his expression with a placating smile.

"Nothing. I just realized I'd never lived with a woman before, other than my mom. I'm a little anxious about what it's going to be like. Is your makeup going to be all over the bathroom counter? Do you leave your wet towel on the floor? Will I drive you crazy with some of my OCD tendencies?"

She smiled and turned around to face him. "You have OCD tendencies? Like what?"

He thought about it for a second.

"I guess I'm just very particular. I like things neat and orderly. Vacuum tracks have to line up; the bed should be made in the morning; everything has its place."

Reagan moved to place the ascot around his neck and help him tie it.

"Well, you are in luck. I have wood floors and a robot vacuum that moves in circles so it doesn't leave marks on the area rugs. I always make the bed unless I wake up late, and I tend to be pretty tidy." She smiled before kissing his cheek, then, with her hands on his shoulders, whispered in his ear. "It's going to be fine. I promise."

He looked up at her and smiled.

"It's going to be perfect, sassy pants."

****

Reagan

The driver showed up precisely on time.

"Is this your usual driver?" he asked when they walked through the villa gates. She knew he was armed; she'd seen him put the holster on before putting on his suit jacket.

"Yes, his name is Carlos. He's been driving me all week."

"Okay," he said and opened the back door for her.

They were quiet throughout most of the drive, although he twined his fingers through hers. Every time she would glance over at him, he would catch her eye and wink with a smile.

"Thank you again for coming. Meeting you is all my mother has talked about since she found out you existed."

"How did she find out?"

"She was worried about me staying at the villa alone, so I mentioned you were there with me."

"And tell me again how I came to be at the villa?"

"You were so relieved once you found out I was safe, you had to fly here to be with me."

"And why am I on crutches?"

"Car accident."

"Why haven't I met your mom before today?"

"I didn't know how serious we were."

He grinned at her. "And how serious are we?"

She returned his smile. "Madly in love, moving-in-together serious."

Mason wrapped his arm around her shoulder and pulled her against his side.

"Well, at least you're not completely lying to your mother."

They pulled up to the estate, and she took a deep breath before sliding out the car door.

"Here we go."

Mason hobbled out then stood with the aid of his crutches, and they went up the front stairs together. It was amazing how well he got around on those things.

"Reagan, you made it!" her mother, dressed in a tight red mini-dress, cried when they walked through the door. She suspected Delilah had been waiting at the window for them. "And this must be your young man."

"Mama, this is Mason Davis. Mason, my mother, Delilah Jones."

Fuck. She hoped that was the last name he'd told her to use. He had so many aliases, she had asked him to use the one with his real first name because she felt certain she was going to slip up with that.

Her mother, never one to recognize social cues, hugged Mason, making him stagger under his crutches.

"So nice to meet you, Mason," Delilah gushed, oblivious to almost knocking the man on crutches on his ass.

To his credit, he adjusted and hugged her back as best he could.

"Great to meet you, too, Ms. Jones."

"Please, call me Delilah. Or mom."

Oh my god.

Thankfully, Bella walked in with the baby just then. Her sister looked stunning in an ivory lace dress that flattered her amazing post-baby figure, her dyed-brown hair piled on top of her head. Baby Maddie was in a traditional white taffeta and lace-applique christening gown that flowed at least a foot past her tiny feet. A large bow headband completed the ensemble.

"Mama... you're going to scare the poor man off with talk like that," her sister scolded, then smiled warmly at Mason.

"Glad to see you're doing better. I have to admit, I was surprised you were feeling up to coming today."

Reagan knew that was Bella's way of admonishing Mason for what she thought was him being reckless with his cover.

"I knew it meant a lot to Reagan."

She decided a change of subject was needed, and quick. She made a demonstrative face at Madison and took the baby from her mother.

"How's my goddaughter? Are you ready to be baptized? Look how beautiful you are."

Madison smiled a big toothless grin in return.

"Can you say hi to Mason? Isn't he handsome in his new suit and tie?"

He reached out and offered the baby his finger and a big smile. Her ovaries were in heaven.

The little girl gurgled in response, and Bella was quick to wipe her face so she didn't drool on the gown.

"You don't even wanna know how much Dante spent on this dress," she said rolling her eyes as she made sure to get the baby's face clean. "I think Father Castellanos is setting up out back if you want to take your seats. Rosa and Maria are preparing brunch for afterward, so the kitchen is kind of crazy right now, but there's a punch bowl and waters on the patio."

Before Reagan could hand Madison back to Bella, her gorgeous brother-in-law came down the stairs in a suit and tie, and his daughter smiled broadly the sight of him.

"I guess she's a daddy's girl," Mason chuckled as Dante took the baby.

She watched the Mexican man beam with pride at his progeny as he held her in one arm, his other hand firmly wrapped around his wife's waist. They were the picture-perfect family.

"I think someone already has her daddy wrapped around her finger." Reagan smirked.

"It's easy to do," Dante said as he kissed his little girl's wispy hair. "You wait and see how Mason is when you two have one."

Surprisingly, Mason smiled and winked at Reagan, not taking his eyes off her when he replied, "I'm sure I'll be the same way."

Bella made a choking noise and started coughing uncontrollably; Dante patted her back.

Reagan's tummy started to feel warm, and she found she couldn't stop smiling, even as her sister seemed to be choking to death at the thought.

"Do you need some water, Bella?" Mason asked. The amusement in his tone was so subtle, Reagan wasn't sure if anyone else caught it.

"No, I'm fine," her older sibling gasped.

The doorbell rang with more guests, so they took the opportunity to escape to the backyard with Delilah in tow.

"We are going to have beautiful babies," he murmured in her ear once they sat down in the front row.

There was that tingling in her tummy again.

"I think so, too," she whispered back and pecked his cheek.

****

Mason

He looked around at the guests and immediately recognized some big names in the cartel world. Miguel Hernandez—El Rey, a supplier from Tucson who was slowly making a move into San Diego—was with his oldest daughter, Laila a few rows back. John Turner, Dante's right hand man out of San Diego, was upfront serving as godfather next to Reagan as godmother. Ramon Guzman, the new head of the Guzman family, was sitting next to his brother, Jesús, Dante's father.

Bella, who was sitting next to him, saw him looking around and leaned over to ask, "Do you feel like you voluntarily walked into the lion's den?"

"Something like that," Mason admitted.

He heard her chuckle—it sounded just like Reagan.

"Don't worry. As long as you behave yourself, and you're a guest of my sister's, your cover is safe here. At least on our end. Speaking from experience, it's your end you should be worried about."

The guest list was minimal; Dante had gone to great lengths to protect Bella's identity, so Mason doubted there were any double agents in attendance. And if there were, the CIA agent thought he was deep enough undercover that he wouldn't be recognized. He doubted anyone would pay attention to him anyway, as the date of the squeaky-clean, artistic godmother from Fargo.

Bella continued quietly as she prepared to stand, "But you should give a lot of consideration to what it would mean for my sister if your cover were to be blown."

The priest called Madison's parents forward, so the conversation was over.

Mason knew Bella was just looking out for her baby sister, and if he were being honest, knew her misgivings about him were valid. Spies didn't have real relationships. Everyone in the agency knew that unwritten rule. Because loving someone meant possibly putting that person's life in danger.

But as he stared at his date while she held her niece in front of the guests in the backyard, he couldn't fathom being without her. Was he being naïve thinking they could be together? Or selfish?

His answer would come soon enough.

Chapter Twenty-Five

Reagan

She hadn't known it was possible for her heart to be this full, but watching Mason in his suit, holding her niece, and making her giggle with laughter, Reagan had never felt happier.

He was going to be a great dad someday. To *their* children. She felt it in her soul that he was Mr. Right.

Mason glanced over and saw her watching him and Maddie. His dimple when he smiled at her made her toes curl.

She felt like a schoolgirl whose crush just noticed her for the first time—which was sort of wonderful because not once in school did one of her crushes ever notice her. She was one of the poor redheaded Jones girls whose second-hand clothes were either too small or too large, and who was always the class charity case.

She stole another glance at the gorgeous blond man, and he held out his hand toward her.

Scratch that. It wasn't like her crush noticing her, it was like the star quarterback just asked her to be his girlfriend.

Is it possible to die from happiness?

She sat on the expensive velvet sofa next to him and began talking to Madison, who cooed and giggled in response. Mason subtly hooked his pinky finger through Reagan's and gently squeezed before letting go.

Bella appeared before them.

"I need to feed my daughter," she said with a smile as she reached down to pluck the smiling baby from Mason's lap. Her niece was equally happy to see her mother, and Bella whisked her away to the nursery in order to breastfeed in private. Reagan wasn't surprised when she noticed Dante disappear, and knew he'd gone to be with his wife and baby girl for some quiet time together.

She loved how much her brother-in-law adored his little family. Not more than ten days ago, Reagan had found herself wondering if she'd ever have someone look at her the way Dante looked at Bella. Feeling Mason's arm come around her shoulders, she leaned against him and sighed with contentment. She'd found him... or maybe he'd found her.

"Do you mind if I head back to the villa soon? I'm getting a little tired and probably will take a pain pill."

"I'll go with you. Thank you again for coming today. I'm so glad you got to be here for the baptism and to meet my mama. Although now she's going to want to have dinner with us in Fargo at least twice a week."

He laughed and kissed her forehead.

"Thank you for inviting me. I'm glad I got to be a part of the festivities and meet your mother. Of course we'll spend time with her when we get back."

She noticed he didn't commit to twice-a-week dinners—not that she blamed him. But she did like the way he used *we*. '*We'll* spend time with her when *we* get back.'

She was part of a *we*.

"You're pretty amazing, you know that?" she said with a sigh.

"I'm flattered you think so—especially when you consider how we met."

Oh, that.

"You had your reasons."

"Selfish ones."

"*Legitimate* ones," she corrected. "And you were never anything but kind to me. I knew you'd never hurt me."

"Bella can't say the same."

"It seems like you two have made your peace, or at least reached an understanding."

He nodded. "I think so. I certainly am seeing things a little differently than I was a year or so ago."

"I hope that's a good thing?"

"It is. My world isn't so black and white anymore—there's room for some grey."

Reagan nudged his shoulder with hers.

"Aw, I was hoping you were going to say there was now some color in it."

He smiled and wrapped a curl of her hair around his finger.

"Well, I love that the color red is in my world now. It's by far my favorite."

His words made her feel giddy. *Giddy.* She was such a sucker for this man, and he knew it.

Hook, line, and sinker.

****

Mason

If ever he'd wanted time to stop, or at least slow down, it was now over the next two days. They were cocooned in the villa, isolated from the rest of the world without a thing to worry about other than what they were going to have for dinner. It was perfect.

Mason imagined their time together in Fargo was going to be blissful, but nothing like this. Reagan would be back to her reality—working, visiting her mother, getting into her normal routine. She'd make room for him in her life, sure, but he was also going to have to get back to work, and he wasn't sure how that was going to go over. It was going to be asking a lot for her to be patient while he disappeared for months at a time with little to no word from him. She'd have no idea where he was or what he was doing.

He wouldn't be able to handle it if the roles were reversed.

So he was going to milk this time with her for everything it was worth.

"Let's not get out of bed today," he murmured against her hair early Monday morning.

The sun had barely risen but Reagan was awake, which was unusual.

"I don't think the nurse would like that," she sighed as she snuggled against his side with her eyes closed.

"I canceled with her today. She's not coming until tomorrow."

Her eyes flew open.

"Why? Do you think that's a good idea?"

"I'm healing nicely—she even said so herself during yesterday's visit. I think it's okay if we skip today."

"But why did you cancel?"

"I told you; I want to stay in bed with you all day."

The look she shot him indicated she didn't have a lot of faith in his abilities.

"Baby, you're a rock star in bed—even with bullet wounds, but I think even for you, *all day* is a bit of a stretch."

He smirked.

"While yes, I am planning on rocking your world multiple times today, I thought it'd be nice just to lay in bed together—preferably naked—and talk, maybe watch some movies. Just enjoy being together for the short time we have left before getting back to the real world."

Her crooked grin was filled with joy.

"Aw, I would love that. That sounds like the perfect day."

"Good, but I think we should start with sex. And I'm really craving the taste of your pussy, so be a good girl and sit on my face."

She swallowed hard and raised her eyebrows.

"You want me to sit on your face? Aren't you worried I'll hurt your neck?"

He scooted down the bed and put two pillows under his head.

"I want you to sit on my face, sweetheart, not my neck."

"Um…" She didn't move.

"Now, Reagan. I haven't tasted you in five days. That's way too long."

"But I'm worried I'll hurt you."

He grasped her hand.

"Baby, I promise if it hurts, we'll figure out a different position. But I'm eating your cunt right now, so…" Mason swatted her hip, urging her forward. "Chop-chop."

His cock was already hard just thinking about it.

With a skeptical look, she kneeled, gripped the headboard, and brought one leg across his head, settling in so her pussy lined up with his mouth. He wasted no time in swiping his tongue up and down her middle. Smiling when he heard her gasp and felt her lean forward on the headboard, his mouth found her clit, and he began to suck on her hooded knot. She pressed her hips down on his mouth, and Mason slid a finger inside her pussy to find her already wet.

"Mmm, that's my girl," he uttered against her pink folds then began lapping at her while moving his finger in unison with his tongue.

She began to lightly rock her hips against his mouth while starting to whimper sweet words of surrender.

She escalated from rocking her hips to grinding her clit against his tongue, and he thrust a second finger inside her. She was absolutely soaked; the sounds of her wetness echoed off the headboard along with her moans.

Mason rapidly flicked her jewel, moving his head side to side as he began to finger-fuck her faster. He felt her pussy clench around his fingers, so he buried his face between her pussy lips and assaulted her clit with his tongue as he continued fucking her.

Her whole body tightened, and she let out a long moan, followed by her body spasming around his head as the climax shook through her.

He continued licking and fingering her, although slower now, until she squeezed her thighs around his head and flopped awkwardly to his side, her head near his knees and her cute toes at his face.

"Holy fuck," she panted. "The things you do to me, mister…" She rolled onto her back, her knees in the air. "Oh my god. That was awesome."

"You are so damn sexy," he growled, tracing a finger up and down her glistening slit.

"Mmm, only because you make me feel sexy," she purred as she sat up with an evil grin.

Reagan licked her lips and stared into his eyes as she crawled toward his hard cock.

"My turn," she whispered before running her tongue up the entire length of his shaft.

It was going to be a terrific day.

Chapter Twenty-Six

Reagan

They literally stayed in bed all day, even eating their meals in the bedroom. The only exception was to use the bathroom and brush their teeth, and they did take a shower break in the middle of the afternoon after their third round of sex.

It was the most perfect day she'd ever had. It seemed like she'd thought that on several occasions since being kidnapped by this beautiful man.

Kidnapped by this man.

Probably not something they were going to tell their children.

"What should we tell people about how we met?" she asked as she sat lotus-style on the bed wearing only one of his t-shirts. She took a bite of the tortilla soup Maria had sent over. "Oh my god, you have to try this," she moaned, gesturing to the bowl in front of him.

He dutifully tried it, savoring it before responding, "Oh, that's good."

She pointed her spoon at him. "Right? Anyway. What are we going to tell people about us?"

"I suppose the truth isn't an option."

Reagan shot him a look. "Probably not."

"How about we met online?"

"What, you just happened to be trolling through Fargo's Tinder from... Oh my god, I don't even know where you live!"

"I have a place outside of Boston where I crash when I have some downtime. And are you really on Tinder?"

"What? No—of course not. So you just happened to be in Boston looking for a date on... I don't know, Fargo's Farmers Only and there I was? That makes no sense."

"Okay, okay. How about if we met in a chat room and spent the last year just chatting and getting to know each other without ever meeting? Then we decided to meet and knew we were meant to be so I'm moving to Fargo to be with you."

"What chat room?"

"Fuck, sassy, I don't know. Does it matter?"

"I think we need to be prepared because people are going to ask."

He seemed to contemplate it for a moment, then suggested, "Well, one of our first conversations was about how horrible your taste in hockey is, so how about that hockey site, For Puck's Sake?"

"Oh, I like that. That's believable, right?"

"I think so, sweetheart."

Then it dawned on her he'd insulted her. "Hey! I do not have horrible taste in hockey!"

He smiled tenderly at her. What was it about this man that constantly made her want to crawl into his lap?

"God, I love you," she said wistfully. Then she muttered, "Even if your team sucks."

"Hockey season's coming up. Name the stakes, little girl," he said confidently.

"Oh, you're on. I'll have to think of something good to bet though."

"You've got time. Whatever you decide. I ain't scared."

She set her bowl on the nightstand and crawled toward him.

"Good. I'm not either."

He pensively set his bowl down and waited for her to be near enough, then pulled her into his bare chest. He was naked except for his underwear.

They'd had sex three times already today—dirty, naughty, steamy sex—but as he stared into her eyes, she knew they were going to make love. Like their last night on the yacht.

"I love you, Reagan Elizabeth."

"I love you, Mason... Hey, what is your middle name?"

"Edward."

"Edward," she repeated solemnly, then tried it out. "Mason Edward Hughes. It sounds very regal."

"I like the sound of Reagan Elizabeth Hughes, myself."

Undercover CIA agent say what?

"Um..."

He laughed out loud. "Don't worry, sassy pants, that wasn't a proposal. But for the record, I am going to ask you to marry me someday, sooner rather than later, because I'm planning on making you my wife."

"Noted. Let the record also reflect that when you ask, I'm planning on saying yes."

His smile spread across his face, revealing that indentation on the side of his cheek that made her swoon.

Are dimples hereditary? Will our children have dimples?

Wow. She went there. How could she not, after everything that had transpired the last few days?

He pulled her under him, his lips hovering over hers as he rested his weight on his forearms.

"It's on record now, so you can't change your mind," and began to inch the t-shirt up with his hand.

She wrapped her arms around his neck, staring into his eyes.

"I'm not going to change my mind. I am so in love with you—I've never felt like this before."

"Me neither," he whispered, then captured her lips with his, as if sealing the deal with a kiss.

Mason pulled the fabric over her head so she was naked beneath him. She noticed he was resting most of his weight on his arms and left leg; she pushed on his shoulder so he flipped over, his back and shoulders against the headboard, and straddled his hips.

"Aren't you getting tired of doing all the work?"

"Oh yes, it's just been horrible having to ride this sexy stallion of a man." She looped her arms around his neck. "I don't know how I'm even coping."

He threw his head back and laughed. "I'm a stallion? That's awesome."

She sighed. "You are the sexiest man I've ever met. No contest. I love being with you; I don't care what position we're in."

He brought his hand behind her head and brought her forehead to rest against his, his eyes closing on contact.

"I don't deserve you," he murmured softly.

Reagan leaned down to kiss his eyelids, her fingers tightening in his hair as she moved down his cheeks until she reached his lips. She sucked his top lip, then his bottom, then enveloped his mouth with hers, rocking her naked pussy against his clothed dick.

His arms came around her back, and he held her tightly while deepening the kiss.

They came up for air, and his mouth immediately found her boobs. He sucked seductively on her nipple while he moaned against her skin.

"God, I love your tits," he growled before tugging on her pink bud with his teeth.

She wrapped her arms around the back of his head.

"Oh, that feels so good," she panted, not wanting him to stop, like maybe ever.

Mason leaned her back, setting her between his legs on the bed, then crawling on top of her as she scooted down the mattress toward the footboard.

"Wait. Aren't you—"

He silenced her by putting his mouth on hers while he tugged his underwear down his thighs, breaking the kiss when he leaned down to remove his boxer briefs from around his ankles and tossing them on the floor.

"Are you sure you can…"

He answered her unfinished question by thrusting his cock inside her. *I guess he can.*

Resting his forearms on either side of her head, he brushed her hair away from her face, staring into her eyes and dipping down to kiss her as he moved in and out of her pussy.

"You feel so good, sweetheart," he murmured.

She could only whimper in response.

He pulled out of her and dropped to his left side, turning her on her side as well, her ass facing him. He cupped her tits and pulled her onto his cock, sliding one hand up around her throat while he kissed her shoulders and the back of her neck.

Reagan arched back against his chest with her eyes closed, her arm reaching behind his head with her mouth slightly open in ecstasy. What he was doing to her was erotic as fuck.

He reached down to find her clit, rubbing her little knot in circles as he continued thrusting in and out of her, his other hand still around her neck.

Panting harder, she clenched her body as her orgasm started creeping up from her toes.

"Mmm, that's my girl."

She loved being his girl. The idea of belonging to him pushed her over the edge, and she began coming as he continued fucking her. For her fifth orgasm today, it was more powerful than she expected, and definitely the most sensual—she loved it. Not that hard and dirty didn't have their place...

He began to grunt, and she knew he was about to come. Listening to him come was the sexiest, most carnal sound she'd ever heard, and let out a soft whimper as another mini-orgasm hit her.

"Oh, baby, baby, baby," he moaned against her shoulder, then collapsed on his back with his eyes closed. "I think you have officially worn me out."

She knew she was going to be sore too, but teased, "Aw. That's a bummer."

He lifted his neck and chest to look at her, one eye open. "Seriously?" Then he slumped back on the bed.

She turned over, giggling, and laid her cheek against his shoulder. "No, not seriously. I'm probably going to be sore tomorrow as it is."

"Fuck, sweetheart, I'm sorry."

She put her fingers to his lips and smiled. "Totally worth it."

"Without a doubt," he agreed.

Laying there silently, limbs tangled and not cleaning up or even moving for that matter, they fell asleep with the lamp on and didn't wake up until the middle of the night.

Best day ever.

Chapter Twenty-Seven

Mason

The buzzing of his phone woke him early the next morning, but he quickly silenced it without even looking to see who was calling.

It immediately started buzzing again.

"Goddammit," he grumbled, fumbling for the phone while still lying on his stomach with his head on the pillow.

"Yeah," he snarled, his words a hoarse whisper.

"Hey, I've got something you need to see." It took him a second to recognize Jacob's voice on the other end.

Mason sat up, taking a quick glance at Reagan to make sure he hadn't woken her. She was still sound asleep, naked except for the sheet tucked around her chest with her hair fanned out along her pillow. *Fuck, she's beautiful.*

"Hold on, let me call you right back," he whispered, and disconnected the call without waiting for a reply.

Setting his feet on the floor, he paused to get his bearings after being woken so abruptly from his sound slumber. The dawn's light was coming in through the high windows, which didn't have blinds, so he was able to see his crutches leaning against the wall, as well as his boxer briefs lying next to the bed. He slipped the underwear on, hopped the distance to where his crutches were, and tried to quietly make his way to the living room and call Jacob back.

The early morning made the house chilly, so he wrapped a royal blue velour throw around his shoulders and sat down on the couch once he dialed the phone.

"This better be important," he said dryly once Jacob answered.

"It is. Kennedy has a car en route for you."

He heard sharp whispering in the background, then it became more muffled—like he'd covered the phone. Jacob came back on, mumbling, "Jesus Christ. *Bella* has a car en route for you."

He was trying to piece together what was happening.

"Are you still in Ensenada?"

"Yes. I'm in Bella and Dante's office."

"I'm assuming I'm going to meet you there? Should I bring Reagan?"

"Yeah, you're coming here, and no, don't bring Reagan yet. We'll send someone for her later once we get shit figured out."

His mind was racing as to what the hell could be wrong that would prompt Jacob to make an appearance at the Guzmans' so soon after Bella warned him never to contact her again.

"Wanna give me a hint what the fuck this is all about?"

"I think it'd be easier to explain in person," Jacob replied cryptically.

He sighed and ran his fingers through his hair.

"'Kay. I'll be there soon."

"The car should be there in ten."

Mason hung up without saying anything further. He was pissed. This was his last full day with Reagan before they headed back to reality and Fargo, and he didn't appreciate the intrusion—he didn't give a damn what the reason was.

Still, for Jacob to be involved, Mason knew it was big.

He thought about leaving a note but imagined that wouldn't go over well when she woke up, so he gently shook her shoulders once he'd gotten dressed and brushed his teeth.

"Sweetheart," he murmured.

She scrunched her face up and whimpered in response, never opening her eyes.

"Reagan, baby. I have to go to your sister's; I'll be back as soon as I can."

There was a lapse from when he said the words to when her eyes flew open—like it took a moment for her to process what he said. She sat up quickly and threw the covers off.

"What's wrong? Is the baby okay?"

Mason grasped her wrist firmly and tried to speak soothingly while keeping her in place.

"Madison's fine. Your sister's fine. Everyone's okay. Jacob just called and said there was something I needed to see."

"And he's at Bella's?" she asked incredulously.

She'd also witnessed her sister's not-so-subtle threat that Jacob never contact her again, so she knew something big had happened.

Reagan shrugged off his hold and was scrambled toward the closet housing her clothes.

"I'll get dressed."

"No, sweetheart. You stay here. I'll come back and get you once I know what's going on."

He knew the minute he uttered the words he had as good a chance of that happening as if he'd told the sun not to rise.

She snorted sarcastically from the doorway of the closet, "Yeah, okay," as she shimmied into a pair of yoga pants, then pulled a sports bra over her head, followed by a touristy Ensenada sweatshirt she'd probably found in one of the many shops that catered to the cruise ship passengers on their day trips. She bent and stuffed her feet into tennis shoes without untying the laces, then practically jogged into the bathroom and reappeared moments later, her face washed and hair up in a ponytail.

"Ready?"

He started hobbling with the crutches toward the door. "Your sister's going to kick my ass for bringing you," he murmured as he paused for her to go ahead of him.

"Yeah, well. She'll get over it. She can be mad at me if she wants to be mad at someone."

Somehow, he knew it wasn't going to work like that.

****

Reagan

Bella gave Reagan the fake smile she usually reserved for stupid people who were getting on her nerves because they weren't doing as she instructed. That instantly put the younger sister in defense mode—she was not stupid and too fucking bad if Bella didn't want her there.

"Can you go check on the baby?"

Reagan leaned against the ornate mahogany desk in Dante's office and crossed her arms. "No."

That made her big sister raise her eyebrows. "No, you won't go check on your goddaughter?"

Reagan met Bella's raised eyebrows with her own and added a tilt of her head. "No, I'm not leaving so you can talk about things while I'm not here."

"Well, you can't be here for this."

"Why not?"

Mason stepped forward, his hand going to the small of her back while glancing at Jacob and Bella before looking down at her. His placating tone pissed her off. "It's for your own safety, sweetheart. The less you know, the better."

"I think we're past that point, don't you? I'm in this as deep as you are."

"This has nothing to do with Cartagena," Jacob interjected. "And you really can't be privy to what we're about to discuss. This is nothing personal, Reagan; it's just the way it has to be."

"You can't be here," Bella repeated. "What we're about to discuss doesn't include you. You need to go."

She shot one last pleading look at Mason, hoping he'd have an epiphany and insist she be included, but he didn't. Instead, he averted his gaze. The quarterback was ashamed to be seen with her.

"Your sister's right, Reagan," he said quietly.

Reagan was embarrassed and angry that Mason was siding with them, and excluding her in the process. It was like she was being uninvited from the cool kids' table at lunch.

"But…" She looked at Jacob imploringly, almost desperate. "You said, at the hospital… *I'm* the one who saved Marcus. Not Bella, not Mason, not Jacob—*me*. I've earned a right to be here."

Jacob snorted like she was amusing him. "Getting kidnapped and being held on a yacht for four days doesn't make you qualified."

"Only sometimes," Bella added with a laugh.

"I'm still in awe of your abilities," Mason chuckled back, completely ignoring Reagan's observation that she deserved to be there. All three of them now looked at her like she was entertaining them.

Now they're fucking laughing at me?

She thought she'd proven herself and could be a part of Mason's life when he went back to work. Not part of his missions, but at least be allowed to know where he was and what he was doing.

Obviously that was a fantasy she'd created in her head. *Whatever.*

She could honestly say she'd never felt more angry or embarrassed. She was seeing red, which was probably why she ignored the almost-always working filter in her brain and snarled at the three of them, collectively, "You're so hilarious. Fuck. You," and stormed out, slamming the door behind her.

The tears were already streaming down her cheeks before she reached the end of the hall. A tiny part of her was expecting Mason to come after her. When he didn't, she escaped to the guest bathroom and sobbed into one of the thick embroidered towels that hung on the rack—more for decoration than actual use.

She'd proven herself last week dammit—no matter what they were saying now. She at least warranted an invitation into the room. Instead, they were making fun of her for being kidnapped; saying she didn't belong with them and their little spy-clique.

They wanted her to leave? Oh, she'd leave all right.

"I'm outta here," she huffed out loud. She was catching the next flight back to Fargo; the X-Men could eat a bag of dicks in their secret meeting.

Chapter Twenty-Eight

Mason

The hurt look on Reagan's face before she stormed out of the room gutted him.

I should've gone after her.

I should have insisted she be allowed to stay.

I should have been on her fucking side.

But Jacob and Bella cited her safety as being the reason she couldn't, and keeping her safe was more important than anything, so he did nothing. Still, his gut was telling him he'd made a huge mistake.

"So what the fuck is going on?"

Jacob produced printouts with his name and some of his aliases highlighted. Kennedy's name was also highlighted with the word DECEASED in all caps next to it.

"What's this?" he asked as he shuffled through the papers.

"The Dark Web's version of *Wanted* posters. Seems there's a bounty on your heads. Well, yours anyway."

"For Cartagena? How were we even identified? You picked up the cameras in the warehouse—I saw you. And the shell casings. Did you miss one? Is there a bounty out on Marcus?"

Bella shook her head. "It's not from Cartagena. It seems we were both part of the same counterterrorism team in Paris three years ago."

He had been loaned out to the French government to infiltrate a terror cell intent on planting a bomb in the city center of Paris on New Year's Eve. He'd known there was a female operative also working on the inside, but he'd never met her.

"Wait—*you* were Red Riding Hood?"

"And apparently you were Robin Hood."

A lot of fucked-up shit had happened on that mission—stuff that PTSD therapy sessions are made of. The day after the terrorists were arrested, he was supposed to rendezvous with Red Riding Hood. On his way to her hotel room, he had intercepted and killed an assassin sent to murder her. Red got away before they had a chance to meet. As was customary, Mason debriefed with his handler and was sent home to wait for his next mission, having never known his counterpart's real identity.

Well, fuck me—Red Riding Hood was Kennedy Jones.

"That only slightly makes up for the fact you were going to kill me—and my little girl—last year," she said with humor in her voice.

"Bella, I didn't know. I was led to believe you'd switched sides." Which, he guessed, was technically true.

"I hadn't done anything to compromise the agency or its agents. I didn't deserve a death sentence. Even now, I only work on Dante's legitimate, legal businesses."

"I told you last week, I'll take your secret to my grave."

"Which may be sooner rather than later if we don't come up with a plan," Jacob interrupted.

"*We*? I'm not sure I can afford you on this, Jake," Mason said with a smirk.

"Well, too bad, asshole. You're stuck with me. I'll put it on your tab. You can make monthly payments."

"Do you take Visa?"

The fixer laughed out loud at Mason's joke. "Cash only."

"I hope you have a houseful of kids whose college tuition I'm funding. Or at least their orthodontia."

"Nope, it's just my private island you're helping pay for."

"Then I better get an invite to come stay for a week," Mason grumbled.

"You know the rule: Never mix business with pleasure." Jacob dramatically looked back and forth between Bella and Mason and made a disapproving face. "Although it appears you two were both absent the day they taught that."

"You should try it sometime; you might like it," Mason goaded.

"Nah, I'll continue living the shallow, one-night-stand playboy lifestyle. Thanks anyway."

"Gentlemen, can we get back to the issue at hand?" Bella said, rolling her eyes.

"Sorry," they said in unison.

"First things first. You need to get away from Reagan—you can't go to Fargo with her. She wouldn't be safe, and you know it. Bounty hunters wouldn't hesitate to use her to get to you. "

He knew she was right. The idea of letting Reagan go killed him, but he knew it was only way she would truly be safe. Still...

"Okay. But don't get too excited. It's only temporary—until this threat is neutralized."

Her smile was empathetic—or maybe sympathetic; he couldn't decide which. Either way, he didn't like it, or what she had to say next.

"Agent Hughes, there will always be another threat around the corner. Reagan will never be safe, and she deserves better. She deserves stability, and someone who will love her and be there for her. Someone she can come home to every night and have dinner with. Go on vacation with without him having to use an alias or constantly look over his shoulder. Have babies with. She can't do that with a spy."

He wanted to be that man and do all those things with her. No one would love her more than he did.

"I *do* love her, and I *will* be there for her."

"I don't doubt you love her. That much is obvious. But how can you say you'll be there for her?"

"What if I wasn't a spy anymore?"

She narrowed her eyes at him. "What are you saying?"

"What if I take a medical retirement, once this Paris threat is taken care of?"

"And do what?" Jacob asked.

He shrugged. "Open my own restaurant in Fargo. Or San Diego. Or anywhere Reagan wants to live."

"Let me know if you need an investor, man. I'm loaded," Jacob said with a wink.

Bella rolled her eyes and sighed. "Let's figure out what you're going to do about this threat, and then worry about Reagan."

Mason nodded his head, but the truth was, he was worried about her now.

He ran his hand across the scruff on his jaw. "We should bring her back in here. She needs to understand what's going on," he said quietly.

Bella steepled her fingers under her chin and contemplated his assessment.

"You might be right," she said, then picked up the phone on the desk and hit two numbers.

"Rosa? Can you ask Reagan to come back to my office?"

A scowl spread across the older sister's beautiful face.

"Oh. When?" *Pause.* "And who drove her?" *Pause.* "Okay then, will you let me know when he returns? Thanks."

She hung up and looked at the two men. "She went back to the villa."

Mason grabbed his crutches and stood. "I need to go and get her."

It was Jacob's turn to scowl.

"I'm on an hourly rate, here, my friend. A very hefty hourly rate. And I've got a plane to catch in ninety minutes, so let's get a plan in place. Then I'll be on my merry way, and you two can fill her in without me."

Mason sighed and sat back down. He was already going to have to grovel—he doubted an hour would make much difference.

"What do you suggest?"

****

Reagan

She considered asking Carlos to wait while she packed but decided it would be just as easy to call a cab when she was ready. Too bad their little meeting hadn't happened yesterday; she could have hitched a ride with her mama on Dante's private plane. The last-minute ticket back to Ensenada was putting a big dent on her credit card balance, but it was a small price to pay for her pride. She hoped she felt that way a month from now when she made the first Visa payment and figured out how much the interest was going to cost her before she paid it off.

Maybe she'd get a bartending job on the weekend. It'd keep her busy, her mind off Mason, and she'd earn some extra money to boot.

Reagan walked out the tall wooden gates just as the cab arrived, pulling her luggage behind her like she owned the villa. Her sister had taught her long ago that the key to not getting hassled by people was to act confident. Not one security guard questioned why Carlos wasn't driving her or asked where she was going—although given the suitcase, they could probably assume.

She did leave Mason a short but heartfelt note. If she were being honest with herself, she was holding onto a glimmer of hope that he'd come after her and try to make things right, but she wasn't betting on it. Still, she purposefully didn't slam the door completely.

Dear Mason,

Thank you for giving me the best week of my life—especially yesterday, which will live in my heart forever as the most perfect day.

I wish you a lifetime of happiness and love.

Always,

Reagan

As she stood in line to board her flight, her phone dinged with a frantic message from Mason wanting to know where she was. Her anger had subsided with the drive to airport, and now she realized how ridiculous she was being. But she was committed at this point. Going back now would mean swallowing her pride and losing face, and she wasn't about to do that. They'd *laughed* at her, she could only imagine how amusing they'd find it if she came back with her tail between her legs now.

Nope. Reagan was past the point of no return. She shut her phone off and stuck it in her purse.

Did she know she'd regret it? Maybe. But she honestly didn't know what else to do.

Surprisingly, she didn't cry or break down again until she walked into her house in Fargo twelve hours later. Looking around at the little white brick ranch, she was reminded of what she had been planning to do in order to accommodate Mason's crutches, and how she was going rearrange her bedroom to make room for him and his belongings.

Her shame and embarrassment at overreacting reared its ugly head. As the tears streamed down her face she thought, *well hey, at least this way I don't have to worry about losing him anymore—I've basically guaranteed my fate with this stunt.*

Which was probably a good thing. There was no way for them to be together—they led two completely different lives. He'd made that abundantly clear today, and that she had no part in certain aspects of his life. Which was bullshit; she had proven herself worthy. She wasn't asking to go on another mission with him, but she had earned the right to know what the hell was going on. What they were discussing this morning was obviously not classified or top secret, since Bella and Jacob were involved in the conversation.

And she certainly didn't deserve to be laughed at for wanting to be included.

Sitting down on her bed, she mustered the courage to turn her phone back on. Part of her dreaded seeing the texts she assumed would be there, and another part was terrified there wouldn't be any. Her phone began to ding with message after message. Three were from Bella, one was from her mama, and thirty-six were from Mason.

Granted, some of his messages were just one or a few words, like:

Are you there?

Sweetheart?

Where are you?

Please come back to the villa.

At least let someone know you're okay.

She could tell when he'd figured out she'd left because his texts got longer and more urgent, and perhaps more contrite.

Babe, I know I fucked up. You should've stayed. I'll tell you everything that's happening, just please don't get on that plane.

Please don't leave. There's a lot I need to tell you. Please.

Don't make me sleep alone tonight.

That one really got her because she was dreading doing the same thing.

I'm assuming you're halfway home by now, since you haven't come back. I love you, and I promise I will tell you everything once I get this cleared up. I don't know how long that will be.

All I can tell you over text is be careful and pay attention to your surroundings. Lock your doors. Buy some pepper spray and apply for a CCW if you don't already have one.

I'm hoping you already have one, considering Kennedy was your sister.

Please let me know when you get home safely. Remember: pay attention and trust your instincts.

He didn't mention when or if they were going to see each other again or what he was going to do now that he wasn't coming to Fargo. Did she dare ask?

Her phone dinged in her hand with an incoming message.

Reagan, I know you're angry with me, and you have every right to be, but baby you gotta let me know you're all right. At least tell someone you made it home okay.

Well, now what the hell was she was supposed to do? Had she ruined her chance with him?

She'd made a complete fool of herself, and she wasn't sure how to go about fixing it. It wasn't like she could show up at his office with cupcakes and no panties and beg forgiveness.

There was a pounding on her front door. *Who the hell could that be at this hour?*

She went to the door and opened it without a second thought to Mason's warning texts that she be careful and aware of her surroundings. She was back in Fargo and in her comfort zone; nothing bad ever happened here.

Chapter Twenty-Nine

Mason

He was going out of his mind with worry.

"I think you're going to wear a path in the carpet," Jacob remarked, not bothering to look up from his iPad as he sat on the couch in the living room of the villa.

Mason paused at the French doors overlooking the grounds and put his forehead against the glass. The feeling of helplessness was overwhelming. Where the fuck was she?

She wasn't answering his texts. Security said she left on her own in a cab with her suitcase a few hours ago. He knew she was mad, and she had every right to be, but it was bullshit she took off like this. Bella wasn't as worried as he'd thought she'd be—or as he thought she *should* be—when he broke the news to her that Reagan had left unaccompanied.

"Did you find anything yet?" he asked, still staring outside at the pink and white flowers.

"Bingo!" Jacob's voice echoed off the Saltillo tile. "She got a flight out of Tijuana to Las Vegas and is making a connecting flight there to Fargo."

At least he knew she was safe in the air.

"So how far is Fargo out of your way to New York?"

"Well, considering just three hours ago you agreed *not* to go to Fargo, it's pretty fucking far."

He tilted his head back, looking at the ceiling with a sigh.

"I know, but I need to see her in person and explain shit, then I'll go."

Jacob looked at him skeptically.

"You're so full of shit. Once she sees you, she's going to beg you to stay—or the other way around, and you're not going anywhere."

Yeah, that sounded plausible.

"No, I know I need to stay away from her for her own good. It will be incentive to get this threat taken care of."

Jacob smirked. "Except, conveniently you still need rehab before you can really do much." His breath through his nose sounded like a low growl. "When Bella finds out about this, I'm going to tell her you stowed away on my plane. I'm not going down for you. And, by the way, you probably should just reconcile with the fact that you're naming your firstborn after me, because there's no way in hell you're ever going to be able to repay me what the fuck you owe. This delay for the pilot alone is going to cost me a couple grand, not to mention it'll be at least five figures to deviate from the original flight plan."

"I'll make monthly payments for the rest of my life. Just give me a ride."

"It's your funeral, dude."

"Why are we planning his funeral? I thought we came up with a plan to circumvent that?" Bella asked as she walked into the living room, looking very much like she could have a starring role in the *Real Housewives of Ensenada* in her silk blouse and pearls, tailored pants, and stilettos.

"Jesus Christ, where did you come from?"

"I used the entrance in the kitchen."

Mason was certain she'd done that to eavesdrop, and he was willing to bet she'd heard his and Jacob's entire conversation, so there was no point lying to her.

"I need to talk to Reagan. In person. She went back to Fargo."

A wry smile formed on Bella's lips.

"I figured as much. Dante already said you can take the jet."

"I think it's safer if I hitch a ride with Jacob. His plane is rented and less traceable."

The Guzmans were more comfortable traveling to North Dakota since they'd gotten confirmation that Bella/Kennedy was now officially considered dead, but considering they'd just delivered Delilah Jones to Fargo yesterday, it might rouse some suspicion if they returned a second time that week. That was part of the reason he and Reagan were going to fly to Minneapolis instead on Thursday. They'd planned on renting a car and taking their time driving back so she could show him some of the countryside where she grew up.

Mason didn't want to have to rent a car and drive from Minnesota by himself with his leg still healing—he wanted to get to his sassy pants as soon as he could.

Bella clicked some buttons on her phone.

"I just transferred twenty thousand to your account, Jacob."

"I'm not a charity case, Ken—er, Bella," Mason interjected.

She smirked at the blond man. "You forget I know how much you make—or don't make, and I'm betting you're not going to put this on your expense report. And, since I don't want my oldest nephew's name to be Jacob Smith Hughes, and I married a man with more money than he knows what to do with, I'm happy to cover it. Under one condition..."

Mason *knew* she'd been eavesdropping. He'd talk about reimbursing her later—when Jacob wasn't around. He had more than enough money—obviously not as much as the cartel, but he'd invested an inheritance wisely when he was younger and had only continued adding to it. He could retire today and live comfortably for the rest of his life—but Mason had a feeling if the fixer knew that, the cost for his services would double.

"What's your condition?" He was ready for her to tell him he needed to stay the fuck away from Reagan.

"You make sure my sister is safe. That is your number one priority."

Well, that wasn't what he had expected.

"And you name your firstborn after *me*," she said with a grin.

Definitely not what he was expecting.

"But… earlier you were adamant I get away from her. You practically tailored the plan around that detail. And, I have to be honest, I think you were right. Until this bounty is taken off my head and I'm out of the agency, if I'm with her, she's in danger."

She crossed her arms.

"Are you part of a different agency than I was? Because I seem to recall getting exemplary training at becoming invisible. Maybe you went to the B Team school?"

He'd let the jab go. He'd gone to the A Team school all right. He'd managed to capture *her* ass not more than a year ago—not to mention saving it in Paris.

"Then you'll also recall the danger of being in one place too long. Or having relationships with people you actually care about."

"If all goes according to plan, you'll be breaking ground on your restaurant in four months. Are you saying you can't stay hidden for four months?" She tsked. "And with help, even?"

Mason looked at her and smiled. "Why the sudden change of heart?"

For the first time he'd ever seen, she looked vulnerable.

"My entire childhood, it was Reagan and me against the world. We were all each other had—she was the only one I could rely on and vice versa. When I joined the Marines, I felt like I'd abandoned her, and it only got worse when I became part of the agency. I want nothing more than for her to be safe and happy, and I've realized I've never seen her happier than these past few days with you. I'll admit I doubted your intentions, given how you met her. But my husband reminded me today about how he and I met, and that love works in some mysterious ways. Seeing how upset you are that she's gone... I don't doubt how much you love her, and I know you'll care for her and protect her with your life. Maybe I'm being selfish because I find comfort knowing someone's looking out for her again, since I can't be there to do it anymore. And our mother, bless her heart, doesn't have the capacity to take care of her—only be taken care of."

He was silent—not knowing how to respond. Bella was trusting him to be with her sister.

Jacob's voice interrupted his thoughts. "We need to get going if you want to be in Fargo by the time she arrives. She's got a good head start on us and only a short layover in Vegas."

He only needed five minutes to get packed and out the door.

"Hey, Mason?" Bella called from the doorway as he maneuvered down the front steps.

He paused and looked back at her. "Yeah?"

"Anything happens to her..."

"Yeah, yeah... fish food. I know. Don't worry, it won't." He took another step, then turned one last time. "Thanks, Bella. For everything."

Her genuine smile escaped, even as she pressed her lips together to try and disguise it. "Remember: your firstborn. Kennedy Alicia Hughes."

"What if it's a boy?"

She put her hand on her hip and dropped her head briefly.

"Fine. Your firstborn girl."

He grinned and winked at her.

"It's a deal."

"Safe travels," she said, then stepped back inside and closed the door.

****

Jacob was unusually quiet on the plane, not even arguing with Mason when he brought up how great the New England Patriots were going to do this year. He put in a jab about the New Orleans Saints, and the dark-haired man didn't even take the bait.

"All right, man, what the fuck is wrong with you?"

Jacob have a humorless chuckle. "I'm trying to figure that out myself."

"Wanna talk about it?"

"I'm conflicted. I don't think you're doing the right thing by staying in Fargo. You're putting the woman you love in jeopardy, and I disagree with that wholeheartedly. She's got spunk, I'll give her that, but she's not Kennedy Jones. She wouldn't stand a chance if her life were in danger. You being with her increases the probability of that happening by about a thousand percent."

Mason didn't have a response, so Jacob continued.

"It doesn't help that I've met her, and I like her. I think she's adorable."

What the fuck was he getting at? Was the mercenary carrying a torch for Reagan?

"I watched you two together, just like I've watched Kennedy and Dante—or Bella, whatever. I had that once. And I walked away—for her safety, even though it gutted me and broke her heart. I'm sitting here on this jet, flying you to be with the woman you love—a woman that I like and would never want anything bad to happen to, and you think somehow it's going to work out. So I'm left wondering if you're making the biggest mistake of your life—or if I did, years ago when I left Taren."

Mason was floored that Jacob was telling him all this.

"Do you still love her?"

"I will until the day I die."

"Do you know what happened to her? Did she marry someone else?"

"Yeah, she did. Eventually."

"That had to hurt."

He sighed. "It did, but it also felt like confirmation that I'd done the right thing."

"Just because she moved on doesn't mean he's the better man for her. I guarantee no one could love Reagan better than me."

Jacob's eyes grew wide and his mouth parted in surprise—like Mason's words were a revelation. Then his expression immediately turned somber.

"You better get this bullseye off your back, man. It'd be a shame if I had to marry your girl because you're dead."

Mason tried hard not to snarl at the man he knew was teasing him.

"Tell you what, you ever talk about marrying my girl again, you'll be the one who's dead."

"Then you probably better get this taken care of. Or not—I can wait. I guess I'll just have to be content with my millions and a different woman every week until she's available," Jacob said with a smirk.

"Maybe instead of lusting after Reagan, you should check in on Taren. Just to make sure she's doing okay."

Jacob's smirk fell, and he shook his head. "No, I wouldn't want to upend her life again."

"How do you know it wouldn't be a welcome upending?"

He could tell Jacob was giving it some thought, but then he shook his head again with a sad smile.

"Sometimes it's best to let sleeping dogs lie."

He shrugged. "You never know."

"No, I do. I would never want to hurt her again. She's happy—I need to leave it alone."

"But what if she's not?"

"Drop it, Mason."

With a sigh, he sat back on the leather couch as they cruised at thirty thousand feet across the US. Watching Jacob reading something on his tablet, Mason realized he'd just discovered the man was actually human—with feelings and everything. He would bet Jacob had never told anyone about Taren.

As if reading his thoughts, the fixer said without even looking up, "By the way, what I just told you…" He tore his glance away from his iPad and looked Mason in the eye. "I recommend you forget all about it, because if it *ever* gets out, I'll know the source and will respond accordingly." With a smirk, he added, "*Then* I'll marry your girl *and* knock her up."

"Your secret's safe with me, asshole. But you really should check in on *your* girl."

Jacob stood. "She's not my girl anymore. She's someone else's wife now," he said, then turned toward the small galley, effectively ending the conversation.

Two weeks ago, he would have understood why Jacob had walked away from the woman he loved. Now it seemed unfathomable. He'd cut off his left arm before he walked away from Reagan. But he was going to do as the man requested and drop it. This was Jake's business, not his.

He'd been a lot more active today than he was used to since he'd been shot, and his leg was starting to throb. He popped a pain pill and laid his head back on the couch cushion, dreaming of his sassy pants as he slipped into a light slumber.

****

Mason still hadn't heard from her, despite sending her what felt like a hundred texts. He fired off one more from the backseat of his Uber on the way to her house.

Still no response by the time his car pulled up outside her tidy ranch home. He immediately noticed some security improvements he wanted to get started on tomorrow, then remembered he was still somewhat incapacitated. Maybe he'd hire it out.

That is, if she even let him in the front door.

He was prepared to grovel to make that happen.

Taking a deep breath, he knocked loudly on her sky-blue front door, observing the matching white planters on either side of the doormat. He'd be willing to bet money there was a spare house key under one of those items.

He heard her coming to the door, and wondered how he was going to respond when she asked who it was, and what he'd do if she refused to open the door when she learned it was him.

He needn't have worried; she opened the front door without asking who was on the other side. They were going to chat about that later.

She gasped when she saw him standing there with his duffle bag in hand, crutches on either side of him.

"Wh-what are you doing here?"

He tried to make light of his uninvited appearance on her front door.

"Well, you wouldn't text me back."

As if on cue, his phone dinged.

"I just did a minute ago," she said with a small, polite smile.

He glanced down and saw her name on his phone screen, but didn't open her message.

They stood there awkwardly, neither speaking, and she didn't move to invite him inside.

"Um, can I come in?"

She crossed her arms in front of her, not moving.

"Why?"

Ah, there's my sassy pants girl.

"Well, I traveled two thousand miles to talk to you."

She didn't budge, simply repeating herself, "Why?"

Mason could tell she was itching to give him a piece of her mind. Something he deserved. But he was tired and didn't want to fight with her tonight. Not ever, actually, but definitely not tonight. And certainly not while standing on her front step.

It was time to grovel.

"Because I was wrong, and I wanted to apologize to you in person. I was hoping to do it this morning at the villa, and then spend the rest of the day between your legs begging for forgiveness, but you sort of modified those plans."

Her arms relaxed in front of her, and the corner of her mouth went up, emboldening him.

"I'm prepared to spend the night between your legs begging for forgiveness instead," he said with a lazy grin.

She stepped to the side, allowing him in.

"You can sleep in the guest room," she said, closing and locking the door behind him.

Oh, no, no, no. He wasn't sleeping anywhere but with her wrapped in his arms.

He paused and reached out, touching her arm.

"Sweetheart, I'm so sorry. Can we please talk?"

She shrugged and wrapped her arms around her middle. Mason knew she was hurting. He dropped his bag and set his crutches against the wall, then pulled her into him. Thankfully, she didn't resist, because he wasn't very steady on just one leg.

She burrowed into his chest and began to cry quietly.

"Oh baby, don't cry." He began to stroke her hair. "I fucked up. I should have insisted you stay. I'm so sorry. Please forgive me."

Her little shoulders began to shake. It was killing him.

"Aw, sweetheart. Talk to me. Why are you crying?"

He tried to pull away and make her look at him, but she squeezed his middle harder and wouldn't budge as she sobbed softly into his shirt.

"Can we sit down so I can at least hold you properly? I don't feel very stable on one leg."

She pulled away, sniffling, and whispered, "Let's go in the living room."

Mason grabbed his crutches and followed her into a cozy room with the same wooden floors as the entryway and a large Oriental rug in the center. It looked like it was straight from the pages of *Better Homes and Gardens* with its overstuffed, vintage furniture in soft, feminine colors. Her decorating touches were ones he'd never even think to consider in his condo. It was very Reagan-esque, and he immediately felt comfortable.

"This is a great room," he said as he looked around. "It's very you."

Her face was splotchy from crying, but she smiled and murmured, "Thanks."

He sat down on the couch, setting his crutches on the ground, then leaned back and sprawled out, gesturing to the cushions at his side.

"Come here, baby. I need to hold you."

She immediately complied, and he wrapped his arms around her.

"I was so scared I was never going to see you again," she confessed. "I was mad—which I had every right to be, by the way. But I acted irrationally, and that's on me. It wasn't until I was in the air that I thought about the fact that Jacob had shown up for a reason, and you might have to disappear without me hearing from you again."

"First of all, I would never disappear without telling you first. Never." He tapped her chin and gave her a disapproving look. "Something we need discuss about you doing, by the way." Then hugged her again. "And as far as why Jacob showed up..." He sighed, suddenly more exhausted than he'd felt in days. It was probably the relief that she was going to forgive him washing over him after a long-ass day. "I'll tell you everything that's going on—tomorrow, I promise. Right now, I'm just really tired. Can we go to bed? Together? Please?"

He felt her smile against his chest.

"Yeah, we can do that."

Of course, he had to push the envelope.

"Naked?"

"Still impossible," she murmured, moving to sit up.

"Always," he said with an unapologetic grin.

Chapter Thirty

Reagan

She didn't know if she was supposed to forgive him this easily, but didn't really care. She'd already softened after reading his text messages apologizing. When he had shown up at her door not more than fifteen minutes after she'd arrived home, what was she supposed to do?

Wrap her arms around him and feel loved that he had chased after her, that's what.

So that was what she did.

He felt even better lying next to her in her bed, naked.

"Your place is so cozy," he said when he walked into her bedroom. She would best describe it as shabby chic, with the wrought iron bed she'd found at Goodwill that she'd painted white, to match the furniture she'd picked up at yard sales and secondhand stores and also painted.

She'd splurged on a mattress and bedding though, something Mason seemed to appreciate when he sank down between the sheets, already stripped naked while she stood fully dressed in the middle of her room.

"Maybe it's because your bed smells like you, but this is fucking heaven. I think I feel more comfortable here than I do my own place."

"Good, since this is going to be your place, too."

He looked away with a frown.

Oh god, he's not staying.

"Isn't it?" she asked. "At least for a while? Has that changed?"

"No, I'm staying. If you'll still have me. I'll explain everything that's going on tomorrow, sweetheart. I promise. Right now, you need to get your ass in bed and snuggle next to me."

"Just let me lock up and wash my face. I've been traveling—commercial, not on a private jet—for ten and a half hours today."

"Hurry back," he called after her as she headed to the main part of the house to make sure the doors were locked and the lights off before coming back and getting ready for bed in the master bath adjoining her room.

She debated putting on the oversized t-shirt she usually slept in, just to hear him growl at her to take it off, but decided against it. Instead, she shut the light off and ventured into her bedroom stark naked. A feeling of happiness bubbled up through her—she was going to fall asleep next to Mason again.

His soft snoring as she slipped between the covers indicated he'd beaten her to it. When she snuggled in beside him, his arm immediately wrapped around her waist, and she fell asleep feeling safe and protected. And loved. So loved.

****

Mason

He woke up early the next morning feeling content in Reagan's bed. The morning light let him look around her bedroom as she lay next to him. From what he'd seen of her house, it reflected her personality to a T, and he loved it. He was going to be really comfortable here over the next few weeks while he healed.

Probably too comfortable. He knew leaving her was going to be a bitch when the time came, but he'd cross that bridge when he came to it. Right now, he was going to enjoy his life with Reagan Jones, and get a glimpse of how things were going to be permanently once he neutralized the price on his head and broke ties with the agency.

The physical therapy appointment he'd booked wasn't until Friday; he had two entirely free days—and at least one was going to be spent having makeup sex.

Maybe both.

Just then a beeping noise filled the room. Reagan groaned and rolled over, fumbling for her phone on the nightstand and shutting the sound off.

What the hell? She set an alarm?

She stroked his forearm where it was wrapped around her.

"I'm sorry if that woke you up," she said softly.

"I was already awake."

That elicited a giggle. "Of course you were."

"Did you mean to set an alarm?"

She sighed then reluctantly sat up.

"Yeah, last night. I have absolutely no food in this house for breakfast, and I have to get you coffee. Actually, I'll need to get a coffee maker or Keurig thingy for you, unless you like instant coffee?"

"No instant, but a coffee maker or Keurig works."

"Which would you prefer?"

"Why don't I go with you?"

The idea brought a smile to her face, then she paused. "Wait. Is it still okay if you're seen with me?"

"As long as we stick to the story."

"So why did Jacob come back?"

He blew out a breath. "To let Bella and me know there's a bounty on our heads. Well, your sister's has been cancelled. She's listed as deceased."

As he expected, panic flashed across her face. He'd seen it too many times in the short time he'd known her.

"Oh my god. What are you going to do? Is it safe for you to even go out? You should stay inside. I know there's physical therapists who make house calls."

He smiled at her concern, causing her to hit his arm.

"Mason, this is fucking serious!"

He stroked her cheek, trying to dampen his smile.

"Sweetheart, I know it is. This isn't the first there's been a price on my head, but hopefully, it will be the last."

"Why? Are you going to fake your death like my sister?"

"Something like that."

"*Something* like that? What the hell does that even mean?"

"It means after my wounds are healed, I'm going to headquarters and meeting with my bosses about my resignation. Since I'm no longer going to be in the field, I'm hoping they'll work with me about listing me as dead. Then I'll go back to using my birth name all the time."

She shook her head as if trying to digest everything he'd just told her.

"Time out. One—why do you have to wait until you're healed to go in? Two—what's going to happen to your pension and health insurance if you're listed as dead? Three—your birth name?"

"I'm waiting until I'm healed because there's going to be a cost. Probably a hefty one if I'm asking to be considered deceased."

"You'll have to pay to quit?"

He shook his head. "Not with money. With a dangerous assignment that I normally wouldn't take otherwise. After I do their bidding, they'll probably give me a lump sum that will modestly cover me through retirement, and send me on my way. Unfortunately, I'll have to be on my own regarding health insurance. And yes, my *real* name. The name on my birth certificate and on all my diplomas. The one that only people with the highest clearance know about. That was my stipulation when they recruited me to become a special agent—I be given a new 'real' identity in addition to the multitude of fake ones I've acquired."

"I don't understand."

"I have two identities that are considered authentic by the government. I file two sets of income tax returns; I have bank accounts in both names, property in my real name, brokerage accounts in both names—"

"How are you able to do that?"

"Like I said, it was part of my negotiations before I agreed to go undercover. I wanted an exit strategy before I even entered, and I wanted to keep my parents and siblings safe."

"Wow," she whispered. "It's kind of like the witness protection program."

He chuckled. "Kind of."

"I'm assuming Marcus did the same thing?"

"Yeah, except he's not listed as dead so he'll be getting his pension direct-deposited into his account, along with terrific healthcare."

"Will he go back to using his birth name, too?"

"Probably not. It'll be safer for me if he doesn't."

"So are you going to tell me your birth name?"

"Afraid not, sweetheart. Not until I'm completely out and going by it."

That seemed to hurt her feelings. "Why? Don't you trust me?"

"The fact that you know Hughes isn't my original last name means I trust you. No one but Marcus knows that."

Reagan continued to pout.

"I'm sorry, baby. It's safer for everyone right now this way."

She sighed and stood up, leaning over to peck him on the lips. "I know you're right. But I also think it's safer if you stay put while I go get some groceries. Nothing like riding around in a motorized shopping cart to draw attention to us."

Mason hadn't thought about that. God, he couldn't wait to be walking normal again. He was going to be the most dedicated physical therapy patient ever.

He reached for her hand. "Do you have to go right this minute?"

She smiled and let him pull her back onto the bed. "No, but I just thought you'd be starving this morning."

Rolling over so he enveloped her frame with his, he growled, "I'm starving all right. Just not for food."

He expected her to giggle, but instead she ran her fingernails down his back and seductively murmured, "Mmm, what do you have in mind?"

"I think it's easier if I show you," he replied with a smirk and a wink.

He dipped his head to kiss her, and she cried out, "Wait!"

He pulled back instantly, worried he'd hurt her. "What's wrong?"

"I have to brush my teeth," she said as she scampered out from under him.

He flopped back on the pillows, watching her naked ass walk toward the bathroom. "Are you serious?"

"Absolutely," she called over her shoulder.

Goddammit, now he was going to have to get up and hobble into the bathroom to brush his teeth, too. As he watched her tits bounce while she moved the toothbrush up and down, he tried to suppress his grin.

Totally worth it.

Chapter Thirty-One

Reagan

She lay panting as he crawled up her body with a satisfied grin after making her moan out his name as she orgasmed.

Damn, did that man know how to lick her pussy.

He leaned down and kissed her so she was tasting herself on his tongue. Pussy and toothpaste, what an erotic combination. She'd had no idea.

"You're getting around better," she observed as he maneuvered around the bed.

"I had incentive."

She pushed on his shoulder so he was laying on his back and began to kiss his chest, her nipples grazing his core as she worked down his stomach toward his cock. His delicious, hard-as-steel, perfect cock.

"God, I love your cock," she whispered in awe, slowly stroking his shaft. Beads of precum collected at the tip, and she dipped her head to run her tongue around his helmet, looking into his eyes as she did.

She'd never considered herself sexy until she met Mason, but something about being with him brought out her inner vixen. He never disappointed in showing his appreciation.

"Fuck, that is hot," he growled as he watched her intently.

With his cock between her lips, she smiled and took him as deep as she could—still staring in his eyes.

"Holy fuck," he shuddered and briefly closed his eyes with his head thrown back.

She began to bob her head up and down his cock while she fisted his shaft from the base to meet her mouth in the middle. Her rhythm started slow and seductive, but as his breathing became shallower, she picked up the pace.

She glanced up and found him watching her, mesmerized. He tenderly tucked her hair behind her ear and let out a long groan when she took him deep in her throat again. His cock was nice and slippery when she popped him out of her mouth and resumed stroking him. Sucking him back into her mouth, she started to moan around his dick. She knew that turned him on.

"Fuuuuck!"

He started to thrust his hips subtly in tempo with her rhythm, and she continued slurping and moaning.

"Baby," he panted, "I'm going to come."

Reagan didn't stop, and he started to grunt while slightly pushing her head down as he began to spurt in her mouth. There was too much cum to swallow, and it dribbled out the sides of her mouth onto his shaft while she continued sucking and stroking him until he began to jump under her touch.

"Okay, okay," he laughed, jerking away from her like she was tickling him as he tried to catch his breath.

She smiled and made her way to the bathroom for a towel, feeling his eyes on her as she did.

"I think we should have a rule," he said when she returned and began to clean him up.

She paused her wiping and looked up at him. "What kind of rule?"

"No clothes allowed when we're in bed—ever. Or in the bedroom at all, for that matter."

"Not even underwear?"

"God no. *Especially* not underwear."

Lying naked next to Mason every night—her skin touching his? *Gosh, twist my arm.*

"I think that can be arranged," she said with a sly grin and finished cleaning him.

He tugged her next to him and lazily ran his fingers down her spine.

"We should probably also dedicate at least one day a week to not getting out of bed. Starting today."

She lifted her head to look at him.

"We already had one day this week that we spent in bed, remember? It was the most perfect day I've ever had."

Mason kissed her hair.

"Mine too. But the week restarted when we left Ensenada."

She smiled against his chest. "But today, I really need to go to the grocery story, unpack and do laundry. Not to mention rearrange my closet so there's more room for your things. How about if we designate a weekend day?"

That would work better for when she started back teaching anyway.

He sighed dramatically. "You drive a hard bargain, Ms. Jones. But how do you feel about couch sex? Or counter sex? Or on the washing machine?"

She rolled her eyes.

"Tell you what. If your physical therapist approves it, I'm all for it."

"Oh, he'll approve it, all right," he said confidently.

"You're incorrigible," she said, pecking his lips than crawling off the bed.

"Is that better or worse than impossible?"

Reagan headed toward the bathroom, calling over her shoulder, "Worse."

"But in a good way, right?" he yelled from the bed.

She peeked her head around the door jamb, the sight of his muscular, naked body lying in *her* bed causing her to catch her breath.

"Of course."

****

Mason

Reagan left to go to the grocery store, leaving him alone in her quaint three-bedroom.

"Look around, get familiar with the place. I have no secrets from you. My sex toys are in the cabinet of my nightstand," she said with a wink as she walked out the bedroom door.

Of course he checked them out the minute he heard the garage door close. There were definite possibilities of incorporating some into their playtime. He wondered if she'd let him fuck her ass and use a dildo in her pussy? His cock moved at the idea.

He'd seen the living room, so he explored the other parts of the house. Opening one door, he found a guest room with floral bedspread and sparse furniture. He wondered if it got used very often, and if so, by whom? Another door led to her office/studio. Some of her paintings on the wall he recognized from his online search. He walked in and approached the first one he came to, studying it carefully before moving on to the next—they were even more impressive in person. His heart filled with pride as he realized just how talented his little sprite was. Her work was expressive and beautiful, and a little sad. He wanted to hug her and take away whatever stirred that emotion in her.

Mason paused in front of an easel with a piece that she was in the middle of working on, tracing his finger on the stool in front of the canvas. He gently spun the seat while his thoughts turned to picturing her sitting there hard at work— her hair up in a messy bun and paint smudges on her face while he fixed dinner for them. Their kids descending on the house after sports practice, creating loud, happy chaos. Her smile lighting up the kitchen when she came out for dinner.

He could see their future so clearly, making him more determined than ever to close this chapter of his life as soon as he could so he could get on to the next one.

With a smile, he glanced around the room once more before closing the door, then headed to check out the kitchen. It was very clean and orderly. Reagan had done a nice job of modernizing it, but it had obviously been on a budget.

His girl was independent, no doubt about it. One more thing he loved about her.

He chuckled when he opened the refrigerator after inspecting the pantry. She wasn't lying about there being no food in the house.

Mason headed back to her bedroom to unpack. She'd made space in her closet before she left and even consolidated her undergarments into one drawer to give him a drawer in the dresser. He didn't need much; he only had a duffle bag of things. Maybe he'd do some online clothes shopping when he graduated to a cane and didn't have to wear loose pants to accommodate the bulky bandages on his leg. His wounds were healing, and he'd been able to hobble and hop around the house without his crutches, so he knew with a few rounds of physical therapy, he'd be ready.

One step closer to his new chapter.

Reagan had been gone a long time, and when she finally pulled into the garage and opened the hatch on her little, red Ford Fiesta, he understood why.

"Good grief, woman, did you buy out the grocery store?"

"Nope, I even have money left over from what you gave me."

She smiled and reached into her front jeans pocket, pulling out two one dollar bills, a ten, and some change and proudly putting it in his hand.

"Change back and everything," he teased.

That wasn't saying a lot, since—unsure of the cost of groceries in Fargo—he had given her three hundred dollars. Judging by the overflowing hatchback and backseat that was filled to the brim, she was either a very good shopper, or groceries were a lot more inexpensive than what he was used to. Probably both.

"You're very sexy and manly, but why don't you go sit down in the kitchen while I unload these. No offense, but you're kinda in the way."

He grabbed as many bags as he could just to prove he was capable and hobbled into the house—regretting his decision the whole way, especially when he realized he'd picked up the bag with eggs.

As he helped unpack groceries and learned where she put things, he couldn't help but smile. She'd even bought him toiletries—deodorant, men's shampoo and body wash, and a new toothbrush.

"I wasn't sure how long you'd been carrying yours around. I figured you could use a new one," she explained when he raised his eyebrows after pulling it from the bag.

This was his new reality, at least for a little while—Reagan was going to be looking out for him and taking care of him. He was going to be sharing his life with her. The simple act of putting groceries away with her made it feel real, and he fucking loved it.

She caught him smiling at her while she stacked the pasta in the pantry and did a double take.

"What?"

He moved behind her and wrapped his arms around her middle, resting his chin on her shoulder.

"Nothing. I just love being here with you. Being a part of your life."

She turned so she could put her arms around him.

"I love you being here." Her smile faltered momentarily, and she looked away, suddenly very interested in her countertops.

"But?" he asked.

She looked back at him, tears glistening in her eyes.

"But I worry I'm fooling myself. You can't possibly be happy here for long. Me, my life, Fargo... we're about as vanilla as it comes. You're going to be bored to tears within a week."

"I already told you, sassy pants. Vanilla is my favorite flavor. I'll supply the syrup and toppings, okay? Believe it or not, I'm looking forward to normal and predictable, as long as it's with you."

She rested her head on his shoulder and was quiet for a beat, then whispered, "I just worry I'm not going to be enough."

Mason pulled back. He still had one arm around her waist, but there was now space between their chests. He tipped her chin with his thumb when she darted her eyes from his.

"You will always be more than enough, sweetheart. I told you, once I chose a flavor that was it. *You're* it. Don't doubt that."

Her expression told him that was exactly what she was doing.

"Reagan Elizabeth Jones, from the second you sat down in the backseat of my car, I was smitten. Then I fucking drugged you—I *kidnapped* you, baby, and you still managed to not only forgive me, but love me in spite of it. If either of us should be worried about the other changing their mind, it's me. I'm just waiting for you to come to your senses, and praying like hell you never do."

The redhead looked away with a small smile, pressing her lips together to disguise it. He'd seen her sister do the same thing.

"Not a chance. You're far too good-looking, not to mention talented in bed," she teased, her eyes shining with mischief when she looked up at him.

"Are you saying you only love me for my cock? What if it quits working someday?"

Her eyes grew wide and she let out a dramatic gasp, acting as if the thought horrified her as much as it secretly did him.

"Then you better stock up on the little blue pills, big guy," Reagan sternly warned, subtly squeezing his middle to emphasize her veiled threat.

He pushed her hair behind her ear and kissed her forehead.

"Sweetheart, I don't think you'll ever have to worry about that. I'll be chasing you around the nursing home when we're old and grey."

Chapter Thirty-Two

Mason

Reagan had left for her first day of work for the fall semester—her students would be starting on Thursday, and Mason was getting ready for his second physical therapy appointment. Reflecting on spending all day yesterday with her in bed, he concluded, *Naked Sundays are the shit.*

They'd done two naked days within the span of a week, and he would recommend them to everyone. It wasn't just about the copious amounts of sex—which was fucking awesome—it was about unplugging from everything else and focusing on each other. Talking, sharing, laughing, and, in their case, getting to know one another better. But he could see it, in the future, being a good way to reconnect and catch up on their lives.

He fired off a text to her: *I decree Sundays to be Naked Sundays from now until eternity.*

Her response was immediate: *I love it! But what brought this on? Aren't you supposed to be at PT?*

Mason: *Just thinking about yesterday. And, yeah, my Uber should be here soon.*

Reagan: *Have a productive session!*

Mason: *How's your first day back? Any idea when you'll be home?*

Reagan: *So far, so good. They might add another section of my 104 class, so many have signed up for it. I should be home around 4.*

Mason: *That's great, sweetheart! Congratulations! I'll have dinner started when you get home—Italian okay?*

Reagan: *Have I mentioned how much I love having you there?*

Mason: *I love being here, baby. See you tonight.*

He was proud of her for having so many students want to be in her classes, but the selfish part of him didn't want her being away at work *more*. He would have preferred *less*. Not that he'd ever tell her that; he was almost ashamed to admit it even to himself. But what could he say? When it came to Reagan Jones, he was selfish as fuck.

That probably wasn't going to change. Ever. He'd waited too long to find her to want to share her. Except maybe with their kids.

****

Reagan

They'd settled into a perfect routine. Well, as far as she was concerned, it was perfect. School was in full swing; she worked until one p.m. on Tuesdays and Thursdays, and four p.m. on Mondays and Wednesdays, plus her class at the community center on Friday afternoons. Mason would have dinner started when she arrived home after five, or he would quietly start cooking it when she was home and working. He always shooed her away when she offered to help, so she would usually just sit and lust after him while he moved about the kitchen. There was something so sexy about watching him concentrate on preparing a beautiful meal for her—which he delivered every time.

She loved snuggling into bed next to his hard body each night, and how he just seemed to know if she needed to be held, made love to, or fucked.

Oh, and he put the toilet seat down.

Hello, dream life.

She knew it wasn't going to last, though. He had graduated to a cane, and was doing physical therapy three times a week. She was also sure he was bored out of his mind—and she couldn't blame him. It was only a matter of time before everything changed.

What she wasn't prepared for was how quickly it did, or the manner in which it happened.

Chapter Thirty-Three

Mason

It would have been easy to let his guard down; living with Reagan was perfect, and Fargo was comfortable and felt nonthreatening. He'd taken steps to improve the security at her cozy ranch house, and when Reagan was home, he was able to completely relax—a byproduct of her calming effect on him. But he was still vigilant, especially when he left the house, and was always aware of his surroundings.

When he walked into physical therapy on a Wednesday afternoon and an unknown therapist greeted him in the workout room, he was immediately on edge.

"Where's Jimmy?"

"He's out sick today," the burly man replied nonchalantly. *Too* nonchalantly. Mason had never seen him in the three weeks he'd been coming here. Something was definitely not right.

"You know what," he told the man, not even putting on the pretense he was going to stay as he started edging toward the door. "I think I might be coming down with whatever he has because I'm not feeling very good either. I'm going to go home and rest." He was out the door without another word.

The thing about Fargo was there wasn't a cab on every corner he could just hop into. When he had first realized that weeks ago, he'd thought it was charming, but at the moment, it was annoying and inconvenient as fuck.

Mason ducked into the coffee shop next door to the PT office in the strip mall and made his way to the back door, startling some of the workers as he limped through the employees-only area. He poked his head out the steel door and found the alley empty, so he proceeded outside. Looking around at the dumpsters, he thought about ditching his phone, but hesitated. It had never been out of his possession when he was in public, so he felt confident it wasn't compromised. Still, Uber was not a safe option.

Fortunately, the charm of Fargo also meant people were trusting, and the second car he tried was unlocked. Less than sixty seconds later, he'd hotwired it and was on his way back to Reagan's little house he'd grown to love.

Mason parked the car two streets over and made his way through the neighborhood and to the back of the house by cutting through people's lawns, the sound of fallen leaves rustling under his feet. His leg was hurting like a bitch but he pushed through, finally reaching the back door. Once inside, he quickly grabbed his duffle, which was already packed. Having a go-bag prepared and ready to go—much like an expectant mother would—had been instilled in him from the second day of undercover training. He'd also bought two burner phones a few weeks ago, just in case the occasion arose. He slid one under Reagan's pillow like he'd told her he would if something were to happen, and moved quickly down the hall to the kitchen where his pain meds were, popping one and swallowing it without turning on the faucet. He pocketed the prescription bottle before stealthily maneuvering to the entryway. He planted a camera so it was pointed at the door, then snuck back down the hall and placed another pointing at the door leading to the garage.

He'd at least be able to keep an eye on things and make sure she was okay.

Grabbing his laptop, he took a long look around her bedroom and sighed. His time with her had been the stuff dreams were made of, and he was pissed off that it was ending so soon—and not on his terms.

Definitely not on his terms.

He gave a determined sigh, and the Terminator's voice rang in his head.

I'll be back.

****

Reagan

She knew something was wrong the minute she walked in the house and didn't smell dinner cooking.

"Mason?" she yelled, setting her bag down on a chair in the kitchen, then walked through the rest of the house, calling, "Babe?" She peeked her head in the bedroom, repeating, "Babe?"

No Mason.

Maybe his physical therapy appointment got changed. She was walking back to her bag in the kitchen to see if there was a text when she heard knocking at the front door. *Did he forget his key?*

Reagan tentatively walked to the front, trying to keep her footsteps light. She jumped when the knocking resumed as she neared the door.

She called out, "Who is it?" in her most authoritative voice. Mason had discussed the importance of not appearing timid, right after he'd finished scolding her about not asking who was at the door before opening it.

"Fargo Police, ma'am. We'd like to talk to you."

Uff da. Fer fuck's sake. She knew half the officers on the force, and they were going to *ma'am* her?

She quickly unlocked the door and opened it, immediately recognizing the two men standing on her doorstep, Brian Kurtz and Ric Casper. She had gone to school with both of them.

"Brian, Ric," she said, putting her hand on the door casing and nodding to them. Then she squinted her eyes and scowled indignantly, "Did you seriously *ma'am* me?"

They seemed flustered at her question, exchanging looks as if unsure how to respond.

"You both graduated a year ahead of me." Reagan pursed her lips and crossed her arms over her chest. "That's just rude."

"Hey, uh, Reagan, right? We didn't know it was you. Sorry," Ric said sheepishly.

She raised an eyebrow, unimpressed with his explanation.

"Honest, we had no idea. Can we come inside and talk to you?"

She reluctantly stepped aside and let them in, shutting the door behind them but making no effort to leave the entryway and invite them in further.

"What's going on?" she asked suspiciously.

"We'd like to talk to you about your roommate," Brian started.

She cocked her head as if confused.

"Roommate? I don't have a roommate. You mean my mom? She doesn't live here."

They shook their head in unison. "No, Mason Davis, the man who's staying here," Brian clarified.

"Mason? Davis? Who?" She shook her head in bewilderment. "I have no idea who that is. I live alone, gentlemen." She held up her left hand, and wiggled her ring finger. "Nobody's living with me unless they put a ring on it."

Reagan had purposefully been trying to make them feel uncomfortable and thrown off their game since she opened the door. It seemed to be working.

"There's not a man staying here? About six feet, blond hair, limping?" Ric asked.

She looked at them like they were crazy.

"Limping? No, no man here—limping or otherwise."

"Are you sure?"

Reagan scoffed. "Pretty sure I'd know if there was a man living here."

Ric took a step toward the hall leading to the kitchen. "Mind if we look around?"

"Um, yeah. I do."

"It's for your safety, Reagan. There's a man who listed this as his address with his physical therapist."

"Well, like I said, I think I'd know if I were living with someone. It sounds like he either gave a phony address or he made a mistake when he gave it. But that hardly seems like an offense to call the police about. Did he skip out on the bill or something?"

"No, he's been paying in cash for his appointments. The manager just noticed he had bullet wounds when he was at his last appointment and is worried maybe he's a fugitive on the run or something," Brian responded.

Oh geez, only in Fargo.

She pressed her lips together, trying not to laugh. "I think maybe the manager has seen too many true crime TV shows."

Ric smiled appreciatively at her observation. *Too* appreciatively, as he eyed her up and down.

"You're probably right. So what are you up to these days? Didn't you join the Marines?"

"No, that was my sister, Kennedy. God rest her soul."

Brian rocked on the balls of his feet and when he coughed politely into his hand, she noticed the gold band on his left hand.

"I, uh, read about her accident. I'm really sorry for your loss. I had no idea she was working for the CIA."

She smiled. "Thank you. It's been a hard year without her." That was true.

"I can only imagine."

Brian bobbed his head awkwardly and rocked on his feet again, glancing at Ric, almost pleading with his eyes for his partner to say something so they could leave.

Ric took the hint, produced his card, and handed it to her.

"If you hear anything strange—day or night—call me." He opened the front door and turned toward her. "You can also call me if you don't hear anything. Maybe I could take you to dinner sometime?"

Reagan hoped this wasn't his A-game—although that might explain why he was still single. She followed him out and stood on her doorstep, her smile pained.

"I'm not really looking to date anyone right now. I'm still grieving for my sister and trying to keep it together enough to still do my job. But I promise, if I see anything suspicious, you'll be the first call I make."

"Okay, please do. Don't hesitate—doesn't matter what time it is." He walked a few steps behind his partner, then turned back with a smile. "It was great seeing you again, Reagan. Let me know if you need anything."

Two months ago, she would have taken him up on his offer for dinner. He was muscular with a shaved head and mesmerizing eyes. And she really liked his smile.

"Good seeing you, too, Ric. You too, Brian. Stay safe, guys."

Reagan hadn't meant it when she said she would contact him if she saw anything suspicious, but she meant that. She would feel terrible if anything happened to either of them.

She shut the door and locked it behind her, then waited at the picture window in the living room until they drove off. Once their car was up the street, she ran through the house, trying to figure out just where her boyfriend had disappeared to, and if the visit from Brian and Ric had anything to do with it.

Her phone started ringing, except it wasn't her ringtone she was hearing. Had the recent software update reset her ringtone? Reagan went to the kitchen and dug through her bag to find her cell. Once it was in her hand, she looked down to realize there was no incoming call—yet the ringing persisted. Following the noise into her bedroom, she remembered him saying something about leaving a phone under her pillow and ran to find it before the ringing stopped.

Discovering it right where he said it would be, she frantically started pressing buttons to answer it.

Her "Hello?" came out a little breathless.

Goosebumps covered her arms when she heard his deep voice chuckle, "Hey, sassy pants."

"Hi, baby. Are you okay?"

"Yeah. I see you had some visitors."

She looked around the room, like she would find him in the corner watching her.

"Yes, how did you know?"

She could tell he was smiling as he replied, "I planted a couple of cameras to keep an eye on things while I'm gone."

Reagan smiled, picturing his grinning face. But then his words sank in, and her smile turned into a frown. She knew— he wasn't coming back any time soon.

"So you're gone then?"

"I'm afraid so, sweetheart."

She slumped down on the bed.

"Why? I think they believed me that you're not here."

"Just them coming there means it's no longer safe for you. Who knows if they did an online search, and if they did, what they searched. It could trigger anyone monitoring those databases. I can't risk it."

She sighed in resignation. "But... I need you here with me."

"I know, baby. I need that, too." His voice was low and gruff.

They sat in silence for a moment, then she sat up straighter.

"Where are these cameras you planted?"

"The front door and the garage door."

"Oh. Nothing in the bedroom?"

"No," he snarled. "Why?"

"Oh, no reason. Are you the only one watching the feed?"

"As of right now, yeah. Again, why?"

"No reason," she sing-songed.

"Reagan…" he warned.

"Maybe I'll just give you a reminder later of why you need to come back soon," she teased.

She heard him take in a sharp breath.

"Dammit, woman. That would be cruel. And sexy as fuck."

"But how will I know if you're watching?"

"You'll know," he reassured her.

"Hmmm… well, then maybe you'll see me later. If not, I hope we at least talk soon."

"We will. Keep this phone on you, but hidden, okay? Don't let anyone see you checking it. I'll only call if I know you're home alone or if it's an absolute emergency."

"Okay," she said softly. "I wish you were here."

"Me too, baby. Soon. I promise. I love you."

"I love you, too."

They hung up, and she didn't move from where she sat on the bed, the tears streaming down her cheeks as the feelings of loneliness overwhelmed her. How could she miss him so much already?

Chapter Thirty-Four

Mason

He wanted to stay close for a few days, but knew he couldn't stay *too* close, so he drove his stolen car to Minneapolis, parked and locked it at the airport, and rented a hotel room a few miles away. He could rent a car by using one of his aliases if he absolutely had to get back to Fargo, or he could get on a plane and fly to headquarters.

When he saw her red eyes on the video stream when she walked through the entry into the living room, it killed him not to go back and comfort her.

He'd been so fucking proud of her when the two Fargo officers showed up at her doorstep. She had been cool as a cucumber and didn't miss a beat, even turning the tables on them and making them squirm. He was relieved to learn it was Fargo PD who were looking into him, and not his agency, or worse, a bounty hunter. But their showing up still lit a fire under his ass to get moving and resolve things. Admittedly, he'd grown comfortable with his life with Reagan and hadn't been in a hurry to change it, even though he knew it was necessary. But he also knew it was necessary to rest his body and let it properly heal; it'd only been a month since he'd been shot. It wasn't exactly like he was milking the time off— just enjoying it. Enjoying the fuck out of it, actually.

Then Ric fuckin' Casper went and asked Reagan out to dinner after he finished questioning her, reminding Mason that he needed to get his shit squared away so he could properly claim her. He planned on being so obviously present in her life, only someone with a death wish would be dumb enough to ask her out. Right now, he'd give the cop a pass—he didn't know she belonged to Mason. But that shit needed to be remedied soon.

After she passed by where the camera was, he began to regret not planting more, because he'd have loved to see what she was doing right now, and if she was okay. At the time, he'd worried they were too intrusive, but justified it by telling himself he was only putting them at the doors, and was keeping her safe by knowing if anyone came inside.

As if he'd channeled his thoughts into action, she reappeared on the entryway camera. It was apparent she was looking for where he had positioned the device. She paused in front of the door, obviously determining where the best angle for the camera would be, then followed the line of sight right to where he had hidden it. He couldn't help but smile at her satisfied look when she plucked it from its hiding spot.

"Hi baby," she said mischievously into the camera as she walked back into her bedroom. He was getting seasick watching the jostled feed until she set it down on something at the end of her bed—giving him an unobstructed view of her body when she reappeared and lay down. In white lingerie and thigh-highs.

That sexy little bitch.

"I don't even know if you're watching," she purred as she traced her fingers over the thin material covering her tits.

He sent a text to her burner phone: *I'm here, sweetheart.*

"Oh, good. You can hear me too," she said out loud with a naughty smile.

He dialed the number, and she answered right away. "Well, hello there, sexy man."

"Put me on speaker and set the phone down," he growled.

She quickly obliged, placing the phone on what would be his pillow. What *should* be his pillow.

He turned the volume down on his receiver to prevent the echo from the video feed, which was delayed by a half a second.

"You look beautiful, baby," he crooned, and was rewarded with her shy smile.

"You always make me feel beautiful."

"And sexy as fuck."

She giggled. "You always make me feel like that, too."

"Good; then I'm doing my job."

She didn't respond, just lay there while her hands leisurely roved her body over her lacy garment, giving him a show.

"Let me see your tits," he urged.

Seductively, she lowered the lace until her perky boobs popped out, her pink nipples pebbled, and she squeezed them together in her hands.

Mason groaned out loud. "Fuck, that's hot."

She traced circles around her puckered skin and arched her back slightly, moaning softly as she brought her knees up with her toes pointed in those goddamn, sexy-ass stockings on the bed.

"Pinch your nipples for me." She immediately complied, and he snarled, "Pull them away from your tits. Hard."

When she did as he demanded, his dick created a big enough tent in his sweatpants that he could have camped in it. He tugged them down to his thighs, along with his boxer briefs, letting his cock spring free and immediately fisting it while keeping his eyes glued to his monitor.

"Spread your legs, baby."

Reagan took her time, but spread her legs wide.

"Pull your panties to the side. Let me see how wet you are."

She did, and he could see her pussy glisten through the camera. What he wouldn't give to be there to taste her.

"Fuuuuuck," Mason drawled as he slowly started to tug his shaft up and down.

"Touch yourself," he demanded gruffly.

She let out a little whimper as she ran her finger up and down her slit with one hand, her other hand still holding her underwear to the side.

"Mmm, yes. That's so sexy. Now, take your panties off."

Reagan brought her legs together and lifted them up high—giving Mason a front-row seat to her exemplary ass as she shimmied her white panties off, then twirled them around her index finger before tossing them to the floor.

"Fuck, you're beautiful baby. Open your legs for me."

Her pussy was fucking soaked.

"Play with your clit." His voice was a little raspier than it'd just been.

He watched, mesmerized, as she moved her middle finger in circles around her knot. His dick was leaking and her soft moans were not helping.

"You're driving me crazy, you're so damn sexy. Put a finger inside your pussy."

She slid the finger circling her clit down to her opening, and he coaxed, "No, no. Keep touching your clit, too."

Using her other hand, she plunged one finger inside herself while continuing to play with her pearl. Mason began to move his hand to match her rhythm, then he remembered the dildos in her nightstand.

"Are you touching yourself?" she purred.

"Fuck yeah, I am. Get your purple rabbit from your nightstand, baby. I want you to fuck yourself with it and imagine it's my cock."

Reagan casually turned over and raised onto all fours, stretching down to the cabinet while keeping her ass on full display for the camera, her shimmering pink slit peeking out. He knew she was doing it on purpose, and he loved it.

"You. Are. So. Fucking. Hot," he groaned appreciatively while smearing the precum around his tip.

Producing the lavender dildo, she turned over on her back and looked straight into the camera with a sexy smirk. He had to let go of his cock or he would've come right then.

"Spread your legs, sweetheart. Let me see you."

She ran the toy up and down over her folds, teasing both of them in the process.

"Put it in your pussy and turn it on," he urged and began to tug on his cock again when she complied.

"Mmm, good girl," he groaned at the sight of her laying on her bed, legs spread and pussy drenched, while she fucked herself with her dildo as he told her what to do.

"Now put the ears on your clit and turn that on."

She let out a long moan and began to pant.

"That's it. God, you look so sexy," he growled. "Keep touching your clit."

He could tell, just by her noises and the way she arched her back, that she was getting ready to come, and he began to jerk his cock harder.

"Are you going to come, baby?"

She whimpered, "Ye—yes."

"Good, come for me sweetheart. Let me see your wet little pussy quiver around that dildo. Pretend it's my cock fucking you," he urged.

Her back bowed off the bed, and she let out a long drawn-out, "Ohhhh fuuuuuck yessss," as her tummy began to make jerking movements. Watching her come undone was the sexiest thing he'd ever seen, and he was quickly spurting his own release onto his stomach, grunting loud so she'd know what she'd done to him.

He sat trying to catch his breath as he watched her shut her toy off, set it aside, and lay there with a smile that matched his own.

"I fucking love you," he snarled into the phone, making her smile grow bigger.

"I love you, too." Her smile turned into a pout. "But now I wish you were here to hold me."

"Soon, sweetheart. Soon. I promise."

Chapter Thirty-Five

Reagan

She'd just put on a virtual peep show for Mason. It was so slutty of her, yet she'd never felt more sexy or desired.

And being told what to do—and then actually doing it without a second thought?

Oh yeah. Hot as fuck.

Apparently she was a submissive exhibitionist. She'd had no idea.

Actually, it was probably his appreciation for what she was doing, and the effect she knew she was having on him, that turned her on the most. Even though she was taking orders from him, she felt powerful because she knew he was coming undone watching her as she followed his commands.

"We definitely need to do that again," she whispered out loud as she moved to stand up from the bed and put her pajamas on.

Her burner phone dinged with an incoming message.

Mason: *Agreed.*

She'd almost forgotten that he could still see and hear her after they hung up. She looked up at the camera and smiled as if he were actually in the room with her.

"I love you, baby. But the camera is going back to its original spot. As much as I wish you were here holding me, it'd be creepy having you watching me all night."

Her phone dinged again.

Mason: *I'll be back soon. Delete these messages, sweetheart.*

She made a show of deleting them while she was still in front of the camera, then laid the phone on the bed and went to get ready for bed. It was still early, so she thought she'd do some work for her classes in bed before turning in.

Her phone dinged again after she put her pajamas on and had washed her face.

Mason: *Don't move the camera yet, please? I feel better being able to look at you and know you're okay.*

She looked at the camera with a grin. "Weirdo." But she left it while she sat lotus-style on the bed with a pencil tucked behind her ear and quickly got lost in her work, soon forgetting it was even there.

Her eyes began to grow heavy, and she slid between the sheets then shut off the light. Only when she snuggled into her pillow—and reached for him out of habit and he wasn't there—did she remember that she hadn't moved the monitoring device.

"Don't watch me sleep all night like a creeper," she murmured with a smile, her eyes closed. She wasn't sure if he'd heard her, but something told her he had.

Just knowing he was still looking out for her made sleep come easier than she'd anticipated. He managed to make her feel safe, even when he wasn't physically present.

****

Mason

He stayed in Minneapolis for two days before getting on a plane to Virginia, but continued monitoring Reagan's doors, especially during the day when she wasn't home. There were no more visitors.

They'd talked on the phone every night, and she would always move the camera into her bedroom, like he asked. He liked being able to check on her and know she was safe. There hadn't been another episode of video sex, but just the memory of it made his cock hard.

Fuck, he missed her, and couldn't wait to have her in his arms again. Which was why he so readily agreed to the next mission. As he had suspected, it was one he normally would never have taken, but he was able to negotiate leaving the agency with a lump sum settlement then being listed as dead—just like he'd predicted. Once that happened, he would be free to be with Reagan. Marry her, have babies with her, maybe open a restaurant. They could feature her art, and she could be the face of the business so he could still maintain a low profile. Even though he was going to be free to do what he wanted, he still needed to be smart. He wouldn't be running for office, or even having a social media presence anytime soon.

Maybe he'd grow a beard.

His burner phone alerted, letting him know Reagan was home from work.

"Hi, baby," she said as she walked inside, making him smile. She often talked out loud like he was home with her. Even though it filled him with longing to be there with her, he loved it. It was the next best thing.

"I have dinner plans with girlfriends tonight, so if you're going to call me, it's going to have to be either before I go or when I get home. I'll send you a text in a little while to let you know when I'm leaving, just in case you're not watching."

He was always watching. In a *I'm not a creeper* kind of way. Or maybe he was? He assumed it didn't bother her, but maybe that was a conversation they should have. If the cameras made her uncomfortable, he needed to take them down. If that was what she wanted, he'd probably still try to talk her into keeping them outside.

Hopefully, with him about to leave for his last mission, she'd leave them intact. It was going to be his only form of communication with her, and it wasn't going to be mutual. The burner phones they had been communicating with had outlived their purpose of secure, anonymous communication, and Mason was going dark, but with CIA-security level phones and computers, so he'd still be able to monitor the CIA-grade cameras in her house.

He got her text and waited until she finished getting ready and made an appearance in the kitchen, where the camera facing the door leading to the garage was mounted, before calling her. His redheaded beauty was dressed in dark jeans that were tucked into her knee-high black boots, and a tan peasant blouse that was cut lower than he liked with him being so far away. She had disappeared from view when he picked up the phone and dialed her number.

She answered with a sweet, "Hello handsome. Have I mentioned today how much I miss you?"

He smiled. "You haven't, actually."

"Well, I do."

"I miss you, too. You look beautiful. Where are you off to?"

"Oh, you saw me? Just dinner with some friends and then bowling."

"Ah, yes. I seem to recall you mentioning something about your mad bowling skills and mopping the lanes with me."

She giggled. "That's right. And the challenge still stands."

"Soon, sweetheart," he sighed wistfully.

"I know, you've been telling me that for almost two weeks now. How much longer?" There was a subtle whine in her tone. Not that he blamed her.

"I don't have an answer for you. And I'm going to be going dark soon."

"Dark? What does that mean?"

"It means you won't be hearing from me."

"Oh," she said softly. "When?"

"I don't know that either. But I promise I will let you know before I do."

"Okay. Well, listen, I'm kind of running late… can you call me when I get home? Will you be around? I don't even know where you're at or what you're doing anymore."

Or who you're doing.

She didn't say it, but he knew it was in the back of her mind.

"I'm still in the country, doing some intel for my next mission. And I hope it goes without saying, but I'm sleeping alone."

"I know. But thank you for affirming it. A girl can get insecure, especially when her boyfriend is so sexy."

"You don't ever have to worry about me, Reagan. I picked my flavor."

"Well, hurry back and cover me with chocolate already!" she teased.

"Don't forget the whipped cream. Go. Have fun. I'll call you back when you get home."

"Bye, babe."

Minutes later, his phone alerted to movement on the camera, and she blew him a kiss before walking out the door.

If he made it through this mission alive, coming home to her every night was going to be worth the hell he was about to endure.

Chapter Thirty-Six

Reagan

They had two more conversations, and then Mason Hughes vanished from her life.

He had asked if she wanted the cameras moved outside, but when he told her he'd still be able to monitor them, just not able to respond, she decided she still wanted them in the house. She'd gotten used to having one-sided conversations with him, and it made her feel like he was still a part of her life.

It was going on five weeks since he left Fargo, and three since she'd heard from him—the same amount of time they'd actually been together. She knew from when Kennedy would disappear for months that this was normal, but Reagan decided to reach out to her sister for reassurance anyway.

"There's no telling where they've sent him, honey. If this really is his last mission and he wants to disappear with their blessing, they're going to make him earn it," the former CIA operative told her when she called.

"I know. That's what he said."

"Did he…" Bella hesitated.

"Did he what?"

"Did he also tell you it was going to be dangerous? Way more than a usual mission. These are ones where the agency may not have to lie when they say he's dead. And because you're not listed as his next of kin, unless Marcus or Jacob reach out to you, you won't even know. Did you two come up with a contingency plan—like so you'll be sure to be notified by someone he trusts, and establish a code for how you'll really know if he's dead or just listed as dead?"

"Well, um, no. He had to leave in a hurry. He was worried his cover was blown."

"And was it?"

"I don't think so. It was Ric Casper and Brian Kurtz who were investigating."

"So Fargo PD then. Well, that's good, I guess. Better than anyone else."

"Yeah, but he said there was no telling who was monitoring databases if they did a search using his alias."

"He's not wrong. He did the right thing by leaving like that."

"Maybe, but it still sucks."

"I know, little sister. But he only wants to protect you; you can't fault him for that."

"I know. I don't."

"Listen, Madison is hungry and starting to get fussy so I gotta go. But if you need to get away, you're welcome to come stay with us anytime. We're back in San Diego for a few months while Dante opens a new dispensary on the East Coast. Say the word, and I'll send you a plane ticket, even if it's just for the weekend."

"Thanks. I'll think about it."

"I'm here if you need me. I love you, Rea."

"Love you, too, Ken—er, Bella."

She hung up not feeling any better. If anything, she felt more worried. They'd left so many things hanging, and worse, now she was left with the knowledge that if someone showed up and told her Mason is dead, he *might not* really be dead. How the fuck was she supposed to deal with that?

She came to the conclusion it would be best for her mental health if no one showed up to tell her that. Period.

Still, she talked into the air that night in her kitchen in case he was listening.

"So if Marcus or Jacob show up and tell me you're dead—am I supposed to believe them? We never came up with a code for something like that, but I've been told on good authority that was something we should have established. So, tell you what. If you're not really dead but I'm going to be told that you are, can you have Jacob be the one to show up and tell me?"

Never mind that Jacob probably wouldn't know either if he was really alive, or that Mason would have no control over how she was notified of his death, whether it was real or not.

So when Jacob showed up at her house ten days later, she had no idea what to think.

****

Mason

The war zone he'd been dropped in was the ultimate shit show, and he wondered if the agency had found out about his involvement in Cartagena and was setting him up as retribution.

They wouldn't do that. Right? Marcus had come home alive with good intel and the yacht was returned no worse for wear. No harm, no foul. The CIA would protect one of its own—especially one as successful as he'd been.

Kennedy Jones had probably thought the same thing on the yacht in Ensenada. Right before he got orders to terminate her.

His taxi was pulling up to a white, battle-weathered ten-story building in Damascus. It was one of several that were still standing, even though three streets over, all the buildings were in ruin. The street was deserted, and looking around at the surrounding buildings, there were no signs of his backup. Shit did not feel right in his gut, and as he walked into the office building for a meeting where he was posing as an arms dealer, it hit him: Did the CIA know he had fucked up the Ensenada mission, that Kennedy was alive and well and now going by Mrs. Dante Guzman? Was this all a retaliatory setup? Did they know about Reagan?

Fuck. Every cell in his body was screaming, *Abort!*

He and the agency were parting ways at the end of this mission, no matter how it ended, so before he left, he'd made sure his retirement funds had been transferred into his

Mason Hughes bank account. That account was quickly emptied and disbursed into various accounts, and his brother had been given strict instructions that Reagan was to get it all should something happen to him. He also quietly deposited nine thousand, nine hundred and seventy-five dollars into her account—just under the ten thousand dollar limit that would require her bank to file a currency transaction report with the Financial Crimes Enforcement Network. The money was obviously clean, and he'd gone to great lengths to hide the trail to his Mason Hughes account, but he didn't need anyone poking around trying to trace its origin and connecting the dots between Reagan and a CIA agent. But maybe the connection had already been made.

If so, it wouldn't be safe for her—or her sister. It could possibly expose Kennedy's secret. Having a known relationship with Reagan would raise too many red flags for the agency to ignore. As he sat across from terrorists, promising to deliver weapons of mass destruction with the uneasy feeling that something wasn't quite right, he had a strong inkling that relationship had already been discovered.

When an explosion rocked the building, and no backup arrived to pull him out, his suspicions were confirmed. He had been expendable bait to bring down terrorists. He was hurt and bleeding, and left on his own to survive.

He pictured Reagan's face just before he blacked out. Maybe that was what gave him the will to regain consciousness. He crawled out of the rubble just before another explosion brought what remained of the building down, leaving little chance of survivors.

Chapter Thirty-Seven

Reagan

In her heart, she didn't feel like Mason was really dead.

"Help me understand this. He's not really dead, right? It's just like how Kennedy is supposed to be dead. That was the plan," she asked Jacob hopefully.

He brought his arms around her and pulled her in for a hug.

"This is what I know. His body hasn't been recovered, but there was confirmation he was in the building before it came down. I'm sorry." She let out a little sob, and he stroked her hair. "I hate the idea of being the one to steal your hope, but I don't want to give you false hope, either."

"Why are you here telling me, not Marcus?" She was desperate to cling to anything that would mean Mason wasn't really dead. She'd told him to have Jacob be the one to tell her he wasn't dead if he wasn't truly dead. She didn't care that she had no idea if he'd even heard her tell him that.

"I'm the only one who knows your real identity, so I volunteered. Although, Mason's trust is being transferred to you, so as the executor, Marcus is going to need to know who you are and your vital statistics."

"Wait, his trust? I don't understand."

"He created a trust with all of his assets and made you his sole beneficiary, after all his debts are paid."

"He did *what*?"

Reagan knew he'd been the one to transfer the almost ten thousand dollars into her account last month. It had been confirmed when she received a card in the mail a few days after the money appeared—no signature or return address, just a note that said, *Promise you'll buy the flowers I never had a chance to get for you. And some sexy lingerie for when I get back.*

She went out the next day and did both, making sure to keep the vase of roses in view of the camera in case he was watching—which she knew in her heart he was. She had diligently made sure to keep fresh flowers at the house ever since. It was her way of keeping the faith alive he would be coming back to get her the flowers himself someday.

"I don't want his money," she said quietly as tears streamed down her face, then broke out into a sob. "I just want him."

Jacob hugged her tighter and rocked her, murmuring, "I know you do. I'm so sorry, honey."

Reagan took a deep breath and pulled out of his embrace, wiping her tears with her fingertips.

"He's alive. I know it in my heart. This was exactly what he wanted—everyone to think he's dead. I just need to be patient. He'll show up. It's all part of his plan."

Jacob's smile was sympathetic, like the one he'd given her in the cafeteria of the Cartagena hospital when she'd told him she and Mason were in love. He didn't believe her.

Well, he was wrong then, and he's wrong now. She just needed to be patient and keep the faith that the love of her life was going to find his way back to her.

Chapter Thirty-Eight

Reagan

It was already almost dark out as she made her way home from the Friday class at the community center. Next week was the last one of the year, along with final exams for her students. Reagan stopped at the stoplight and looked at a couple in the Christmas tree lot. They were happy and smiling, holding hands while strolling through the lot looking at trees. Suddenly, she burst into tears.

The car behind her began to honk, and she realized the light had turned green. She began to move forward, even though her vision was blurred with tears.

There had been no word from Mason. No call or cryptic text from an unknown number. No anonymous card or letter to let her know he was alive and watching. Nothing. The realization that he was really dead was becoming harder to deny with each passing day.

What made it worse was that she had to put on a smiling face every day. Other than Delilah, no one in Fargo even knew she'd had a boyfriend—how was she supposed to explain why she was grieving? She'd told her mama they had broken up even before he left. It was safer for Mason that way.

Despite her protests, Marcus insisted on transferring Mason's trust. She didn't want it and dragged her feet sending him her information. It wasn't her money. When he told her just how much was in it, it made her want it even less. The money he'd put in her account had made her uncomfortable enough; what was she going to do with millions? She still hadn't touched a dime of the almost ten thousand, other than to buy the flowers.

When she got home, she realized she'd let the ones in the vase die without replacing them. He was slowly fading away.

Maybe it was time to stop this and let him go.

With a heavy heart, she threw the roses out, washed the vase, and put it in the cupboard. Then she put her pajamas on, curled up in her bed, and cried the rest of the weekend. It alternated between sobs so hard she couldn't breathe and a steady stream of tears. She neither ate nor drank, and any texts or calls were ignored. She was finally mourning Mason; it was gut-wrenching and horrible—and long overdue.

When her alarm clock went off Monday morning, Reagan woke feeling prepared to face the day. The weekend had been cathartic, and she was ready to take on finals week. Maybe even handle the holidays alone.

On second thought, she wasn't that strong yet. She was going to take Bella up on her invitation to spend the holidays with her. Her mother had left when the weather turned cold.

That afternoon, Reagan got a text from Amy, one of the women in her small group of friends.

Happy Margarita Monday! It's been too long since we've seen your pretty face! Meeting at 5:30 at The Pub for dinner and pre-bowling drinks, bowling alley at 7:00. Hope you can make it.

She'd been avoiding going out, afraid Mason would call—or better yet, show up—and she'd miss him. Taking a deep breath, she slowly exhaled before replying. It was time to start living again.

Reagan: *I'll be there! First round's on me.*

****

Mason

Good Samaritans had found him near the fallen building. Fortunately, they were vehemently opposed to the insurgents, and seemed to understand he was one of the Americans fighting them and not his arms dealer persona. As they slowly nursed him back to health, they never questioned who he was, or whether he had played a role in the bombing near where they found him that had killed several high-level terrorists.

Mason hadn't, of course. Not directly anyway. But his government had; he was sure of it.

Throughout his entire recovery, all he could do was worry about Reagan's safety. He'd lost his phone—his connection to her—so he had no way of knowing if she was okay or what she'd been told about him. She'd have to have been given the news by now that he was dead. How long would she hold out hope that he'd show up? He hoped there would be no backlash for her connection to him, and he hoped Marcus kept his word and followed Mason's instructions about her inheriting his trust.

When he had first made the decision to leave her his money, it was with the intention that he'd be returning to her—so basically, he'd still have it, it'd just be under her name. Or, worst case scenario, he'd be dead, and she'd be taken care of.

But now, Mason realized her life would be in jeopardy if he showed back up in it. Not to mention his—again; her sister's cover would be in danger of being blown as well. It had been months since he'd left, and they'd only been together less than a month. Had she moved on? Was someone new reaping the benefits of his trust? He'd give anything to access her cameras again—if she even still had them up.

He needed to get out of the country and back into the US. There were only two people he trusted to know he was alive, and only one had the means to help him.

"Jacob Smith," came the man's curt greeting when Mason's call showed up from an unknown number.

"Jacob, you sexy son-of-a-bitch. How the fuck are you?"

The fixer sat in stunned silence for a moment before replying quietly, "Well, I'll be damned."

"Think you could help a buddy out, for old times' sake?"

"What do you need?" he responded without hesitation, his voice stronger now.

"I need a ride. Out of Syria."

"Let me see what I can do and get back to you. How long is this number good for?"

"Until I hear back from you."

****

Jacob was able to transport Mason on a cargo plane out of Syria into Athens, Greece. From there, he was getting onboard a chartered jet leaving for America. Slow-moving, he stutter-stepped in disbelief when he saw the fixer waiting for him on the plane.

"What are you doing here?" he asked as he carefully sank down next to Jacob.

"I was in the neighborhood taking care of business when you called. Thought we could ride back together, and you could fill me in about where you've been the last two and a half months. Thought for sure I was going to be able to marry your girl after all."

Mason laughed, even though it still hurt to, and it turned into a hacking cough.

He took the water bottle Jacob offered and gulped, choking out, "That's not funny, fucker," between swallows.

Jacob lifted his shoulders in response. "Who says I was trying to be?"

Mason screwed the cap on the bottle and narrowed his eyes.

"Have you seen her? How is she?"

"About as good as you'd expect her to be. Last time I checked, she was still holding out hope you're alive."

That helped settle him down. His imagination had been fucking with him lately.

"So, she's not shacked up with some guy spending all my money?"

Jacob gave a wry smile. "She won't take it—she's been avoiding your brother, refusing to take his calls or give him her information so he can transfer it."

He wished he could say he was surprised.

"Stubborn woman," he muttered under his breath.

"Yeah. She's going to be over the moon to see you. Just in time for Christmas."

Mason shook his head with a sad smile. "I think it's best for everyone if I stay dead."

Jake shook his head in disgust. "Are you fucking kidding me? You're just going to let her go—just like that?"

"It's for the best."

"Whatever, man. Then you won't mind years from now when you find out she's married to some asshole who doesn't give a damn about her. Knowing she's miserable when you could have made her happy," the dark-haired man spat out.

Suddenly it was clear: Jacob wasn't just talking about Mason and Reagan.

"You checked in on Taren," he said quietly.

"Yeah," he scoffed. "I did some digging. Almost wish I hadn't—thanks a lot for the suggestion, asshole."

Mason shrugged. "So fix it."

Jacob tipped his chin at him. "Remember you said that."

"It wouldn't be safe for Reagan if I showed up, and you know it. And what about Bella? That wouldn't be a neon sign or anything that she was alive. The team leader shacking up with the sister of the woman he was sent in to terminate and whose body was conveniently lost at sea."

"All I'm saying is, as far as the agency is concerned, you're dead. Keep a low enough profile for a few years and there'll be enough turnover that anyone who would even remember you to begin with will all be retired or moved on. The question is—do you keep the low profile with the woman you love, or let someone else do it so when the time comes to be with her, you've been replaced."

"She loves me—she's not going to move on so easily," Mason said confidently. More confidently than he really felt.

"She thinks you're fucking dead, dumbass."

Chapter Thirty-Nine

Reagan

A night out with girls was just what she needed. It felt good to laugh and let loose for a while—to actually talk with other three-dimensional people who weren't her students. Talking to a dead man through a camera in her kitchen was just sad. More than sad—pathetic.

The women were in the middle of their first game of bowling, with Reagan strutting back to the group after having bowled a spare, when she noticed a new group had sat down to occupy the lane next to theirs. It was none other than some of Fargo's finest, including Ric Casper.

"Hey, Reagan. Nice to see you again," he called over from the table where he sat putting his rented shoes on.

"Hey, Ric. Good to see you as well," she said with a wave.

He got up and left in search of a ball, and Amy not-so-subtly elbowed her in the side.

"Oh my god, he was totally checking you out when you were bowling."

Reagan shrugged with a smile. "We went to high school together."

"He's hot. You should go for it."

"I don't think so," she said, sitting down at the little round laminate table and picking up the double-sided menu displayed in an acrylic stand.

Amy sat down next to her, mouth agape.

"*You don't think* so? Why the hell not? He's handsome, has a job that assures you he doesn't have an arrest record, and he's obviously interested. Give me one good reason why you shouldn't go out with him."

"I'd be interested to know the answer to that, too," a deep voice interjected. She looked up to find Ric standing there with a smile, eyes twinkling.

Because I'm mourning a man I can't even tell anyone I lost.

"I just don't know if I'm ready—"

Their other friend Caitlynn joined the conversation after finishing her turn and picked up her drink off the table. "Ready for what?"

"To go on a date," Amy helpfully provided.

"Why wouldn't you be ready?" Caitlynn asked with her lips around the skinny red straw.

"You should go." Denise, who had been listening from the bench, came forward. "It's time for you to get out there and have fun."

Reagan had thought that was what she was doing tonight with her girlfriends. Now, instead, she was feeling ambushed.

She gave Ric a smile that was far brighter than she was feeling, hoping he'd take the hint and drop it. Which, thankfully, he did.

He smiled and gave her a wink. "When you're ready, you know where to find me," he said, then rejoined his group.

Her friends descended on her like the plague.

"You're a fool. Look at him. He's hot."

"I've known Ric since we were kids. He's a really good guy."

"Why aren't you interested?"

"Oh my god, are you dating someone?"

"Wait—are you gay? My cousin's gay, maybe I could set you up."

Reagan buried her head in her hands. They were right. Ric was hot—and a good guy. Mason was never coming back; maybe she *should* go out with the Fargo police officer.

"Oh my god, if I say I'll go on a date with him, will you all stop talking about this?"

"Yes!" they cried in unison.

"Fine. I'll go on a date with him."

They stood there grimacing.

"What? I said I would go out with him."

Amy raised her eyebrows and motioned with her head in Ric's direction.

She whirled around, expecting him to be standing there listening. Instead, he was chatting with a cute brunette at his table.

"Oh. Well, then there you go. Can we please bowl now?"

Reagan wasn't necessarily jealous, but she did wonder if she had blown it by not taking Ric up on his offer to go on a date. It wasn't like Fargo's streets were lined with single, handsome, good men over the age of thirty.

Fortunately, before the night was over, she was given another chance. She was putting on her boots when he sat down next to her.

"Look, I know you're not ready to necessarily go on a date, but maybe we could meet for coffee or lunch sometime. We don't have to call it a date, just two friends getting food or having a hot beverage."

His eyes were really pretty. And kind. But he wasn't Mason. Yet, that was the point, wasn't it? He was alive and sitting next to her, and offering to be her friend.

"I would love to have lunch with you. Are you available tomorrow? Is that too soon?"

A smile spread across from face.

"Yeah, I'm available. Let me give you my phone number."

She pulled out her phone and programmed it in, sending him a text immediately so he'd have her information.

Looking forward to lunch.

"I'll text you in the morning, and we can figure out where to meet," she said as she put her phone in her purse.

"That sounds great." He put his hand on his knee like he was going to stand up, then paused and chuckled. "You know, it's funny. I wasn't going to come tonight, but changed my mind at the last minute." He gave her a poignant smile. "I'm glad I did," he said, then gestured to his phone. "I'm looking forward to lunch, too."

"Me too." *He knows—you already said that, doofus.*

As she watched him walk away, she realized: She meant it.

****

Mason

Reagan's camera streams were still online. He wasn't sure if they would be; they were battery-powered, and he'd never monitored one in the same place for that long, so he hadn't been sure about the battery life.

They were out of frame though—especially the one at the front door. Probably because that was the one she used to take to her bedroom with her.

He closed his eyes at the memory of her ivory skin against the sheets, her auburn hair spread out on the pillow in beautiful contrast to it.

"I just want to make sure she's okay," he told himself before checking the video feed. Part of him was nervous about what he was going to find.

Her house was empty and dark, except for the light she always left on above the stove at night. The streetlamps from the street streamed in the windows at the top of her front door, bathing the camera in the entryway in yellow light.

He had no idea if she was even home or out, and let out a long breath as he sat down at the kitchenette table of his cabin in northern Michigan. The plane Jacob chartered had touched down in New Orleans last night, and Mason had declined the fixer's offer to stay at his house—although he was curious to see the man's place.

Just as Jacob said, Reagan hadn't touched his money, so he was able to access a small sum to buy a plane ticket to Grand Rapids, rent a car, and buy supplies. Jacob provided him with secure electronics. Funny thing about being in the spy business; you had that kind of shit stockpiled.

He turned on the television and found that his favorite movie, *Warning Track,* was on one of the stations he could get with the antennae. The movie was almost over when his phone alerted him to movement on the camera facing Reagan's garage.

Mason's breath caught when he saw her, dressed in dark jeans tucked into black knee-high boots and a simple black cowl neck sweater, her hair loose around her shoulders. That was the face that had kept him going these last few months.

His heart was urging him to get in the car, drive to the airport and hop another plane to Fargo so he could be holding her by morning. His cock was screaming, *What are you waiting for?* But his brain told him he needed to stay away. Watching her on camera was as close as he could get.

He smiled as she moved about the kitchen, putting water in the tea kettle and pulling out a hot chocolate packet she emptied into a mug. Then she rummaged around the pantry and triumphantly produced a bag of marshmallows.

Her victorious hip shimmy as she sauntered her way back to the table with her mug was all it took for his brain to be overruled, and he was gathering his things to go to Fargo.

Except hopping a plane from Grand Rapids, Michigan to Fargo, North Dakota wasn't quite as easy as catching a plane from Boston to D.C.— there wasn't exactly a flight available every hour. By the time he reached the airport, the only flight he could get out of Michigan was either to Atlanta, Houston, or Chicago. He boarded the Chicago plane and slept in the airport to catch the first flight out in morning. That was going to get him into Fargo around nine; she'd already be at work by then. He'd have to settle for holding her by tomorrow night.

Chapter Forty

Reagan

Lunch with Ric was nice. He was funny, and nervous, and sweet. Best of all, he didn't put any pressure on her for a 'date.'

"So, I'm thinking about getting a dog," he confided as she took a bite of her tater tot hotdish in a corner booth at Cracked Pepper.

"Oh yeah? When?"

"Maybe after work today."

"What kind?"

"I don't know. I haven't really decided; I'm trying to leave myself open and thinking I'll just know when I see him or her."

"I'm assuming you're going to the shelter?"

"Yeah, of course."

A dog. She'd never had a dog, although she always wanted one when she was a kid. But she and her sister barely ate on a regular basis; adding a dog to the mix would never have worked. She nodded thoughtfully before asking, "Want some company?"

His smile was genuine. "Really?"

She shrugged. "Yeah, sure. Maybe a dog is exactly what I need in my life."

Suddenly the idea of being a dog owner seemed like the best thing in the world, and she perked up in her seat. Reagan did a quick search on her phone. "They're open until seven, so can you meet there at five?"

"Absolutely."

Her mood was happy for the rest of lunch. She was going to have a four-legged companion to come home to every night. Maybe it would make it feel less lonely when she walked in the door. It wouldn't be Mason making dinner, but there'd be someone happy to see her at the end of the day. Her new normal. What did Amy call her ninety-pound German shepherd? A *fur baby*. Reagan was getting a fur baby.

****

Mason

He was sitting in his rental car in the parking lot of the grocery store down the road from her house, watching his iPad screen for movement. He had slipped inside Reagan's house and adjusted the cameras in order to have a better view of her moving about when she was home. He'd thought about just staying and waiting until she came home to find him there, but decided against it.

He was second-guessing his showing up in Fargo at all. He had no idea how to proceed. As Jacob had so eloquently put it, *She thinks you're fucking dead, dumbass.*

How was he going to let her know he was alive without sending her into shock, or worse? Sitting at her kitchen table when she walked in from the garage after work didn't feel right. Nor did knocking on her front door. But calling or sending a text seemed too impersonal.

He buried his head in his hands. *Fuuuuck.*

His phone beeped with an alert of movement at her front door, and he put the car in drive. She wasn't home yet, there shouldn't be activity at her front door. He pulled in three doors down from her house and watched.

Reagan opened the door and was beaming. *Beaming.* Then she stepped aside as a floppy-eared black hound with tan ears bounded through like a bull in a china shop. She tugged on the aqua-blue leash attached to an obviously new matching collar with shiny tags as the purse over her shoulder slipped, tangling with the full Petsmart bag looped around her wrist. She unceremoniously dropped the items next to the door.

"Hold on a second, Walter!" she giggled as she adjusted the lead, then directed her attention outside.

Another dog walked politely through the threshold, wearing a new pink collar and leash. This pup was black and white with a long, flat coat and withers. It appeared to be a spaniel of some kind and had what looked like freckles on its nose. And attached to the other end of the leash was Ric fuckin' Casper.

"Why is Daisy so much calmer than Walter?" Reagan asked with a fake cry.

Ric shrugged. "She's a female, and she's been spayed. Plus I think she's older than he is. Once he goes in for the surgery, he'll calm down a lot. I think he's just excited to have gotten the hell out of the shelter." He tapped Reagan's nose. "Not to mention his new mom is a knockout. Can you blame him?"

Her smile was polite, and she dropped to her knees to rub her dog's floppy ears. "Thank you again for letting me go with you."

Ric kneeled down so he was eye level with Reagan.

"I had a lot of fun today. I'm glad we were able to go together, and I'm even more thrilled that you adopted Daisy's kennelmate so they'll still be able to spend time together."

Okay, Romeo, let's move along.

"We definitely need to get them together again once Walter is recovered from his surgery."

Ric stood and offered his hand to help her up.

"Do you need help getting the rest of the stuff out of your car?" he asked.

"Nope, I got it. Thank you though."

They stood there awkwardly. *Please don't kiss him. Please don't kiss him.*

Ric coughed into his hand. "Okay, well, let me know if you need any help with him at the vet. Otherwise I'll just give you a call tomorrow after work?"

She rubbed his bicep, making Mason's fingers curl into a fist. "I appreciate the offer, but I got it. I'll talk to you tomorrow."

More awkward silence as he didn't move to walk out the docr with his stupid dog. Then he leaned down and kissed her cheek, whispering, "Talk to you tomorrow," before finally leaving.

Reagan watched him walk to his car, then closed and locked the door, turned to her new dog, and, with her voice an octave higher than usual, cooed, "Okay, buddy. You wanna see your new home? Come on, let's go."

Mason couldn't help but chuckle as his sassy pants girl talked to the dog like it was a human and showed him around the house. He could hear her even when he couldn't see her on camera.

"And you'll be sleeping in here with me. Oh, let me go get your bed out of the car."

She walked into the garage, leaving the hound alone in the kitchen. He watched as Walter promptly knocked over the garbage can and began digging through its contents.

Reagan staggered through the door with a dog bed in one hand and her other arm wrapped around what looked to be a fifty-pound bag of dogfood. She really needed to learn how to make two trips.

She set it down with a thud when she saw what the pup had done.

"Walter, no! Bad dog!"

With a sigh, she righted the trash can. "I guess I'll be needing a heavier one of these with a more secure lid." She started picking up the mess, including what looked like dead flowers.

"Mason got me these," she said wistfully as she brushed the petals in a pile with her hand. "You would have loved him. I think he would have loved you, too. But I don't really know." Her laugh was filled more with sorrow than joy. "I guess I'll never know."

She continued cleaning up, talking to the dog. "But Ric seems like a nice guy, right?"

Mason almost closed down the app and drove away right then. The cop was a good guy, from what little he could find out about him. Maybe she was better off with him.

Then she slumped down on her butt with her back against the wall and began to sob softly into the dishtowel she'd pulled from the oven handle. Poor Walter looked on, whining and trying to nuzzle his way under her leg.

"I just miss him so much," she whispered as she wiped her eyes and scratched behind the dog's ears. "It's not fair. Why did he have to leave me? He was *the one*, ya know?"

She glanced up at the camera and paused, doing a double-take before standing up and slowly walking toward the camera to inspect it closer. She'd obviously noticed it had been adjusted.

"Mason Edward Hughes, I swear to god, if you're alive and watching me right now without letting me know you're all right—"

He had already been on his way to her door the minute he saw her on the floor crying. It was serendipity that she uttered her warning just as he quietly opened the door leading from the garage. He was going to have to talk to her about closing the garage door behind her so not just anybody could walk in. Ric should have warned her about that— further confirmation that Mason was the better man for her.

Chapter Forty-One

Reagan

She let out a little gasp, startled at the sight of seeing someone in her kitchen when she wasn't expecting it, then blinked hard and shook her head, as if she were imagining things.

Mason was standing in her kitchen. He looked gaunt—at least twenty-five pounds lighter—and pale, like he hadn't seen the sun in months, but there was no doubt it was him.

Unless it was a ghost.

Walter started barking at the perceived intruder, and she reached down to grab his collar.

"It's okay, boy."

Turning her attention to the man standing five feet in front of her, she didn't know what to say. Why was he here after all this time?

"I thought you were dead," she whispered.

He held his hands up, like he was reassuring he wasn't a threat, and walked slowly toward her.

"There were times I thought so, too. Then there were times I just wished it. It was touch and go there for a while."

"What happened? Where have you been?" Her tone was more accusatory than she'd intended.

"Syria. I was in an explosion."

Tears filled her eyes. "And you were hurt."

He nodded, less than a foot in front of her now.

"Pretty badly. I would have died if some good Samaritans hadn't found me and hid me while nursing me back to health."

"How long have you been back?"

"In the States?" He looked at the nonexistent watch on his wrist. "About thirty-six hours."

A sob escaped her lips. "And you came back to me."

Slowly, like she might bolt if he moved too quickly—either that or he might get bitten by her new dog—he touched her cheek with the back of his hand.

"I came back to you."

At that, she launched herself on him, wrapping her arms around his neck, legs around his waist, and burying her face in the crook of his shoulder while she cried softly. His hands came under her ass to support her and Walter began to bark excitedly.

"Walter! Quiet!" his deep voice commanded, and the dog immediately complied, looking almost dumbfounded that this man knew his name.

"How long are you here?" she asked, sniffling.

She didn't want to assume anything or get her hopes up.

He rocked her gently, shifting her weight in his hands.

"For as long as you'll have me, sweetheart."

"Forever work for you?"

"Forever works perfectly," he said with a smile.

"I guess you'll probably want to marry me for my money, huh?" she teased. "I've been told I'm quite wealthy now."

"Sassy pants, I would love to marry you—but not for the money. We can have a prenup that gives you everything. I just want to grow old waking up next to you every morning and going to sleep next every night with you in my arms."

She unwrapped her legs and dropped to the ground, but kept her arms around his neck.

"It's your money—I never wanted it in the first place. And I was just teasing—you don't have to marry me to get it back."

Mason shook his head. "No, baby. I don't want to waste another minute to start our life together. Hell, I'd fly to Vegas tonight and marry you if I thought you'd go."

She narrowed her eyes. "Exactly *whom* would I be marrying?"

"Edward Marcus O'Connor."

She studied his face, her fingers threading through his hair almost subconsciously as she did. Finally, she nodded. "It suits you. You look like an Edward."

He smirked. "Oh yeah? How many have you known?"

She looked toward the ceiling. "Well, let's see, there's Edward Norton, and Prince Edward. Edward Burns. Oh, and don't forget, Edward Lewis."

He tilted his head. "I'm not familiar."

"He was Richard Gere's character in *Pretty Woman*. Can I call ya Eddie?" she teased, quoting Julia Roberts from the movie.

Mason didn't miss a beat when he replied with Richard Gere's line, "Not if you expect me to answer."

Reagan didn't know how, but she might have just fallen more in love with him.

"So, is that a yes on marrying me?" he asked, his tone hopeful.

"Are you really asking? Like, for real?"

He dramatically dropped to one knee—which would have been uber-romantic if Walter hadn't taken that opportunity to plaster his face with dog kisses.

She erupted in a fit of giggles and dropped down next to him to help fend off the slobbering dog, holding onto his collar.

Her smile faded when she looked into his eyes. His expression was sober.

"Will you marry me, Reagan Elizabeth Jones?"

Were they crazy? They'd only spent the equivalent of a month together. But he had once told her he just knew— meeting her had been like combustion. She felt the same way about him.

Tears began to fall before she even got the words out. Nodding her head, she exclaimed, "Yes, I will marry you, Edward Marcus O'Connor."

He pulled her into an embrace, his mouth capturing hers for the first time in what felt like an eternity. Walter tried to get in on the action and Mason/Edward pulled her to her feet.

"Do you have bones in that bag?" he asked hopefully.

"Yeah, why?"

"I'm going to need to keep him busy for at least an hour and a half before he can come in the bedroom with us."

"Oh," she replied, her toes curling in her shoes. "Let me find them."

"Hurry, sweetheart," he urged. "I need to feel you under me again."

She needed that, too.

Chapter Forty-Two

Mason/Edward

He woke when her alarm started going off after sleeping like the dead. It was the first time in months he'd been completely at ease and able to stay asleep for more than an hour at a time. Making love to her until they were exhausted probably also helped.

Today was the first day of his new chapter.

Reagan shut the alarm off but didn't get out of bed; instead she turned over and wrapped her arms around him.

"I can't believe you're really here," she murmured with her head on his chest.

"Believe it. I'm not going anywhere again."

"Does that mean you don't have to hide?"

"That's exactly what it means."

"How am I going to explain you?" she asked with a laugh.

"We'll use the original story we were going to go with. We met online in a hockey chat room last year. We'd been talking the entire time, growing closer, and when we met in person for the first time last summer on the cruise you went on with your mom, we knew we were in love. We'd been doing a long-distance relationship since then but finally, I couldn't be apart from you for another minute and moved here to be with you."

"And why didn't I tell anyone about us?"

He shrugged with a mischievous grin. "You were worried I was too good to be true?"

Her expression was somber. "I still worry about that."

Edward was going to have to remedy that right away. *Trip to the jewelry store* was going to the top of the list of his things to do today. Calling his brother was number two, making flight reservations to see his parents was number three.

"I'm not too good to be true, sweetheart."

Reagan sighed and snuggled closer to him. "I think everyone will believe our story, except my friend, Ric. He was one of the Fargo officers who came here looking for you that day. I actually went to lunch with him yesterday, and then we went to the shelter together last night and each adopted a kennelmate."

And he's interested in me. She didn't say it, but he knew that was the case, and so did she. Yesterday, Mason had been jealous, now he just felt bad for the man; Ric seemed like a good guy. He'd left here yesterday thinking he was making inroads with Reagan, only to not have a chance today.

"Maybe you should meet him for coffee and let him down easy."

"I probably should," she agreed.

Just then Walter started to whine.

"You go get ready, I'll take him out."

As he sat shivering his ass off in his pajama pants and sweatshirt while holding the dog's leash, he decided number four on his list was building a fence off her backdoor.

He had a lot of things to do today.

****

Reagan

She walked into the coffee shop where Ric was already waiting and waved before going to the counter to place her order. He stood and kissed her cheek when she approached the table by the window where he was sitting.

"Did you get Walter to the vet okay this morning?"

Mason/Edward had taken care of that for her, but now wasn't the time to bring that up.

"I'll pick him up this afternoon," was her reply.

"I was happily surprised you wanted to meet this morning," he said with a smile.

She gave a pacifying smile and his face fell, but he remained silent.

"I haven't been completely honest about why I'm not ready to date," she began. "The truth is, I'm seeing someone. It was mainly long distance until last night."

"What happened last night?"

"Well, um, he showed up at my door."

Ric sat up straighter as he slipped into cop mode and began to pepper her with questions about how much she knew about her long-distance boyfriend, how did they meet, and had she run a background check.

Finally, she gripped his hand, which was clenched into a fist on top of the table.

"My sister introduced us. He used to work with her."

She raised her eyebrow to drive her point home without having to utter the words.

His mouth opened when he figured out what she was saying.

"I see. And now?"

"He's retired. I hope I can count on you to keep this between us and no one else. For his safety as well as mine."

"So, the guy doing the physical therapy few months ago—"

"Wasn't a fugitive from the law," she finished for him.

Ric nodded his head thoughtfully as he stared at the ground, then looked up and gave her a small smile.

"Your secret is safe with me. You have my word. And if either of you ever need anything, you can count on me. I mean that."

She believed him.

Chapter Forty-Three

Mason/Edward

They woke up to a foot of overnight snow on Christmas Eve morning, and Mason had to use the snow blower to create a path for Walter to have a place to do his business, but for all intents and purposes, they were snowed in. It sounded ideal.

"How does Naked Christmas Eve sound?" he asked, bringing his arms around her middle while she poured him a cup of coffee.

She shook her head with a smile.

"No. We have to finish making cookies, and I still have your presents I need to wrap, plus I guarantee there will be carolers tonight."

"What if I don't clear the front walk?" he asked hopefully.

"Babe, don't underestimate Fargoans willingness to wade through knee-high snow to sing Christmas songs to their neighbors on Christmas Eve."

He sighed. "Okay, but we're at least having naked Christmas morning."

"We can be naked all day tomorrow," she promised, patting his cheek.

"No, just the morning. I'm making Christmas dinner tomorrow, remember?"

Besides, he was planning on making love to her all night tonight by the light of the Christmas tree after he proposed to her. He'd even stocked up on Busy Bones to keep Walter occupied.

"Oh yes! I hope you're not planning on going to a lot of trouble since it's just going to be the two of us."

"Nothing too elaborate," he assured her. "But it's still going to be a beautiful meal. Maybe next year, we can be with one or both of our families and go all out. Speaking of which… I bought our tickets to Boston for next week—is Ric going to be able to take Walter while we're gone?"

"He said no problem."

Mason was going to show up on his parents' doorstep and let them know he was alive—and with a fiancée in tow. He'd already called Marcus, who hadn't seemed very surprised to hear from him, leaving Mason to wonder aloud if Jacob had called him.

"Nah, I just saw some withdrawals on your accounts and sort of figured it out, based on where you'd made the withdrawals and for how much."

"Oh. Well, I'm going to see mom and dad the week after Christmas if you can make it. I'm going to bring Reagan with me. I'd like to officially meet Susana."

"I'll see what I can do," his brother replied noncommittally, quickly changing the subject. "What are you going by these days?"

"Reagan still calls me Mason, probably more out of habit than anything, but when we're out in public or if I'm doing any business, it's Edward."

"Business?"

"I'm going to open a restaurant," Mason confided.

"I think that sounds like a terrific idea. It's good to have my big brother back."

"It's good to be back."

****

Reagan

They were nestled under a blanket on the living room rug next to the fire in the fireplace, drinking wine while leaning on throw pillows and staring at the twinkling lights on the Christmas tree.

Walter was on his bed, gnawing away at a bone Mason had given him.

Mason—er, Edward moved to sit up straighter, her head now resting in his lap as he entwined their fingers. Reagan suspected his injuries made it harder for him to stay still for very long. While his face remained almost flawless, his back and chest bore the scars of the explosion that day in Syria, on top of his previous scars and bullet wounds. He looked like the walking wounded when he got out of the shower in the morning, and it made her heart ache for everything he'd been through.

"Were you serious about marrying me, sassy pants?" he asked quietly.

"Of course," Reagan whispered, squeezing his fingers in hers. She was about to bring his hand to her lips when she realized there was a diamond shimmering on her left ring finger and gasped.

"How did you do that?"

"Once a spy…" he said with a smirk as he cloaked her body with his.

"Our poor kids aren't going to be able to get away with anything," she giggled.

"Speaking of… when are we going to have one? Not that I'm opposed to just practicing until you say the word, but what do you think?"

"Let's get back from getting married in Boston next week, then I'll go see my doctor about having the implant removed."

His eyes got big. "So there's a chance we could have a baby by next Christmas?" Then he realized what she'd said and shook his head. "Wait, did you say you wanted to get married in Boston next week?"

"Well, assuming your family likes me, I thought I could talk Bella and Dante into bringing Mama for New Year's… it seemed like as good a time as any."

"But Boston, sweetheart? It's cold there, too."

"I'll wear a pretty white fake-fur wrap around my dress."

He stared at her with a soft smile, then bent his head within inches of hers.

"I'm gonna wife you so hard," he warned just before capturing her lips with his.

She couldn't wait.

Epilogue

Edward/Mason

He had his restaurant opened by September the following year, and it didn't take long for him to become an honorary Fargoan—probably thanks to his native wife, who was the face of the company. That allowed him to stay out of the limelight. The community embraced Sassy's Bar and Grill from the first hour it opened, making it an instant hit. They loved seeing one of their own succeed.

Reagan's pregnant belly in all the newspaper and magazine articles more than likely helped. It had just popped out a week before their Grand Opening, and Fargoans were just so damn *nice,* they were rooting for her—and by default, him—from day one. Brianna Kennedy O'Connor arrived December fifteenth, and when she was two and half years old, James Mason O'Connor joined his sister in the world. Edward and Reagan stopped procreating after their son was born—but not practicing.

Standing in the kitchen doorway watching her with the kids on a Saturday morning, he wondered how he'd gotten so lucky. But, as Jacob had pointed out one summer day when Edward was wearing a shirt poolside to hide his scars, it wasn't like he hadn't paid his dues. "You just needed to find your way to where you belonged," the former fixer had told him. At the end of the day, all roads led back to Reagan. Be it in Fargo, San Diego, Key West, Boston... he didn't care, as long as she was by his side.

And there were naked Sundays.

Thank you!

Thank you for reading *Combustion*! I hope you enjoyed Mason and Reagan's story as much as I did writing it. Would you mind leaving me a review wherever you purchased this book? Believe it or not, your review really does help get my book seen by other readers. xoxo

Appreciatively,

Tess

Reignited

Agents of Ensenada, Book 3

He's known as the CIA's top mercenary fixer. But he can't fix this.

Jacob Smith

Seven years.

Seven long miserable years since he'd ripped his heart from his chest and left it on her doorstep when he walked away from her. But, he'd had no choice.

At least, he'd thought he hadn't. He was too entrenched in the CIA's underground world to safely ever have a wife and family.

But now, after turning his CIA dealings into a *very* lucrative mercenary career, here he was, about to embark on a ten-day cruise with his cabin next to hers, not by coincidence—although she didn't know it yet.

He wasn't known as a 'fixer' for nothing. Maybe it was time to try to fix his broken heart, and hers—if she'd let him. And that was a big *if*, given how he'd shattered hers so long ago.

Ignition
Agent of Ensenada, Prequel

Betrayal had always been part of the plan; falling in love complicated everything.

Dante Guzman

He knew within hours that Ruby Rhodes, the sexy little auburn-haired beauty, who just happened to sit next to him at his favorite bar and flirt with him all night long, was not who she appeared to be. Redheads were his kryptonite—everyone knew it, including his enemies who wanted to see the Guzman cartel destroyed. Just exactly who sent her and why was something he was going to have to figure out. At least playing along with her was enjoyable since part of her ruse seemed to entail sleeping with him and indulging his... let's say, *darker* desires.

Or maybe that wasn't supposed to be part of the plan, and she broke the rules.

Falling in love with Ruby was definitely not part of his plan, and Dante was going to have to punish her for making him do just that. Especially after he learns who she really is and why she was sent to seduce him.

Inferno

Agents of Ensenada, Book 1

Kennedy Jones

I'm a special agent with the CIA, and I'm good at what I do. In fact, I'm considered one of the best. I can play the role of anyone and eliminating bad guys without them seeing me coming is my forte—which is why I was chosen to take down the head of the Guzman family.

Dante Guzman is a ruthless, sexy, cold-hearted cartel money-man. And now it's my job to study him, learn his likes and dislikes—in and out of the bedroom—so I can gain his trust and access to his uncle, the head of the Ensenada cartel.

I just didn't count on falling into Dante's clutches.

Every second I spend with him he manages to pull me further and further into his world. And the more time I spend there, the deeper I slip into the darkness with him, the more I realize...

I like it.

Dante Guzman

Don't let my good manners fool you—I'm one cold-hearted SOB, and I control the family's monetary affairs with an iron fist. There's no place for weakness in my world. Show weakness, and you die. As simple as that.

So when a petite, feisty, hot-as-hell bombshell storms into my life, I didn't stop to think about the consequences of keeping her. I wanted her, and I always get what I want. Period.

Turns out, the stakes were too high...for the both of us. And there's going to be hell to pay if we're going to be together, to one form of the devil or another.

Other Works by Tess Summers

Free Book! *The Playboy and the SWAT Princess*

BookHip.com/SNGBXD Sign up here to receive my newsletter, and get SWAT Captain Craig Baxter's love story, exclusively for newsletter subscribers. You'll receive regular updates (but I won't bombard you with emails, I promise), and be the first to know about my works-in-progress.

She's a badass SWAT rookie, and he's a playboy SWAT captain… who's taming who?

Maddie Monroe

Three things you should not do when you're a rookie, and the only female on the SDPD SWAT Team… 1) Take your hazing personally, 2) Let them see you sweat, and 3) Fall for your captain.

Especially, when your captain is the biggest playboy on the entire police force.

I've managed to follow rules one and two with no problem, but the third one I'm having a little more trouble with. Every time he smiles that sinful smile or folds his muscular arms when explaining a new technique or walks through the station full of swagger…. All I can think about is how I'd like to give him my V-card, giftwrapped with a big red bow on it, which is such a bad idea because out of Rules One, Two, and Three, breaking the third one is a sure-fire way to get me kicked off the team and writing parking tickets for the rest of my career.

Apparently my heart—and other body parts—didn't get the memo.

Craig Baxter

The first time I noticed Maddie Monroe, she was wet and covered in soapy suds as she washed SWAT's armored truck as part of her hazing ritual. I've been hard for her ever since.

I can't sleep with a subordinate—it would be career suicide, and I've worked too damn hard to get where I am today. Come to think of it, so has she, and she'd probably have a lot more to lose.

So, nope, not messing around with Maddie Monroe. There are plenty of women for me to choose from who don't work for me.

Apparently my heart—and other body parts—didn't get the memo.

Can two hearts—and other body parts—overcome missed memos and find a way to be together without career-ending consequences?

Also available at TessSummersAuthor.com:

San Diego Social Scene series:

Operation Sex Kitten—Book One

The General's Desire—Book Two

Playing Dirty—Book Three

Cinderella and the Marine—Book Four

The Playboy and the SWAT Princess—FREE Bonus Book

The Heiress and the Mechanic—Book Five

Burning Her Resolve—Book Six

The Boston's Elite Series

Wicked Hot Silver Fox

Wicked Hot Doctor

Wicked Bad Medicine

Wicked Hot Baby Daddy

Wicked Bad Decisions

About the Author

Tess Summers is a former businesswoman and teacher who always loved writing but never seemed to have time to sit down and write a short story, let alone a novel. Now battling MS, her life changed dramatically, and she has finally slowed down enough to start writing all the stories she's been wanting to tell, including the fun and sexy ones!

Married over twenty-seven years with three grown children, Tess is a former dog foster mom who ended up failing and adopting them (and a 75-pound tortoise) instead. She and her husband (and their three dogs) split their time between the desert of Arizona and the lakes of Michigan, so she's always in a climate that's not too hot and not too cold, but just right!

Contact Me!

Sign up for my newsletter: BookHip.com/SNGBXD
Email: TessSummersAuthor@yahoo.com
Visit my website: www.TessSummersAuthor.com
Facebook: http://facebook.com/TessSummersAuthor
Twitter: http://twitter.com/@mmmTess
Instagram: https://www.instagram.com/tesssummers/
BookBub https://www.bookbub.com/profile/tess-summers
Goodreads: https://www.goodreads.com/TessSummers
TikTok: https://www.tiktok.com/@tesssummersauthor